In the channel where a sea floo and haze and showering wate able forms approached. She cau ... appendages, and yawning mouths, blisters of ... eyes and around the massive figures, she thought she saw winged, demonic forms and shapeless others with hints of more massive contours beyond.

The thrill inside her, even as wind whipped behind them and threatened to knock them forward was akin to orgasm mixed with shock and astonishment.

"It's incredible," she said, knowing the word to be almost a joke, an inadequate grunt.

She turned to Liam to see glazed eyes and an expression of amazement. He'd lost awareness of almost everything around him except the witching hour-vision, the death dream, the abyss in front of them.

DISCIPLES OF THE SERPENT

Sidney Williams

About the O. C. L. T. Series

There are incidents and emergencies in the world that defy logical explanation, events that could be defined as supernatural, extra-terrestrial, or simply otherworldly. Standard laws do not allow for such instances, nor are most officials or authorities trained to handle them. In recognition of these facts, one organization has been created that can. Assembled by a loose international coalition, their mission is to deal with these situations using diplomacy, guile, force, and strategy as necessary. They shield the rest of the world from their own actions, and clean up the messes left in their wake. They are our protection, our guide, our sword, and our voice, all rolled into one.

They are O.C.L.T.

Tales of the O. C. L. T.

"They know much about the stars and celestial motions, and about the size of the earth and universe, and about the essential nature of things, and about the powers and authority of the immortal gods; and these things they teach to their pupils."

—Julius Caesar

20 Years Ago

The symbol looked almost like a contemporary set of tally marks. Short slashes angled away from a straight center line but not quite like those they'd seen in class. The slashes were clustered differently and featured additional flourishes at the end of some lines.

Kaity angled her headlamp toward it with an adjustment then gave the mark a couple of careful strokes with the soft round hand brush she'd been given. She wanted to clear dust particles without damaging the edges. Etched along a corner on the old stone wall in a seldom unexplored chamber, it might have gone unseen for ages until her headlamp hit it.

"What have you got?"

Her friend Lizabeth had slipped in behind her, through a doorway of this narrow building, what the professors had called the necessarium.

"A marking. See it?"

Liz laughed. "The monks wrote on their bathroom walls?"

"What?"

"Didn't they tell you where you were working? This was the latrine." Liz giggled. "It really was necessary."

"Well, it's different isn't it? We need to show one of the professors."

"They're off at the truck. Drinkin' coffee or something. Liam is close. Will a student assistant do? That's close to a professor. Why don't we get him?"

That should do, Kaity thought. *Everyone whispered about Liam, who was a couple of years older, and he'd been showing a keen interest in symbols from what she understood.*

Maybe he'd be impressed.

Switching off her headlamp, she stepped from the shadows under the stone out into the light. She blinked a bit before spotting the young man at the worktable under a small tent. He seemed to be cleaning a bit of stone with a hand brush.

With Liz at her shoulder, making slight hand gestures at her side to keep her friend from giggling, she moved across the grassy expanse outside the old monastery wall.

"I think we have something of interest," she said, showing a quick pencil rendering of the symbol.

The young man looked up from his work. "Oh?"

"I think it's a bit odd to have it on a Christian site," she said. "What do you think?"

She hoped she sounded solemn and intelligent. She didn't want him to think she was a twit.

His brow wrinkled.

"These symbols have been found in a lot of places," he said. "Let's take a closer look."

His voice was soft, but deep and serious. He reached for a round-brimmed hat before rising. The hat seemed an odd choice for him. His work clothes were always crisp and perfect, even though he spent his hours working in chambers filled with dirt. He was tall and angular.

Kaity tried to hide her infatuation as he moved past her.

"Where was it?"

"She was workin' in the toilets," Liz said.

Kaity gave her friend a glare to freeze the inevitable giggle.

"It's over here."

She led the way back to the corner where she'd been exploring. There, she turned her headlamp on again, focused it, and pointed, then looked back at him.

His eyes had widened and he looked just a bit mesmerized.

"That *is* different," he said. "May I?"

He gestured toward her headband.

She slipped the light off, and he accepted it, holding the lamp in his hand as he knelt beside the wall and carefully moved a finger along the hash marks.

"This may really be something new," he said.

"Would a Druid sneak in and leave a message on a monk's bathroom wall?" Kaity asked.

"Not sure," Liam said. "I've seen a couple of other similar marks, and I've been talking with some others. We're wondering if there might have been a secret alphabet, maybe something only used in this region. You maybe have found a new piece of the puzzle."

He switched off the light and looked over his shoulder at her.

"Don't tell anyone about this symbol yet, okay? Could be something interesting. Don't want whispers going around too early. We have some thoughts about what we might do with them. You know the African student?"

"Sure."

"He's bloody brilliant. He's been makin' some notes, doing some calculations, and we've been talking, a few of us, about doing something interesting with the findings."

"OK," Kaity said, and she had to fight a giggle now. It felt a little exciting to be part of an ancient secret. What fun.

1

Dublin, Ireland—Today

He had to hurry.

Professor Inerney Burke's heart thundered as he headed down the stairs, but not just from the exertion. A man and a woman had arrived unannounced, and without an appointment. His assistant had called, and he'd said he would be right out—he was pretty sure who the visitors were.

He then rose from his office chair in Trinity College Dublin's Department of History, put on his raincoat, beige tartan scarf and a hat and began to gather printouts, clippings and other materials scattered across his desk. These he stuffed into an accordion folder. He didn't worry about the order. Organization could come later.

In his haste, a small plastic item that had been resting atop a paperweight bounced off his desk, ricocheted off his chair arm and disappeared under a bookcase that stood on legs a few millimeters high.

He let it go as less essential and headed for a back exit. He didn't like leaving without finding coverage for his afternoon class in medieval history. It would be the first time in thirty years he'd shirked a lecture responsibility, but circumstances left him little choice. Things seemed on the verge of getting out of hand again.

His heart rate ticked even higher by the time he reached the gray cobblestones leading into the grassy Library Square. Looking over his shoulder as he passed a row of student bicycles, he checked for pursuit. The lack of it offered no comfort. They'd be coming.

He hurried through the arched stone exit onto the street, ignoring the afternoon rain as he waved for a cab. Failing to capture one's attention, he made a left and hurried along to the busy corner of Grafton and Nassau. Pedestrians filled the walkways, traffic buzzed, and he stepped into the flow to lose himself, keeping the file tucked under his coat to protect it from the rain.

He had intended to scan the drawing that had come this morning, storing it digitally for safe keeping, but he'd had no time. The envelope had arrived in the morning post, a printout of a photograph showing a symbol painted on a metal light pole, location undetermined. It seemed to be a warning from some anonymous ally that activity had resurfaced. Strangers on his doorstep had to be related.

Back in the day, the time of the Old Crisis as he now thought of it, even though he'd disapproved, the ideas had seemed intriguing and exciting. The notions behind it all had been stimulating.

Now, with the theories and hypotheses being discussed and dissected in Internet groups with disconcerting signs of belief, everything felt more like a nightmare. Decisions made then had triggered repercussions that rippled all around him.

He looked back again as he waited for the traffic light. The figures that stepped from Trinity's entrance had to be the pair who'd come to visit. They too wore raincoats, a square-faced man who stood head and shoulders above the crowd, and a younger woman, auburn-haired and dressed in a gray plaid skirt and dark boots that matched her overcoat and sweater. She'd probably be considered fashionable, but that was the sort of thing Burke would have to consult his assistant about. Some trends escaped his notice and interest.

Could they recognize him?

It would be easy enough to check his picture on the college website or from other online sources. Did they know him on sight? He couldn't chance finding out by giving them more than the back of his head.

He had to keep moving, had to take at least some steps in case he was captured. Rushing across the street with the Don't Walk sign still on display, he drew a horn honk. Ignoring it, he pulled his mobi from his pocket, raising an arm to protect its face from the rain while managing to keep the folder tight in his arm pit. Almost frantically he searched through his address book, praying he had not deleted the contact he needed, the name of that man he'd met long ago at a conference.

People jostled him as he scrolled the B's, but he ignored them, slumping his shoulders, cupping one hand over the phone's screen and forging onward, glancing up only to check street signs. He made a right when he saw the street name he wanted, turned and jogged down the less crowded sidewalk until he reached another corner, then another turn. The creak in his knees had to be ignored.

Bells rattled on the shop door when he found it, putting his weight into it. A girl with straw-colored hair, young enough to be one of his students, stood behind the counter. He'd met her. What was her name? Best to be polite.

"Nelda, I'm looking for Mr. Redmond," he said, pulling off his rimless glasses to shake away raindrops.

Her gaze locked on his face for a second then flicked down to the bulging folder under his arm, taking it in. Then a greeting smile flickered onto her lips.

"He's in the back—inventory work. New arrivals and the like."

"Could you get him please?"

She disappeared through a curtain.

Finding the name he sought archived on his phone, he pulled it up and began to tap a message. The students could do these things so much more easily. His fingers felt stiff and heavy, the aches in the joints intensified by the damp cold of the afternoon. He made mistakes, didn't bother to correct them, just concentrated on getting his fingertips to convey enough meaning.

"Inny," came his friend's voice.

He looked up to see a gray-haired figure in a charcoal sweater.

Redmond looked older and thinner than when he'd seen him last. How many months? Perhaps he was recently recovered from an illness. No time for small talk.

"It's been a while," Redmond was saying.

"I wish I had time to chat longer," Inerney said. "Can't."

He pulled the package from under his coat.

"Safekeeping?"

Redmond looked at the offering with a wrinkle of his brow. "What?"

"I'll call you later to explain. Just get this locked up somewhere, and I was never here."

Redmond looked at the girl, then at the professor again, jaw sagging.

"Is this about…?"

Burke didn't want to say more, and he didn't want the package he now held. Inerney just shook his head slowly. *Sorry, Reddy, no other way.*

Finally, Redmond gave a nod, resigned.

"Certainly," he said. He took the package, nodded again to Inerney's thanks then watched his friend head out the door.

Inerney had almost finished his message as he stepped into the rain. He took a second to check for his pursuers. Seeing nothing, he turned again, and headed toward the Liffey.

He checked the words on his screen one last time, cupping a hand to shield the phone. Did they make sense? They'd have to.

Frm Inerney Burke- met at conferenxe. Your attention needed on matter discssed. Mst talk soon!!!

He hit send, shoved the phone back into his pocket and rushed on into the rain.

2

Jobstown, Southwest Dublin

Detective Aileen O'Donnell of Garda's Special Detective Unit ignored the rain pelting her blue-and-yellow coat and checked the Velcro at her waist, making sure her ballistic vest was secure as an officer in front of her readied the battering ram. Her father had died from a bullet that had found an artery in spite of body armor, so she always checked the details within her control. That had never led to her being assessed as risk-averse at the An Garda Síochána's college, however. If anything, she'd come to be known in her training days as someone who'd step onto a high wire if the situation demanded it. That earned her respect with few realizing the dark streak buried somewhere deep inside her. Her father's life being snatched away had led her to feel there was little worth in avoiding danger. If the reaper wanted you, he'd find you.

No counselor had ever scribbled fatalism on her record as an assessment of her personal philosophy, but that might have come close to accuracy. She'd encountered the word in a philosophy class and had tried reading about it until she'd tired of deciphering academic language with all of its propositions and premises and decided to rely on her gut. She'd formulated her own unofficial credo, cataloged and defined only in her head.

Deep down, she found it hard to believe anyone could really influence the inevitable or alter a course of events already set into motion. The best you could do was keep your head low and forge ahead, getting a handle on things you could manage and preparing for likely grim outcomes. Perhaps that was a little more gloomy than fatalism. Maybe she was the truest form of a pessimist.

To combat that, she often reminded herself above all Ireland's police were named as the guardians of peace, and the Special Detective Unit was perhaps responsible in that realm most of all. Counter-terrorism investigation and related duties fell to them. Duties just like these she was engaged in at the moment.

Lifting her walkie she pressed TRANSMIT even as rain began to weigh down her hair's unruly blonde waves. O'Donnell didn't allow herself to be beautiful. Granting her hair its right to be a wild, unkempt array of curls, she mitigated the fine bones and cast of her features with a stern look that struck fear into the hearts of suspects and drew sober respect from fellow officers, those males who might otherwise give her a difficult time. That was the goal. Decrease bullshit.

A few indelicate nicknames had formed behind her back, such as Thundering Bitch, the most polite of the collection. She was aware of those remarks and bore them without second thought, preferring them to any alternative.

"Curtains are drawn." The response was from Daly, who was commanding the Emergency Response Unit. "We can't get a sight inside the apartment, but we know at least two men are in there."

"Should we hold?"

"I can't say circumstances are going to improve but we don't have eyes on them."

"Weapons and equipment haven't been moved?"

"Not unless they have a teleporter. Nothing's come out the front or back."

"We ready to knock?"

"At your command."

She lowered the unit, rested her rifle's retracted stock against her hip and looked at the man beside her, Inspector George Crowell, who nodded back. The Garda's Special Detective Unit had developed credible leads that what the press would refer to as rogue Republican dissidents had a weapons cache in this small, mundane gray apartment just a few blocks from City Centre.

The SDU had rolled out a response team once chatter had developed that either movement of the weapons was planned or that some kind of attack was imminent.

Reminding herself what would happen would happen, she lifted her walkie. "Forward."

A man in black tactical gear slammed the ram into the wooden door, splintering it with seeming ease. The stun grenade flash came a second later, tossed in by the officer at his shoulder. The heartbeat after that, a hasty flow of black-clad men with Heckler & Koch assault weapons ready streamed through the doorway.

O'Donnell held her position, observing, shifting her rifle to the crook of her arm, fingers flexing around the stock. She felt the rush of adrenaline. She could almost sense its flow in the systems of those men in the first wave.

She listened to the movement, to the footsteps, to breathing, to the sound of doors kicked inward, the softer sounds of weapon straps and components rattling. All of it rose above the hiss of the increasing rain.

In another heartbeat, movement in the window of the apartment the men had targeted caught her eye. Her actions began a split second sooner than they might have...

...as shattering glass interrupted quiet precision. She looked upward to the source. The man in the second-floor window clutched a rocket launcher. Compact, black metal. He balanced it in one hand because his other was wrapped in a length of cord.

He stepped into air, swung from the window, the launcher aimed toward the building entrance where a file of police was still moving through the doorway. The blast, even if erratic, would be devastating.

"Reports didn't indicate that level of firepower," George shouted.

O'Donnell's heart pounded. Of course the reports hadn't specified the unpredictable, that some arms dealer would throw in a bonus bit of destruction. You never knew what kind of weaponry was floating around even these days.

O'Donnell was no sniper, but she stayed current on all her qualifications, and she had only seconds. Dropping to one knee, she put the rifle against her shoulder and aimed for his throat in case he wore body armor as well. One of those things they drilled into you.

She hadn't planned on needing to fire any distance. Holding her breath, she squeezed the trigger. Prayed.

Muzzle fire blazed into the rain. The weapon thundered.

And in the next seconds, the slug tore through flesh and ripped arteries, producing a crimson shower that spilled down across the man's chest, soaking his clothes and sending red rain-drops onto the concrete below.

The officers at the rear of the procession looked up at him, raised more weapons, rapid-firing weapons that began to spew. His body jerked, as if he were an odd marionette twisted into an arrhythmic dance. Or a church aspergillum, spreading not holy water, but a spray of gore.

In seconds it was over. The rocket launcher dropped, unfired, into an officer's hands. Good catch.

The riddled remains stilled, except for the dripping blood. That continued.

3

"Why did this go so wrong?"

The silver-haired man's face probably always had a bit of a ruddy complexion, but it had turned redder as he scanned the street across from the police cruiser that had whisked him to the crime scene. Television cameras from beyond a cordon were aimed at the building where the terrorist's body still dangled.

"Why is he still up there? You've had time to collect what you need. Get him down. What are you waiting for? The maggots to come?"

It wasn't clear if he spoke literally or if that was how he felt about the press. O'Donnell had never met him, but she recognized Deputy Commissioner Darce Sheehan, someone high up on the food chain. His formal uniform was flawless, every crease pressed and button in place.

"Who was in charge of the operation?" he demanded, leaning to only a couple of inches from the face of a superintendent who'd been called out shortly after the scene had been secured.

Heads nodded her way, and the man wheeled and stomped toward her.

"How did this go so wrong?" he repeated. "In Jobstown of all places."

He towered over her, and she found herself staring up into his salt-and-pepper mustache, though his hard black eyes were what demanded her focus.

"Didn't you have intelligence up front, to know what these men would be capable of?"

"With due respect," O'Donnell said, "no one expected we were knocking on Batman's door."

"Looks like you found him anyway and strung him up for everybody to see."

A group of officers in yellow jackets had moved in to lower the body to a set of officers and crime-scene technicians in white jumpsuits on the sidewalk.

O'Donnell tilted her face toward her feet as words spilled on her. Self-defense was pointless at the moment. There would be time for that. For the moment, she just needed to be absorbent. The verbal discipline didn't matter. She felt blood rush to her face, knew her skin was as ruddy as the superior's, but she clenched her teeth and willed herself not to show any emotion she could control. And she willed herself not to cry. Definitely not to cry.

She knew, and her father had always told her, a Garda officer, a female officer, couldn't afford that emotional outlet, no matter what the stress, no matter how dire the situation. Never let 'em see you cry.

"We've tried everything from gas to LRADs to quell violence. Couldn't you have just called 'em out?"

That wouldn't have worked here. He knew it, but she reminded herself as the man spat more words that this would pass and the official proceedings were what mattered. She'd acted properly. She'd followed orders. Their goal had been to rein the terrorists in before they did any damage. They'd succeeded in that, and bloodshed had always been a possibility.

They might try to make her a scapegoat, but it wouldn't be easy, and there was no reason to help that cause by counter-attacking. If she could remain calm with someone dangling over her head trying to kill her and her comrades, she should be able to do the same under this rain of verbal abuse.

Let him vent, let them get the body down and let them take her statement. Then she could go home and any emotion that showed there wouldn't matter. She could cry if she needed to.

"I asked if we had an ID on the body yet."

Sheehan had wedged that in amidst the diatribe, and she'd been so focused at remaining stoic it had almost slipped past her.

"He was living under the name Aidan Stephenson, but we believe him to be Rhys Sanders. He's a suspect in a plot related to bombings in Galway last year, and we had intelligence he'd come to Dublin to meet with a rogue group of local boys with cross purposes. They stayed inside when he came out to play, so they're in custody."

"Let's pray he's who you think he is. If he's on a watch list, that might help when the excessive force outcries start in a few minutes."

"There's a cache of arms upstairs that ought to help with that, too. Not to mention the one he had aimed at my men."

"I believe she did a commendable job," a superintendent named Ciarán Donnelly said. He'd always been an advocate and had been standing by, and the moment had finally arisen for him to interject that.

"We'll see about that," Sheehan said, but he'd calmed a bit, and was looking toward the front of the building, assessing what had transpired.

O'Donnell's attention was drawn away from that and the deputy commissioner. A man with red hair and a beard stood near a corner looking on. He had been there for several minutes, a stout man with a stern expression on his upper face.

He wore a dark suit beneath his overcoat and looked official save for the beard, though he wasn't associating with the other officials present, and did not seem to be with the media. What was his interest?

She had to stop contemplating that when she was pulled to a van by a man in a suit. A seat and a paper cup of hot coffee were offered.

"We're gonna take you over to Phoenix Park so that you can provide a statement while events are fresh."

She nodded as she sipped. As the van door slid shut, she saw the red-haired man still standing nearby. He continued to watch as the van pulled away.

"Just give us an order of events," an investigator in a crisp white shirt said, aiming a small digital recorder at O'Donnell's face.

At Garda Headquarters at Phoenix Park, she'd been shuffled into a small interview room. The interviewer had identified himself as Internal Affairs, but crowded behind him were suits and uniforms, civilians from human resources but uniformed assistant commissioners including Sheehan as well. There'd been clamoring for more civilian input on matters like these. She couldn't tell at a glance which ones wanted her head.

She just went over things in order, from the van pulling up and the force piling out to the slam with the battering ram and the swinger's first appearance. From the corner of her eye, she saw that Sheehan had found other things to interest him.

That helped her keep her demeanor calm and her speech matter of fact, but the questions soon strayed into dark territory.

"Do you feel there's anything you overlooked going in?"

"No sir. We were looking for a weapons and explosives cache and we found it."

"Your father was killed in the line of duty?"

"Yes."

"Have you ever found that impacting your judgment?"

That had to come.

"It only makes me more careful."

If they sought a lynch pin for a case against her, she wouldn't make it easy. She sipped the coffee and closed her eyes, slowly drawing in a breath, holding it, then letting go. She'd learned the calming technique long ago. It returned a casual ease to her, and she dealt with the next barrage without betraying any emotion.

Eventually the recorder was switched off and the investigator thanked her, told her to wait for IA to contact her. She'd be seeing a counselor as well. Rest easy.

Sure. And wait for a desk assignment, the expedient solution while things got hashed out. Or, and the pessimism kicked in, while they plotted a way to serve her up.

As they left, she looked for the red-haired man again. She caught no sign of him, but as she walked into the hallway, Sheehan was on the phone, listening to someone.

He looked up as she passed and kept watching, nodding occasionally to whatever was filling his ear.

4

O'Donnell didn't see the man in the black suit again until he arrived on her doorstep early the next morning. As she looked through the peephole, she spotted red beard hair. She suspected she'd have to tell the story yet another time. He'd finished his quiet observation and now stood ready to put her on the grill for one reason or another. Then to usher her into early retirement.

She massaged her eyes and forehead, hoping to clear the numbness of sleep. She'd spent restless hours until sometime past one. Then she'd dozed and drifted into fitful dreams of rushing and carnage. Somewhere in the depths of sleep, the dream had stopped being a repeat of the day's events and become a tempest of pitching waves and dark clouds that masked things peering at her with red eyes. A compulsion to pull back some curtain of gloom nagged at her, as if she sensed the mind of the thing with red eyes, but not much of that stuck with her now.

As her sleep melted slowly, she was left with only lingering and disturbing impressions that she attributed to the after effects of the shooting, something she'd be able to give this guy when the mandatory sessions began.

If he was a counselor. She hadn't expected to begin again so early. Maybe he was another investigator with a report to file. She assessed him as he stepped across her transom, getting a better look than when he'd been standoffish on the street.

Tall, somewhere deep in his fifties, he could have blended into a group of middle-management paper pushers, though he had an ex-military air.

"You want to hear what happened again?" she asked once he'd

flipped some kind of ID that looked reasonably official.

"I need you somewhere else, actually. Immediately. The wheels on the shooting inquiry can grind for a while without you. Why don't you get dressed?"

"Where else, actually?"

"Your … incident frees you up for a special assignment that cropped up overnight and needs someone with your talents."

"What are those?"

"Investigative skills. Proven ability to handle yourself in dangerous situations as they occur. We always have an eye out for good operatives."

"Who'd that ID say you were with, exactly?"

She wore navy lounge pants with a pattern of royal and pale blue flowers along with a loose pullover jersey. She folded her arms now, feeling a bit awkward. Sleepwear had seemed good enough to greet some obligatory counselor. Now she felt like she ought to be at attention and saluting a new boss, as well as pulling her disheveled curls under some kind of control.

"Have you ever heard of the *Aisteach*?"

Ash-tuck. The Irish word rumbled deep in his throat.

"The Garda strange and unusual bureau? I thought it was a joke. Or a conspiracy theory."

"It wasn't. My name is Zachary Rees. You won't find me on the flow charts the public sees, but I'm the equivalent of an assistant commissioner."

She held back an urge to note his full name sounded almost like the possessive of his first. Have you seen Zachary's cap? Have you seen Zach Rees? She folded her lips in to hide the smile.

"That's why you could make a call and get me…?"

"To get you reassigned?" He nodded. "You'll be said to be on administrative leave. That's the boat you'd be in anyway. The usual hubbub's brewin', 'ill-planned, too much force' on our part. A box of South African weapons is unaccounted for after yesterday's carnage. You'll be needin' to lay low and see a counselor, go through the other motions."

He curled one corner of his mouth upward. "But the situation yesterday opens the door for you to serve in a special liaison capacity. Why do you think you were sent home so quickly?"

"I saw my supervisor take the mobi call. Do I have a choice?"

"You can do this or you can sit around here watching *Red Rock* until you're given a desk assignment for the next eon. Want to get dressed and be a police officer or watch a soap about police officers?"

"Join the creepy patrol or sit on my arse? Great options."

She gave her head an almost imperceptible uptick.

"Good, plain clothes, pack your sidearm."

"I hope there's coffee where we're going."

"We'll find some on the way."

He whisked her away from her apartment building in an unmarked car, driving with measured precision. His speed picked up once O'Donnell had a cup of hot coffee from a corner shop.

Her career had moved into shaky territory, so she was handling it with black coffee. Wasn't that how a man would handle it?

That's how her father would have liked it. Right up there with never let 'em see you cry.

She wondered what her mother would have told her. Her mam had passed away when she was so young, memories of her were spotty, and she hadn't had that much of an example of how women reacted to things.

Sliding past buses and around other cars, Rees navigated narrow streets with an experienced confidence, that of a man who knew the turns and knew his vehicle and what it would do in almost any circumstance. He'd been a copper a while. He wasn't concerned with wet pavement. Must've had a fall like hers if he was over the spooky squad.

O'Donnell could respect that.

"You might actually find this interestin'," he said. "We'd been monitoring a potential situation, and it flared up overnight."

"*Seafóid* can grab your attention. Doesn't mean you want to get used to the smell."

Not far from city center, crime-scene tape had been strung in a large rectangle, sectioning off a portion of a grassy area near the statue of the fates in St. Stephen's Green, a grassy park not far from City Centre and major thoroughfares.

The fates, positioned on a block of stone in the center of a small reflecting pool seemed to look on with stoic gazes. Inside the tape, white-clad technical bureau operatives worked busily while uniformed Garda officers and men in suits conferred. An older woman in a sweater stood under an umbrella, holding a dog on a leash outside the tape, talking with uniforms. Her morning routine had clearly taken a grim turn.

Rees led O'Donnell across the grass, past officers and lifted the tape for her to duck under. At the center of the activity, a body was being zippered into a bag.

"Hold on," Rees said.

The tech with a hand on the zipper paused and leaned back, giving Rees and O'Donnell at look at the purple, twisted face on a bloated body. In spite of what she'd seen minutes earlier, her throat clenched.

O'Donnell felt a bit of coffee trying to burn its way back up her throat. One side of the face bulged like a squeezed balloon, while tissue around it faded from purple to black. At the jaw, a portion of flesh seemed to have been peeled back from red layers of muscle. At first she thought the man had been strangled by the scarf around his neck, then she decided it was something much worse.

"What the hell?" O'Donnell gasped.

"Time of death?"

"About two a.m.," said a tech.

"Venom acted quickly?"

"If it's venom, quite quickly," the tech noted, looking back at the man in black. "Like nothing I've ever seen."

"What kind of venom?" O'Donnell asked.

"Possibly snake venom," Rees said. "St. Patrick must have missed one."

5

"That was a thirty-eight-year-old businessman from Ballsbridge two weeks ago," Rees said. "Now on to the next set of photos."

O'Donnell watched the slender visitor in the gray Savile Row suit tap notes into his computer tablet, not changing expression as lurid images of another swollen, purple body zipped into view to replace the previous victim on the large screen at the front of the conference room.

"This one was found near St. Stephen's Green this morning," Rees said. "Elderly Trinity professor."

O'Donnell sat at the end of the table in a small meeting room. They were in an indistinct building tucked away a few blocks from Garda headquarters at Phoenix Park. Outside, the building had looked like a warehouse with no distinct markings or signage. She'd probably been past it before without noticing. That must be by design.

Things had begun to feel a little stranger once they stepped through the front door. A glass case that looked like something out of the Natural History Museum stood as a focal point in the lobby. Inside, an antler headdress rested on a faceless mannequin bust.

As she'd focused on that, a figure in a black robe, almost like a nun's habit had glided past to disappear down a corridor, offering just a glimpse of a hard silver mask that seemed to fit tightly against the face.

O'Donnell had also spotted a pair of men in what looked like hazmat suits rolling a heavy crate with air holes on a dolly through a secured doorway.

Focused on them, she almost stepped on a scurrying form she thought to be a dog. At first. She held a foot in midair and tried to balance, as she looked down at the spherical, glowing blue-green form that scrambled across the tile on little, reptilian feet.

What the...?

She then almost collided with a woman in a lab coat who hurried from the mouth of a hallway, holding a small, hand-sized smart phone of some sort.

"Bodie's in a hurry. Gotta keep up with him."

Rees had steered her forward as she looked back over her shoulder at the scene. What floor of the loony bin had she stepped off on?

Everyone here seemed to wear badges that had to be scanned for access. Everyone except her and the man in the nice suit, who also seemed to be a visitor.

Uniformed officers had accompanied the man in—tall, dis-tinguished looking, silver haired. Aging without seeming too old. He'd introduced himself with a crisp and deep, British accent: "Professor Geoffrey Bullfinch." Apparently a car had picked him up at Dublin Airport while she and Rees had surveyed the crime scene.

He had settled in quickly and seemed to be looking at small details as more pictures scrolled past, offering the St. Stephen's Green victim from a variety of angles on the grassy patch.

"Is this anywhere near the zoo?" someone asked. A handful of men and women in suits and business attire were scattered around the table.

"Not far, but they weren't missing any massive vipers from the reptile house," Rees said.

Some of the staffers tapped notes into laptops. A few seemed to prefer a more old-fashioned approach and scribbled on note pads. They looked more like they belonged in an accounting department than a police station.

"I suppose whatever did that might have dined on a lion or

penguin before it got to a cyclist if it had," one man said, staring at the image.

"Toxicology?" Bullfinch asked.

"Reptile, but not quite matching any known variety. Acts like a neurotoxin, the nasty stuff a North American coral snake delivers."

"Injected?" Bullfinch asked. O'Donnell couldn't quite make out the accent. Was it Northern? Maybe it sounded slightly less British this time. Had he spent a good deal of time in America? Something in the body language suggested that also, although O'Donnell couldn't pin it down.

"Syringe. Needle marks near the base of the skull in each," Rees said.

"Any indication the venom was synthesized?"

"It's hard to tell. The reports are in your data files," Rees said. "And shared with O.C.L.T. labs."

O'Donnell glanced at notes air dropped to her phone. They included a couple of paragraphs. She started reading what O.C.L.T. stood for.

"We were actually checking on that front to see if you had seen anything like it," Rees said, directing his statement toward the professor. "Then the word came through that you were in Dublin, so your people asked that we have you over."

O'Donnell had never heard of the Orphic Crisis Logistical Taskforce before Rees mentioned it on the way in, but then she'd thought the Garda's sub rosa unit for unusual crimes was legend. Modestly funded, she was learning, it was kept quiet since part of its work was to deal with unusual incidents before panic ensued. Almost informally at first it had been dubbed *Aisteach*, the Irish word for strange, peculiar or weird. It was said with slightly more irony than O.C.L.T.'s almost acronym mentioned in her notes: OCCULT.

If this wasn't a loony bin, she'd stepped into a strange corner of the world. She looked toward one exit. An odd blue fish with a pronounced knot on its forehead glided about in an aquarium beside the door. Why'd they keep that in here?

As she looked at it, the fish made a turn in the tank and swam near the glass, one eye focusing on her as if it had sensed her notice. She turned away quickly. Then she felt strange and ridiculous. This place unsettled her.

"So do you think this professor's text to you was related to our strange serpent deaths, Mr. Bullfinch?" someone asked.

"I'm not sure it is, but the urgency and overall serendipity led to my being asked to check it out. I met Professor Burke at a myth and folklore symposium a number of years ago in California."

"The conference referred to in the text?"

"Exactly. He approached me about what he called a folkloric phenomenon he thought might be occurring."

"Did he elaborate?"

"Not with a lot of specifics at the time except to say he was growing mildly concerned about some…ripples, possible paranoia."

"We don't know more than that?" Rees asked.

"Not really. The professor said he was initially interested in it from a scholarly viewpoint, curious, he said, about the nature of belief in phenomenal legend in a rational age."

"How so?"

"Again, he didn't go into detail, but it seemed to focus on the way myths appear to adapt, or how contemporary events or urban myth might be incorporated into belief. Faeire abductions or old hags turn to Grays or Nordic aliens who visit your bedroom at night. Things with pseudoscientific underpinnings become more palatable than supernatural beings to the modern mind."

"I know the link is thin," Rees said, "but I wonder if it could have another impact on the modern mind. Do you think we could have a serial killer acting out some ancient rite? Or anything in that vein? So to speak?"

"Given these deaths, I'd say it's possible."

"Is that like a ritual from any group you've ever heard of?"

"Asian, African, Greek, even Nordic, speaking of. You have a lot of snake-worshipping groups to choose from," Bullfinch said.

"Any of those kill people with venom?"

"Not as a rule of thumb, though you could see how a twisted mind might get from offerings to a giant snake god to a human sacrifice with synthesized venom. The preparation of the toxin might even take on a ritualistic element, though that might be a bit off the wall for an official report."

"Wouldn't synthesizing the toxin we're seeing be a fairly sophisticated process?"

"Somewhat. I'm told O.C.L.T. labs are still trying to break it down to figure out what it would take. Discretion is always helpful in matters like this." Bullfinch kept tapping his screen as he spoke, zooming in on a shot of a body he'd opened. Then he turned his pad around, indicating the spot he'd enlarged. Dirt near a lifeless hand appeared displaced.

"I was looking at this photo provided to me. It's possible those marks were made by fingertips."

"It's not much of a mark," O'Donnell said. "Not a word. Could be just scratches in the ground. Death throes."

"Grass had to be pulled back to give him a canvas. Perhaps a symbol was marked there," Bullfinch said. "Is the crime scene preserved?"

"It's taped off, but that won't be covered or protected because it wasn't noticed."

Bullfinch flipped through all of the photos.

"No other shot gives a better view. Could we take a look before it rains? In case?"

"We have to start somewhere," Rees said. "You two up for a drive back over there?"

His gaze focused on O'Donnell.

"What are you thinking this might be?" O'Donnell asked.

"Let's look for the symbol," Bullfinch said. "If I'm wrong, any contemplation is wasted energy."

20 Years Ago

"*The markings are supposed to be extensive.*"

Kaity smiled, as she watched the young man, Liam, in front of her. He'd been keying data into a computer work station. He turned from the keyboard and screen and looked at the single report page.

"Who else has seen this?"

"I brought it to you first when I took the call."

They'd both been assisting at the main offices of Kilduff-Power Archaeological Trust, and had started riding to the location together on weekday mornings when they didn't have classes.

"No one's explored this site?"

"It's been looked over and documented, but he's saying a wall collapsed."

Liam looked up at her, expression stern and earnest.

"Let's keep it to ourselves for the moment, have a look. Get some pictures, see if it fits into Keon's extrapolations. Maybe it fills in some gaps."

6

Castle Cluin sat on the River Shannon's edge in a spot once defended by Vikings. Rebuilt numerous times over the centuries, it stood as a remarkably well-preserved tower house, walls topped by jagged merlons and crenels. In its day, a defensive fortress of gray stone, now it had become a tourist destination, focal point of a re-created medieval village with actors and livestock giving a realistic though sanitized depiction of the past. Tourists didn't care for growths on the cheek or the smell of peasant folk.

Freya Turnbull had grown up in Ireland, but she learned the terms merlons and crenels from the tour guide as she and her companion approached the castle along a narrow path, blending with the tour group or attempting to as the gaggle strolled from a pair of buses looking anachronistic in the parking area.

Freya had gained knowledge right alongside the tourists including Patty Dowell, Patty from Paddock Lake as some of the other tourists seemed to have dubbed her. Even on the short journey, they talked about her. In whispers. With giggles. Patty was nosey and a know-it-all it seemed.

Merlons were the upright portions of the wall's jagged upper border. The spots where castle defenders could shield themselves as they prepared for onslaughts. Crenels were the notches between the merlons where archers might position themselves to fire. Freya cataloged that tidbit for what it was worth.

Patty said she'd share it with her husband when the tour returned to Dublin.

He was in sessions all day for the economic summit in which he had been sent to participate by his bank back home, which wasn't Paddock Lake but Minneapolis these days. She spilled a lot of details on a short walk.

Freya said Bailieborough was her hometown. Sounded good enough and no one else was from there. She'd left the real town of her birth behind years earlier, and no one on this trip needed to know it. She just needed enough detail to keep Patty happy.

She seemed to be as she spilled more than anyone needed to know about Douglas, her husband who she met at the University of Minnesota where he'd been studying accounting, and she'd been taking courses at the college of design, thinking she might go into fashion design of some sort.

Freya's companion, who croaked the name Jaager if anyone asked, listened to Patty's prattle, as he did most things, with quiet, stoic disinterest.

It was as if he'd left his body, fleeing while Freya had smiled at Patty's tales of how her husband had begun working his way through the ranks at Wells Fargo, cold-calling potential clients in the beginning, a job he hated.

Fifteen years later and here she was, seeing the world at last as she'd dreamed of in Paddock Lake where their sons were freezing their asses off with her parents so she could be here learning about castle defenses.

Quite a journey. Freya's hadn't been quite so far, but her path was going to have more of an impact on the world, soon. They'd pick up on the news of events, even in dear old Paddock Lake.

She just had to keep blending in with the Pattys and others.

That might be easier said than done. As they moved on, Patty kept looking at them. They stepped slowly past decorative cannons just inside the front wall, and she kept trying for a look at Jaager's features hidden in part by large, round rose-tinted workman's sunglasses.

Dammit, something had tipped her despite what should have been Patty's countervailing interest in herself and over-sharing.

That wasn't good. Freya looked average enough. Jaager didn't need extra scrutiny. Certainly not the level Patty was giving him as the group inched into a great hall where a violinist in medi-eval attire re-created a tune that might have been played for some previous resident, though perhaps not on the same instrument. What would have been used? A mandolin?

At least his outfit seemed authentic but neither tune nor authenticity could break Patty's attention. In a way, Freya couldn't blame her. Jaager was a real oddity. More than six feet, he kept the hood from the hoodie he wore under his gray over-coat draped over his head, obscuring his features. Even when he wasn't trying, he gave off a sense of quiet menace.

Freya believed she looked a little more average in compari-son, especially now since she was keeping her scarf over her hair, striving not to leave anyone with distinctive impressions like wavy hair or ruddy cheeks to recall. She tried to appear inter-ested in the music and patter from the tour guide, tried to just blend in.

As the violinist completed his tune, she slipped a small map from her coat and ran a fingertip across it, tracing the castle lay-out. Letting her hands fall to her sides, she nudged Jaager and tilted her head toward a doorway near a tapestry and display of antlers.

As a new tune began, they both looked around a bit. One more turn toward Patty revealed she still watched them. They had to keep moving. Maybe she wouldn't follow.

Exiting into a stone corridor, they hurried to a rounded stair-way then slipped through an entry arch and through slashes of sunlight from a sliver of a window.

Would the fates let Patty take an interest in the next song or would she be headed in their direction? They had a timeline, oth-erwise waiting for a better moment might have been advisable.

As they put the crowd further behind, the tour guide's voice carried as he recounted the musician's credentials which included Julliard. *Fascinating, Patty, stay and take it all in.*

On the next floor, they exited. The narrow rectangular lamp blazed over the glass case, illuminating the stone on display, just where brochures said it would be, a few yards from the stairway mouth. As they approached it, the woman saw a small inscription noting that it pre-dated even the first structure on the Castle Cluin site and that its markings, characters that looked almost like etchings of blades, were not fully understood.

The woman glanced right then left before turning to the man. "It's clear. Go."

The case seemed free of alarms. The man slipped a slender set of lock-picking tools from his pocket and began to work on the simple padlock that secured the lid. The woman stood in a position that partially blocked the view of his efforts, acting as if she were browsing a brochure, just a tour group member thrown off course.

Just as the lock popped open, a single hard click echoed along the corridor. The woman realized it had to be a shoe heel clicking on the stone floor. They'd been followed.

Patty stood frozen a short distance along the corridor. Freya looked her way, and for several seconds Patty just stared, looking like her lungs had stopped working.

Freya smiled. Exploiting Patty's shock at being caught, she stepped forward politely, keeping her body between Patty and the man. Maybe this could be salvaged.

"Lost?" she asked.

"Just looking…"

She was indeed, past Freya at…

…her companion. He held the stone now.

Patty tried to conceal her look of alarm but her eyes betrayed her. She knew she had failed.

The woman slipped toward her, grasping a lapel.

"Now, now, no reason to get upset."

She slipped her right hand into her coat pocket.

"We're on official business. You should get back to the group."

Patty's gaze shifted, moved from eye to contact, tracking downward, lips trembling as she spotted the needle. She froze for a second, breath catching again after it had just re-started.

She knew what was about to happen.

Panicked, she lifted a forearm, raking her lapel from Freya's grasp. Then she spun, hastening toward a connecting hallway, not worrying about her heels clicking anymore. She wanted to get attention.

She had to be stopped before she cried out.

Freya bolted after her, and shot a hand forward. For a second, Patty seemed perplexed that her forward momentum had been interrupted. Then she began to thrash against the hold on the folded-down hood of her coat.

Freya yanked her backward while surprise still offered advantage. She pressed in on her, forcing her against the jagged stone of a wall.

Patty whimpered. "Please, I won't…"

"Hold still."

She flailed arms and worked again at a scream as the protective cap on the syringe needle was flipped away with a thumbnail.

"Wait, I didn't see…"

The needle moved past Patty from Paddock Lake's now-terrified eyes and her cheek, and sent a sting through her neck. In the next second, her jaw sagged.

Something was coursing through her and she knew it. The jaw closed and tightened. She began to strain for air as the cylinder's contents flowed into her bloodstream.

She wouldn't be telling this story back home for the Junior League. People would read about her, but there'd be no quotes explaining the attack.

Her husband back at the economic conference would wonder what had happened. So would anyone else waiting back home…

Freya used her grip on the lapel to lower her to the floor, letting go without gentleness. Then she looked to Jaager with a jerk of her head.

"It was quick and quiet," she said, when he looked on without expression.

Pocketing the stone, he turned to the stairway again.

Better create a distraction so they could get out of here. She shouted.

"Help, help, someone has fainted."

She was moving then, as footsteps began to clack along the corridor.

In seconds, she was on Jaager's heels, taking steps downward two at a time then back to casual for the stroll to the exit.

"Hold on there, we're going to ask that no one leave."

They were near the arched passage to the parking lot when the shout rolled out from a man in a billowy white shirt and brown breeches. In spite of the attire, he sounded no-nonsense and was big enough to matter. A second later he was joined by another man in period dress.

Jaager looked to Freya who gave him a slight nod.

His hand shot under his coat and he pulled out a machine pistol, compact but menacing. He didn't wave it about long. He aimed it slightly upward and spewed a burst into the air. Slugs bit into stone, sending up bursts of smoke and dust.

That froze the peasants and sent a titter through the throngs of nearby tourists. Seizing that moment, they hurried through the exit, not looking back but expecting they had a few moments before they were followed.

7

The crime scene remained cordoned in St. Stephen's Green.
O'Donnell slipped on an official baseball cap and a blue
jacket with gold markings before leading Bullfinch across the
grass toward the lone uniform standing sentinel. The cap served
to make her look official and cut through crap but also to contain
her curls a bit and help her look nondescript in case any television cameras or anyone who might recognize her as the trigger-
fingered officer were looking on. People were keeping back from
the crime scene, but the area was well-traveled.

When they reached the blue-and-white tape that fluttered in
the crisp breeze, she swept up an arm to raise it high for Bullfinch's passage, lifting it over his Homburg and letting him step
under. She took the moment to observe his movements. For his
age, he didn't seem too creaky. She wished she could get a better
read on what he was thinking. Usually she was good at that sort
of thing, but this gentleman was stoic and betrayed little.

"The body was over here…" she began, but Bullfinch already
had his tablet out, using the photo to guide him. After a bit of
pacing in the general area, he found the spot he'd seen on the
photo and crouched.

O'Donnell moved to his side and looked at the patch of
ground he studied. A lot of people would have dismissed it as a
piece of a footprint on ground that had escaped from the grass
covering, but distinct lines were clear in a small marking. It
looked like a variation on a Greek letter like Xi or one of those,
several lines intersected with angles and edges not likely to have
occurred by happenstance.

"Do you think it was left by the victim?" O'Donnell asked.

"Very likely."

"Do you recognize it? Was he trying to say something in a language only professors know?"

"It resembles markings I have seen," Bullfinch said, splaying his fingers a bit among blades of grass, peeling them back just enough to snap pictures with his pad.

Still keeping things close to his chest. If he'd been a suspect in an interrogation room, she'd be ready to take his coffee away about now.

"Ready to share? If you're not speculating any longer?"

She couldn't be sure if he just didn't trust her, had a problem with women in general, or thought she was an idiot. She couldn't help but resent the latter. She'd sweated out her high school test results, but she'd cleared it and the Garda academy. She might not have been as cerebral as a professor, but she managed.

She'd have to quell that. He remained too matter-of-fact for her to determine for sure.

"For the moment, let me say I think this could be cause for great concern. Perhaps we need to talk to someone who'd had recent contact with Professor Burke."

Okay, he needed her badge. Maybe that was a start for working together.

Alison Syn, Inerney Burke's student assistant at Trinity, poured over a stack of essays in a small cubbyhole with a desk. She looked up when O'Donnell and Bullfinch entered the room and introduced themselves, keeping affiliations vague. O'Donnell conveyed police officer without effort and offered a little glint of her shield before putting it away.

"Academics must go on," the girl said, tapping the papers, before she stood to offer a hand.

She was under twenty-five, not terribly tall with shoulder-length hair somewhere between brown and blonde, and less of a librarian type than O'Donnell would have imagined.

The girl's eyes were a pale shade of blue and her nervous smile formed dimples. Firm lips, well-defined features. Smart gray pullover; black skirt; pale, casual jacket. It suggested an effort at being taken seriously while being aware she was attractive. O'Donnell could identify with that.

"The secretary said you were the last person to interact with Professor Burke the last time he was in the office."

"If interact is the right word. He didn't say much before he left again."

"Once he heard strangers had come to see him?"

"Exactly."

"I need you to try to recall impressions, or anything that might help us. Had he seemed upset before that?" O'Donnell asked.

"Maybe a little agitated. It seemed to start with whatever he got in the morning mail."

"And you'd sorted the mail?"

"The secretary would bring his in. I'd open it for him. It's all so routine, you don't hold on to the details, you know? I think I asked if he wanted tea as he went through it, and he waved me off."

"Was he usually abrupt?"

"Usually pleasant coupled with slightly grouchy and, you know, focused on his work. Figured he'd just take his tea at eleven."

"Your best impression of him yesterday morning," O'Donnell said. "Think carefully."

The girl's eyes tilted slightly upward and to one side, searching, then she moved her head a bit, side to side. "Something had caught his attention that morning."

"Do you remember anything about the letter that seemed to set him off?"

She brought a hand to her face, resting it across her mouth as her eyes focused somewhere other than the room. "I didn't pay it much attention. It was one more piece of postage along with magazines and conference circulars."

O'Donnell didn't really like the gestures she was reading, but she let it slide.

"Return address?" she asked.

"Not sure."

"He definitely didn't leave it behind?" Bullfinch asked.

She chewed her lower lip. "I heard him fumble around before he left. I thought he was straightening up since he had visitors waiting, but he must have been making sure he grabbed some things before he made his exit out our back way, although he never really seemed settled in all morning. Something about it had him agitated."

O'Donnell watched her features carefully. Had Burke asked her to withhold something?

"No mention of where he was going?"

"I don't recall him saying anything."

"Did he have any usual hangouts?" O'Donnell asked.

"The library. He loved research. Pub wise? I'm not sure. He was particularly good friends with Professor Shea. He's one who could tell you more."

"Did Professor Burke ever speak of the Nāga? Did you ever hear him mention that or get a research assignment along those lines?"

O'Donnell studied the old guy as well as she could from the corner of her eye. What did he know? Did she need to give him a good shake?

"Never a research assignment. Never a mention that I recall. What's it mean?"

"Just a myth he might have been interested in," Bullfinch said.

"Myth sounds like the kind of thing the professor might take notice of any time, but I never got any word of that."

"All right," O'Donnell said. "We have your name if we need more."

Bullfinch seemed focused on something on the desk, a

doodle on the edge of a bit of notepaper, a memo from Burke on closer inspection. It might have been a random set of pen strokes or scores from a tic-tac-toe game, but the man studied the lines carefully.

Slipping his tablet out, he snapped a photo of the mark, and then his fingers danced on the device's face for a second.

"What are you doing?" O'Donnell asked softly. "Is that in the same family of symbols from the park?"

"Possibly. Maybe made absently. We'll keep a record of it."

"You're gettin' a lot of clues here. You want to tell me dots are connectin'?"

"I'm not quite sure yet. Give me just a little while. Professor Burke spoke with me at a conference several years ago. He didn't elaborate, but he said there was something he was a bit nervous about. He was afraid he or some friends had triggered something."

"Years later he's dead, and you're noting a bunch of cryptic symbols and saying funny words. What did he think they'd triggered?"

"He called it a mythological event. He didn't say more."

"People in Ireland dying of snake venom. Does seem mythic. What the hell have we stepped in here, Mr. Bullfinch?"

"We may be figuring that out together. I know we're outside the scope of the true Garda investigation, but can you get us street-camera footage to try and trace Professor Burke's path? Knowing where he was between the time he left his office and wound up dead in the park might be useful."

"I could agree with that," O'Donnell said. "They're probably scanning Grafton Street cams to see who dropped the body. Let's see what our *Aisteach* unit can come up with."

8

"You're gonna to want to see this," Rees said.
O'Donnell and Bullfinch had just climbed back into the
car when her mobi sounded. Both on her phone and Bullfinch's
tablet, an image materialized a bloated body on a stone floor.
The swelling and purple contortions matched what they'd seen
before.

"Where...?"

"Just in from Castle Cluin."

Rees hit another key on his end, and the screens gave way
to an unsteady YouTube video stream. Tourists shrieked and a
hubbub of voices and chaos rippled through a crowd in a stone
hallway. Via a jostled, unsteady lens, a woman in a gray raincoat
pushed through a crowd. She seemed possibly to be following
another blur, bobbing somewhere ahead of her, opening a path
in the throng.

"This the best we have?" O'Donnell asked. "It's like Nessie
footage."

"Analysts are working," Rees said. "We'll know in a while."

Bullfinch was studying the figures, eyes focused, processing.

"See anything you like?" O'Donnell asked.

"Nothing's clear enough."

"We're searching for other video sources," Rees said.

"Interesting you should mention that," O'Donnell said. "Are
you tracing Burke's path in your shop?"

"It takes time to consolidate the footage, but yes. They're
trying to pick him up outside Trinity. It's a game of 'which way
did he go?' Any thoughts about what they might have wanted

at the castle, Professor Bullfinch?"

"Not at a glance. While your analysts are working, maybe we should have a look around there. Is it far?"

"It's not next door, but I'm up for a drive," O'Donnell said.

"Off you go then," Rees said. "I'll buzz you when we have something new."

Police units blocked the roadway leading to Castle Cluin a little over two hours and a drive through the countryside later. A flash of a badge got them past the perimeter, and in a while Bullfinch was crouched at the crime scene while white-suited technicians continued to work.

No signs or symbols were evident at this location, and the spot where the victim had fallen seemed to be a less-than-spectacular stretch of hallway.

"Nothing?" O'Donnell asked.

"Nothing obvious," Bullfinch said. "But something brought our venom purveyors here."

"It's looking like the victim just got in their way."

"Tourist?"

O'Donnell nodded.

"No obvious ties to Burke or other victims. Patricia Dowell. She's what Americans would call a soccer mom, I believe. Husband's at a conference in Dublin."

O'Donnell had spent a while talking to the local authorities while Bullfinch had moved around the perimeter, scanning the antlers, paintings and tapestries that decorated the ancient walls.

He straightened from the spot where the body had been found and looked a few feet away to an intersection of hallways. His gaze seemed to calculate the number of steps, then he moved to the corner and turned.

"Has anyone been up here yet?" he asked, moving to the edge of the glass showcase.

"An odd bit of stone is missing."

Bullfinch and O'Donnell turned to a man with brown hair

that brushed the collar of his sports coat. *Another scholarly type*, O'Donnell thought. She was outnumbered.

He offered a photograph in a clear protective sleeve.

"I'd just been checking our records," he said. "I'm Hayden McKenzie. Curator for the historical exhibits."

"Mean anything to you?" O'Donnell asked, passing the photo to Bullfinch.

"These markings on it, along the edges…"

"Are undetermined," McKenzie said. "But the characters do seem to be an arrangement suggesting language, but it's not Ogham characters."

More slashes and angles.

"Professor?" O'Donnell asked.

Bullfinch's brow had wrinkled as he stared down at the photo.

"I'd concur with that."

He extended a hand and introduced himself to McKenzie. McKenzie smiled politely. He held O'Donnell's hand a little longer and smiled. She forced a smile back and disentangled her hand. No time for that. Should've worn the baseball cap over the hair.

"Is this an isolated piece or do you have others?"

"It's an odd find from what I understand. A farmer's field in the early aughts. Supposedly there are a few others with similar markings and there's been some effort to study and correlate, but they offer only what you might call snippets."

"Has anyone tried to put them all together?" O'Donnell asked.

"Possibly, but I don't know where anyone is with it. We haven't had any requests for a look at this piece in a while. Scholars often keep things close to their chests. Ever hear of the Facsimile Edition of the Dead Sea Scrolls?"

O'Donnell shook her head. Bullfinch nodded.

"Fragments of the Dead Sea Scrolls were controlled by a group of scholars who held back their publication from the Fifties until the Nineties," Bullfinch explained. "It was only when The Huntington Library in California decided to make embargoed copies available via microfilm that the blockade was broken."

"This could be even closer to the chest. There are rumors of more examples of this secret alphabet held by a secretive group of scholars," McKenzie said. "As you know, Officer O'Donnell, in Ireland you can plow a field and find a Viking ship from twenty-five hundred B.C. Sometimes things get found and sometimes the wrong people get there first."

"What are we talking about here? Private collectors?"

"Or some band of scholars who want to hold onto the knowledge until they've amassed what they want to publish," Bullfinch said. "Or something more insidious."

"Why was this thing in plain view if it was so rare and important?" O'Donnell asked.

"They won a bit of a battle here to keep it local vs. shipping it off to Trinity or somewhere. If we hid it away, we'd be as bad as the scholars with their finds under wraps wouldn't we?" McKenzie said.

"Can I talk to the professor alone just a second?" O'Donnell asked, taking Bullfinch's arm.

She tugged him several paces away from the curator and ducked her head slightly.

"These in the photo look like what you found in the park, right? And the marks on Professor Burke's desk."

"These markings seem to be some kind of alphabet." He tapped markings in straight lines on the photo. Then he traced another set of additional marks. "These others are unclear. Might have been brought out with a little more washing and care. We'll run the photo through O.C.L.T. databases and see if we get a match, but speaking of things that get locked away, we may be in undiscovered country here."

"How come you've never heard of this rock?" O'Donnell asked.

"It's an artifact, dear lady, of an obscure or even obfuscated story. I'm not an expert on every rock in every corner of the globe. I'm a student of mythology. Ask me what Quetzalcoatl or Jörmungandr can do, I can fill you in…"

"Wait, who?"

"Show me a few examples of a potentially lost alphabet; I'm scratching my head like you are."

"What does it mean that these symbols aren't familiar to you? If they represent a myth?"

"Probably that it's an odd and isolated myth tied to whatever Professor Burke was upset about."

"One group of Celts around a campfire?"

"Something like that."

"Whatever the story, maybe we need to figure out the locations of similar artifacts, right? Or I suspect more lives are going to be lost."

"No argument there," Bullfinch said. "And if these people collect what they want, there's no telling what awaits us."

O'Donnell's brow wrinkled into a frown. "What are you suggesting here, Professor? I'm talking about killers with a twisted delusion. Are you saying there's something they might do with a bunch of ancient rocks or marks?"

"I'm afraid I am. I've seen a lot of strange things. If these people are willing to kill, they believe there's a prophecy that can be fulfilled. I've seen enough to know we can't rule out the possibility that they're right."

9

When McKenzie was asked if he had any reference of the farmer who'd found the artifact, he not only confirmed that the man was still alive but produced an address. While O'Donnell had wondered if talking to him was worthwhile, Bullfinch had accepted McKenzie's offer to drive them to the location. He warned it would be hard to find, so they piled into his little red Renault hatchback and cruised along a highway past neat single-family dwellings, then past rolling green fields occasionally dappled by crumbling gray stone walls and remnants of ancient structures.

"When I come back to the isles, the sense of awe returns to me. You can drive past things that are a thousand years old," Bullfinch said. "They don't have quite so much of that on view in America. Everything's new."

After a bit of a drive they moved through forestland where nearby, McKenzie informed them, scenes for the BBC-TV series *Ballykissangel* had been filmed. Not long after that, they passed a field where a huge gray speckled draught horse grazed.

Then they turned onto a winding road that stretched through more verdant territory, and after a few turns and a spin through a tunnel of arching tree branches, they came to a small farm house. It felt like the absolute middle of nowhere to O'Donnell.

In the middle of nowhere chasing spooks. What a difference a day makes.

Alfie Morten was in his late fifties, and as the Monty Python troop might have put it, not dead yet. He looked rather vibrant, in fact, with wind-tossed hair still dark atop his head, though it had grayed at the temples. He wore a heavy blue fleece vest over a couple of layers that didn't include a wool sweater. He did have a black-and-white sheep dog following him around the barn beside his house as well, making him almost right for a postcard pose.

"We have one little field we still plough the old way," he said after introductions, hand shaking and expressions of remorse over the theft. "That's where we turned up the stone. Thought it might be meaningful, so we called Mr. McKenzie's office and the local paper came out."

He rubbed a hand across his chin. "Didn't think it was something to kill for."

"We'd love to see the field where it was planted," Bullfinch said. "How'd you come to turn it over to the castle museum?"

"Right thing to do. Same county where it was found, though the museum of natural history in Dublin would have loved to have it, they said."

He opened a gate and let the dog lead the way, and they strolled through grass still damp with dew toward a distant, fenced portion of land.

"Other Garda authorities will be coming eventually," O'Donnell said. "You'll probably be makin' this trip again."

"If it'll help get the stone back, so be it. If you folks are ahead of the game, glad to show you."

"I'm wondering who might have contacted you besides museums, once the story was in the paper."

"Mostly folks like Mr. McKenzie's predecessor and the people from Dublin. I think it was a while later a few other calls came."

"Later?"

"Couple of years really. A man called wondering what we might have done with the stone. Said a few quid might change hands. Said I could always use some *airgead síos* but the stone was already where it needed to be."

They reached a small gate, and he unlatched a chain and

pushed it open, allowing O'Donnell to follow the dog through to the edge of settled rows. The harvest of the field had been complete a while for the year, and the land rested at the moment.

"I guess you've turned the dirt here enough to know there's not more where the first stone came from."

"I'd say that was safe, though it had been turned a few times before the rock turned up. Was a bit of a surprise, but they said it'd probably been here quite a few years, people who came and poked a bit, that is. Couldn't figure out how it came to be here."

"Given the oddness of the markings, from what I've read in the files, they thought it must date to before the Norman invasion, probably before Christianization or concurrent with," McKenzie said.

"If you had to guess?" Bullfinch asked.

"A broad guess, fourth- to seventh-century range."

"Can we get GPS coordinates on this patch?" Bullfinch asked.

O'Donnell gave a slight laugh. "If there's coverage. I don't see that many cell towers nearby."

"We've got it on record," McKenzie said. "We can almost give you the precise point."

"I'm getting a little juice. What are you thinking?" O'Donnell asked.

"Long shot," Bullfinch said. "Just considering the possibility ley lines. We're still in a realm of inquiry where anything could be relevant."

"I'm new to this realm of inquiry. You're going to have to fill me in on ley lines."

"Lines of energy. Often sacred sites, especially in the British Isles, seem to be arranged along those lines. Bear in mind there's some skepticism about that."

"You can count me in those ranks 'til I know more," O'Donnell said. "But you're thinking this stone found here might be lined up with something else?"

"Speculation, but as I said, at this stage anything's possible, or it could matter to our killers, and that's what's really important." He mulled something over for a moment. "Could explain why an errant piece of rock with a strange marking turned up so far off the beaten path."

"Off the beaten path but along a magical energy highway stretches credulity," McKenzie said. Sounded like he was among the skeptics as well.

"In my circles the unlikely commonly surprises," Bullfinch said. "Fringe is relative. Besides if it matters to…"

"I've got coordinates," O'Donnell said. She'd been pacing with her phone in her palm and now stood several paces from the men.

"Well, one form of magical energy worked," McKenzie said.

"It would seem that way to a sixth-century resident anyway," Bullfinch said. "Your suggestion proves one point, my boy."

Bullfinch keyed in coordinates to his tablet from O'Donnell's screen. "Some things scientific can appear magical. Our phones alone might have gotten us all hanged or burned in some cultures."

A map of the British Isles appeared on his screen after a bit of a wait, and a moment later networks of amber lines zigzagged through the mapped territory. Then a little blue dot began to pulse.

"Ah, the app my friend Mack created appears to work offline with your data," Bullfinch said.

"Is that where we are?" O'Donnell asked.

"The blue dot's where we are."

That dot sat right on one of the large amber lines. Others stretched off in multiple directions.

"We follow those, we gonna find another rock with funny markings?" O'Donnell asked.

"Not necessarily, but if we can figure out anything about our killers' desires, we can see where their work lines up and where it might lead. There are probably sacred sites all along these lines."

"Looks like you've got a lot of choices," McKenzie said. "It's really an antique land here. Deserted medieval villages, churches, standing stones, just what you might expect."

"Yes," Bullfinch said. "Just what we might have expected."

"You want to tell me what you might suspect yet?" O'Donnell asked, once she and Bullfinch were alone, back in the Garda vehicle on the return trip to Dublin. She'd stopped trying to hide frustration.

"I'm not sure what I expect or what I'm seeing," Bullfinch said. "Let's try to get our data aligned and then we can develop an informed hypothesis."

The road didn't offer much shoulder, but she tapped the brakes hard, jolting both of them as she edged the vehicle to the roadside and shoved it into park.

"Look, I'm a copper. We've been thrown into working as partners here. Whatever they told ya, I'm not just a gunslinger riding shotgun, Professor. I'm an investigator and I'm trained in intelligence and counterterrorism. You're acting like these folks are building to something. If it looks like we've got what leans toward terrorist activity, I can't work in the dark."

"In the sense that they're possibly perpetrating something worse than Islamic fundamentalists or the IRA, I'd agree on the terrorism front," Bullfinch said.

"Mass poisoning with this venom?"

"That might be a best-case scenario. That could be contained."

O'Donnell draped a wrist over the top of the steering wheel, keeping the car steady while allowing herself a glance at the passenger seat.

"What might be the worst?"

"I've been studying and doing this for a long time," Bullfinch said. "The world is full of secrets. We don't know the worst until we gather more information so I'm hesitant to trigger a panic that could complicate matters. If they merely think something is possible, we're dealing with human behavior we can contain. If that stone they've taken is part of a bigger puzzle that they can unlock and there's something slumbering they can awaken, we've got real trouble."

"Wait, what? What do you think might be sleeping?"

"Based on this venom, Irish legends like Crom Cruach, some of Professor Burke's verbiage at the conference and my personal experience the last few years, coupled with my luck, I'd say a giant serpent's not out of the question."

19 Years Ago

*M*att Snyder felt his brows converge as oiled cloth folded back from the broken stone. He had to study it only seconds to see that it was probably heavy and its shape and markings suggested the tapering near the upper portion of a menhir, a single standing stone with lines etched into its edges.

"A fine piece, wouldn't ya say?"

The man grinned, parting lips over yellowed teeth.

"It's interesting," Snyder agreed.

He studied the markings along the stone's corner with more focus. They were lined with grit and white dust that made them stand out. The angles of slashes that stretched down to the jagged edge of the break were familiar in style, but he thought some looked different. He couldn't deny he'd like an opportunity to clean the stone and do some careful study to try and interpret them and see if they complemented what he'd assembled so far.

He'd like the chance to do that somewhere quiet under a magnifying lamp, making precise measurements. Not in this man's dusty and dimly lit shed. If a secret alphabet had developed then been scattered, he wanted to understand it and be one of the first to reveal it.

"Where'd you find this?"

"That information would be part of the askin' price," the man said, tilting back his tweed cap with a tweak of the brim. He winked a lid closed over one pale gray eye.

He was in his late twenties, sporting as much of a beard as he'd ever grow, which amounted to stubble. He didn't look like a farmer, but Snyder couldn't detect any clues in his neutral street clothes that suggested useful background detail.

He'd asked Snyder by phone to come to this residence at the edge of Drimnagh, a suburb, for something interesting related to his studies. Accepting had seemed odd and dingy at once, but promises of a major discovery lured.

"I was told this was your area of interest. You know I can go somewhere else. Maybe not to as serious an independent scholar as yourself, but to some rich American who'd like nothin' better than to have this in a case in his den fer his drinkin' buddies to admire."

Snyder wasn't sure that was exactly the kind of American who'd want to pick up an artifact, but this definitely belonged in the hands of someone like himself, amateur or not, someone who understood its importance. Not in a showcase overseas.

"Offer's good fer now. Goes up later. Leaves the table in three days," the man said.

Hard-bargain time.

Snyder could try to memorize the markings, but he'd never be certain he had them right, and the error of an angle could make all the difference in a new discovery.

"The price includes the stone and the details of its original location?"

"Sure. You can go poke around there all you like after we've had our handshake. You won't find no more of it that's what you're thinkin' though. I looked everywhere. Didn't find the rest of it."

At least after this, the area could be looked over by serious searchers and not whatever this man was. Snyder reached into his breast pocket. He'd brought an envelope with cash as the man had asked.

Sometimes scholarship, even his brand, meant dingy deals.

"OK, for this, the stone and a map to where you found it. The location matters."

"Certainly, sir. I'll draw it on the back of your hand if ya like."

"A paper will do if you don't have any better coordinates."

"As you said on the phone, I'm not a serious researcher like you, but you should be able to find the spot for what I can give you."

He found a pad of old, brown paper and began to scribble.

A few minutes after the stone had been lugged out to Snyder's trunk, the man in the tweed cap leaned against the window, looking both ways through the glass to make sure the vehicle had departed.

When he felt comfortable that was the case, he pulled a handkerchief from his pocket and began to wipe the gel from his teeth. He'd been assured at the theatrical supply store that it would not damage enamel, but he didn't want it staying on any longer than he needed it. Likewise, he didn't want to swallow much of it.

Once he'd cleared most of the makeup, he strolled into the kitchen and picked up the telephone to dial a number from a piece of paper in his pocket.

"It's done," he said. "I'm about to clear out of here before the owners get home."

"He paid for it?" asked the guy who'd called himself Liam.

"And took it along. It was heavy, and we had to lug it to his car. You said I could add his cash to my fee. I may need it for my back now."

"Keep it. Did he say where he was going?"

"Nah, just anxious to get away with it. He was interested in the markings like you said."

10

A dark sedan waited behind the deserted roadside restaurant, a vehicle larger than average by Ireland standards, driven by someone unconcerned with petrol costs.

The location had been chosen hastily by phone when the woman called in, reporting mixed news, the mishap with the tourist and the triumph of obtaining the stone.

Jaager parked their vehicle near a back corner of the abandoned building and walked around to let her out. He escorted her to the sedan where he took a post, ready to stand guard, one hand holding his thick wrist as his arms crossed in front of him.

As she climbed in a rear door, a man in the back gave the driver a gentle nod, and a barrier slid up between front seat and back. As the woman settled into a seat, the tall man snapped the door closed and stood with hands folded outside.

"Welcome, Ms. Trumble," he said in the soft voice.

"Sir."

"You may call me Malphas."

That had to be an assumed name, but she nodded. The leader of her section referred to him as The Shepherd. That had always been enough for clarity and sir sufficed for her salutation. She'd been told small talk was not expected, and she'd never been comfortable with it anyway.

He appeared ancient, skin wrinkled and loose at the jaw, hair snowy. The black suit looked like it would be perfect for lying in a coffin. For a wake. She could only imagine the watery eyes behind the black lenses of his sunshades.

She'd wrapped the stone in a silk scarf. Placing it between

them, she folded back just enough of the brightly colored fabric to reveal the markings.

Long, skeletal fingers traced the etched characters, and she detected a slow intake of breath that suggested a positive assessment.

"Better than working with photographs," he said.

He gave an almost imperceptible nod.

Freya shifted in her seat. She didn't want the elation to show. She'd done as ordered in all instances to the best of her ability, but the praise ignited a satisfying burn at her core. She wanted to tilt her head back and raise a song, the zealot in her almost overwhelming the calm, efficient demeanor she'd worked to establish and maintain in all her endeavors. In a closed chapter of her life, she hadn't been quite so successful. She didn't want to lose what she'd gained as a believer with a purpose in this new mission.

"Does this give you enough pieces?"

The old man passed the scarf and stone to the figure beside him, a man in dark clothes and a hood whose hands looked younger and less withered. Her section leader called him The Friar.

"This is Balor," the old man said.

The younger one had been so silent Freya had almost forgotten he was there. He folded back the scarf again and let a beam of sunlight strike the stone's swirls and markings.

After a heartbeat, his head bobbed up and down once, slow and grim.

"Is that enough?"

Balor's head turned side to side. Freya had come to expect theatrics.

"We'll need to proceed with seeking the other pieces," Malphas said.

He slipped a hand into his breast pocket and produced a small, flat phone. His thumb clicked a few times on the screen.

"The data is on your handheld," he said. "I'm sure Mr. Jaager is ready to accompany you. Proceed."

So the quest would continue.

11

"This is the stone found in the farmer's field and stolen from Castle Cluin," Bullfinch said as the image McKenzie had provided flashed on the screen at *Aisteach* headquarters.

A gentle motion with two fingers produced a new image, the symbols from the stone, black on a white background, side by side.

"O.C.L.T. analysts took the photos we sent and produced this representation of the characters, then enhanced them and compared what they found to other known alphabets including Ogham markings and characters found in European caves recently by researchers that pre-date what we recognize as established languages."

Another tap of his finger and some of the markings on screen disappeared, leaving only a pair of the hash-style marks which slid together at the center of the screen to sit side by side.

Bullfinch smiled as he realized he had begun to develop some proficiency with electronics at Mack's direction. He couldn't help but be a little proud of himself.

"Some of the markings on the stone were meaningless, but these were mixed in and bear enough similarities to suggest they aren't random."

He clicked again and another symbol appeared beside the three. The similarities were obvious.

"This is the mark from Professor Burke's desk, enhanced from a photo I took of it and sent off."

"He'd seen these or similar markings," Rees said.

"It would appear so."

He clicked again and a few more symbols appeared.

"Stylistically the three new markings seem in alignment with these that our analysts located through various references."

"Where do those come from?" Rees asked.

"These appeared in letters sent to various scholars in Europe and the British Isles about eighteen or nineteen years ago. The letters claimed a scholar had run across various symbols and was beginning to compile them, but he'd run into difficulties, feared he was being followed by shadowy figures with nefarious purposes, and wanted to get the data into the hands of someone knowledgeable."

On the screen, several points of comparison between the characters were now highlighted in yellow—the slashes, a few serifs, and a few other similar alignments.

Rees wrinkled his brow. "Was any research stimulated?"

"No," Bullfinch said. "The letters were generally regarded as a hoax. The source was never identified. They stopped circulating after a couple of years and were largely dismissed."

A new image flared onto the screen. A line drawing of a coiled serpent. Some of the markings were similar to the images already visible.

"By serious scholars anyway," Bullfinch continued. "O.C.L.T. analysts believe these symbols represent similar markings."

"Where's this one from?" Rees asked.

"An Internet site called Stranger Bazaar."

O'Donnell snickered. "Of course it is."

"Brainchild of a couple of conspiracy theorists from London."

"The site claimed the markings were related to an ancient belief that a giant serpent could be awakened."

"Anything grounded in actual research?" Rees asked.

"No, it's all based on rejected ideas and theories."

"So people inspired by hokum related to snakes who may have scared Professor Burke years ago have resurfaced and are killing people for the marks on our farmer's stones and others," O'Donnell said.

"It would appear so."

Rees shifted in his chair. "All or most of it's from Éire?"

"Some of the letters were dispersed further afield, but the markings seem to originate in Ireland."

"Other than connecting snakes and symbols, how does any of this help us find our venom killers?"

"At the moment it only gives a sliver of possible understanding of their motive. We may find more signs of artifacts in Ireland that can help us get a step ahead of them, but the roots of these symbols are not Irish alone. In India there was a race called nāgá, part serpent. That suggests virulence."

"You asked someone about that. Could some of that belief have made its way to Ireland?"

"Connections don't seem to have been made before," Bullfinch said. "What we do often see if we delve deeply enough into cultures is parallel belief. Many cultures have dragons. We can find reasons for that, but if you like conspiracy theories or *Chariots of the Gods* thinking, you can get to the notion that there's something behind the legends, something real that turned up in diverse locations, appearing to different groups and cultures. There's been a lot of study recently in Ireland about the impact of comets on belief, maybe even that the mythic figure Lugh was inspired by sights of comets."

"The locals did the best job they could of telling about what they saw in the world by reflecting it in their art and stories?" Rees asked.

Bullfinch gave him a slight head tick of confirmation. "Something like that."

"Still, snakes in a land with no snakes?" O'Donnell asked.

"You do have accounts of them being driven out," Bullfinch said. "And who knows what the Celts saw? Who knows what artifacts have gone undiscovered or tucked away in sealed-off Neolithic passage tombs? Or what did the Druids really know and what did they do? We're aware of a ritual involving oak and mistletoe to cure ills from one section of Druids, but that's about all. There haven't been many details uncovered about their other rituals."

"You think someone's pursuing lost Druid knowledge?"

"It's a possibility. Julius Caesar and Pliny the Elder alluded to Druid secrets. With the Roman invasion, a great deal of knowledge was lost or hidden."

"Do we think knowledge has been hidden or suppressed?" Rees asked.

"Perhaps someone's sat on discoveries for one reason or another," Bullfinch said. "Fear of what it might lead to?"

"A conspiracy among scholars?"

"Bullfinch was telling me there's been a bit of proprietary behavior among scholars through the years," O'Donnell said.

"I mentioned the Dead Sea Scrolls controversy," Bullfinch said.

"Could Burke have known of something he kept secret?" Rees asked. "We got word the man killed with venom just before Burke was named Nathan Finch. Graduated from Trinity, but then a lot of people in Dublin did."

"Burke was nervous about something. Maybe the killers just thought he knew something and couldn't get what they wanted out of him, killed him in the process," Bullfinch said. "Everything amounts to enough to get O.C.L.T. interested."

"Maybe you two should be talking to more of his friends," Rees said. "There could well be something Professor Bullfinch might pick up on."

"No word yet on a path after leaving Trinity?"

Rees shook his head. "As you can imagine, it's a process even with facial recognition software…"

"Been there," O'Donnell said under her breath.

"…and it was a rainy day."

"Maybe it's back to Trinity then," O'Donnell said. "To rattle the professors' chairs."

"Maybe so," Rees said. "Just try not to rattle too hard. *Aisteach* doesn't need additional complaint calls."

12

Freya watched the blue dot that corresponded with their car glide toward the pin graphic on her mobi. Its movement was barely perceptible, firing her impatience as they travelled through County Fingal north of Dublin. The goal seemed so close, yet each step was slow and frustrating.

A light rain had set in a few miles back to slow progress even more. It fell harder now, but it didn't seem to bother Jaager, who steered around the twists in the old highway with just a wrist resting atop the steering wheel. His expression suggested he was unaffected by the waves of rain splashing on the windscreen, though the shadows made his cheeks look like they were spotted and melting.

He was as committed to the cause as she, but he didn't say much, didn't make conversation, didn't betray any feelings or hint of his anticipation. He just functioned. She could appreciate that, the efficiency, the calm, but his robotic style made long trips dreary. As the meters rolled on, it seemed they were in some perpetual loop, making no progress at all.

She watched buckets-worth of rain slosh down the windscreen and occupied her thoughts with daydreams of their pending results. If traveling with Jaager was boring, changing the world, upending it, giving it a shake was not.

She'd grown up in a little village not that different from the one they were headed for, and things had never changed. Her father had trudged out into his fields day in and day out, covered up on rainy days, bundled up on cold ones. When the sun rose high and blistering, he put on a hat with a wider brim and mopped his brow with a little more frequency and didn't alter his routine much from there.

When she'd first moved to Dublin—to seek work, to escape— people had made fun of her country accent. She'd started then, building her persona, toughening her outer edge, smoothing out her style and her accent, and she'd started a climb in an office job, taking a personal assistant position that had suited her more than shop girl, and she'd begun to learn the ways of commanding respect.

She'd done well for two years, keeping her boss's diary, tending to day-to-day affairs, never missing a detail even as she maintained a rigorous personal regimen that included a daily physical workout that kept her lean and toned. That compounded her stamina and resolve. When other things had been snatched away, her discipline and that personal power had remained. Even after a client from Australia had torn her world apart. She'd been assigned to see to his needs while he was in town. They'd had different opinions about how far her instructions extended. Ultimately the company had sided with the client. She'd been dismissed, dismissed and devastated.

She reminded herself that was behind her. A new calling had replaced what she had lost. She'd found it in coping with the fallout of her dismissal, and she and Jaager were heading toward the realization of new goals. Far more important goals than she'd held as a secretary or personal assistant.

The car turned onto the dirt road they sought, and Jaager steered through a series of twists and turns, navigating potholes and ruts filled with rain until they were facing a little white cottage with a red door and a thatched roof, just beyond a low stone fence. Hills rolled into the distance beyond the structure, disappearing into the mist and rain.

Freya slipped a knit tam over her hair and did a quick check of her makeup before levering her door open. Time for a bit of charm.

She led the way up the stone path to the front door, rapping gently while Jaager took a position at her shoulder. As always, he looked distracted and nonchalant, but she knew he stood ready to act, ready for whatever might greet them.

As it turned out, it was an old man in a tweed cap and heavy turtleneck sweater who answered the door. He looked out, seeming puzzled at first. Then something flickered in his gray eyes.

"You're the folks from the institute."

"That would be us," Freya said. She flashed a smile. "Copley Institute. We were hoping you could show us the markings you found."

"Jack Patterson. Come inside. I have the old photo."

Jaager's features didn't change, but he looked toward Freya, and she could read his impatience. He didn't care about niceties or finesse, but she gave him a "be-patient" gaze, and they followed the old man into his front room.

The same white stone that formed the outer wall was exposed in his living room, avoiding gloom even though the light through the small windows was gray. A few logs smoldered in his little fireplace, and a coffee pot sat on a black metal pad near the hearth.

"Can I interest ya?" he asked. "Or you could have tea or Guinness."

"Just the photo. We're on a time constraint."

"Mind if I have a cup? Old bones and it's chilly."

Freya said that would be fine. He urged them to seats on a wooden bench then poured sludge into a mug. He added a bit of whiskey from a bottle under a cabinet, hoisted the cup toward them and disappeared through a narrow doorway.

Jaager's muscles were taut. Freya sensed the tension at her side, and she could detect tension in his breathing. She put her hand on his forearm.

"No one has to die here," she said.

He turned, and the lenses of his glasses were like cold stone, or at least they seemed that way.

"Patience," she said, though she reminded herself she'd done the killing at Castle Cluin, not him.

"Here we go." The old man had returned with a ragged brown photo album.

He sat on a little wooden chair across from them, flipped past pictures of his younger self with a wife and a few different dogs then and produced a snapshot that had been tucked back in the folds of the album.

"'Twas a long time ago the wall inside crumbled," he said.

The picture wasn't sharp, but it offered a look at a gray and damp stone wall illuminated by a camera's flash, probably an old-style bulb. Markings were etched into the curved surface, some characters clear, but the message, if it was a message, disappeared into darkness above and below the photo area.

"When did you find this?" Jaager asked in his throaty rasp.

"Years ago now. Ah'd almost forgot about it. Told the professors about it back when. They sent some folks out, had me show them the spot, took some photos and seemed interested then, no more."

"No one else has contacted you over the years?"

Patterson chuckled.

"I didn't say that. Didn't hear back from the professors' folks. Now and then some folks you might say were from, uh, the edge. Figured there was some kind of word of mouth that brought 'em. Heard somethin' from someone who heard somethin' from the professors."

Jaager's face turned in Freya's direction, his lips tight, whitening as he pursed them, and a muscle in his jaw rippled.

"What made them 'from the edge'?" Freya asked.

"They were lookin' for signs of monsters and stuff. Alien hunters.

"What did you tell them?"

"The weird ones. Away, I sent 'em. Comin' round here in robes and funny headgear or with a *fiáin* look in their eyes. First few I showed the spot, then just gave directions; I feared some of 'em would fall in the lough and started sayin' I did it to 'em. So

I just started to play dumb. Figured everyone would forget one more set of stone ruins, 'til I heard from official types like your institute. Took you a little more seriously."

"Can you give us directions or walk us out to have a look?" Freya asked.

"Could walk ya but it's not hard to find. Just out the back door and a few hundred meters through the trees. You'll come to the edge of the lake and you'll see the ruins, and the tower will be obvious."

Freya detected a change in Jaager's muscles. She could read them almost like his thoughts. She closed her eyes, feeling just a bit of pressure at her throat. He'd made a decision. She put a hand on his forearm, but he gently if not politely slipped it away.

"'Scuse me a moment."

The old man had risen to walk back into his little kitchen. Almost without sound Jaager rose. Freya wanted to call out, to urge him to reconsider, but she knew it was a lost cause. He would not be dissuaded.

He stepped through the narrow doorway and stood behind the old man, who was humming a soft tune under his breath as he rinsed his cup. As the tap squeaked off and water gurgled down the ancient pipes, Jaager's long arms folded around the man's body.

One black glove rose to pinch his nostrils closed, and another clapped across his mouth, silencing the humming. The sounds from the old man's throat became low, protesting grunts, components of words he couldn't form.

His arms thrashed a bit, and he twisted. He couldn't escape Jaager's grasp or do more than wiggle. Freya stepped to the doorway, then put a hand across her mouth and folded herself back against the white stone wall. A few tears formed, but she wiped them away. *For the cause*, she reminded herself, for the miraculous awe they had planned.

In the kitchen, the struggle stopped, and Jaager lowered the old man to the floor. No need for the venom here. No need to give those who must be tracking them by now another marker like the tourist.

The venom had been used as an emergency at the castle. When he was found, more than likely the old man's demise would be blamed on a stroke or his heart. She drew in a quick breath as she heard him sag and his body slid to the floor, heavy with a thud.

When Jaager stepped back through the kitchen doorway, she looked up into his stoic features. She didn't expect him to say anything, and he didn't surprise her.

She reached into her purse even though they were alone. Plucking out a compact, she tamped one of his cheeks a couple of times then stepped back to check her work. It looked fine. "Well," she said, "let's hope this spot's as easy to find as he said."

13

Ethan Bransfield, chair of medieval studies at Trinity, carried himself with an energy and poise that seemed more athletic than academic. He wore a tweed jacket and a charcoal-gray tie with a subdued fishbone pattern, but that all looked like it could be peeled off to reveal running clothes beneath. The disheveled brown hair and a hint of shadow on his squared features added a boyish touch of disregard even though he'd hit his mid-forties.

After shaking hands, he settled behind a heavy oak desk in front of bookshelves that looked as if they might collapse at any time under the weight of the thick volumes they held.

Alison Syn, the same young woman who'd met them on their first visit had showed O'Donnell and Bullfinch in. She stood for a moment, looking at them with an almost dramatic hesitancy until O'Donnell's glare prompted closing the door as she exited.

"I've spoken with the homicide investigators," Bransfield said. "This has shocked us all, and we've been struggling to get our minds wrapped around it. I don't know if anything new has come to us."

"Details matter of course," O'Donnell said. "We're interested in your insight into Professor Burke's work. Areas of focus. Professor Bullfinch has helped me understand the Middle Ages constitute quite an expanse of time."

"That would be accurate," Bransfield said with a smile, suggesting indulgence of a lay person more than condescension. He gave a nod toward Bullfinch. "Professor Burke's interest lay in the period we call Late Antiquity through the Early Middle Ages, though his focus was really around the fifth and sixth centuries.

Interesting times in Ireland, but then all times are."

"What was going on then?" O'Donnell asked.

"It was the time a lot of monasteries were forming all the way from Skellig Michael near Kerry in the South all the way to the North. It's when St. Patrick and St. Brendan were at work and when Christianity took hold here."

"So Professor Burke was interested in religious artifacts?"

"Often, yes. And the path of belief. He was a student of how belief impacted human development, and how truth became myth. Students have always loved him."

"Perhaps," Bullfinch said, "he was fond of stories like Patrick's Battle with Crom Cruach or the Voyage of St. Brendan. Brendan set sail in search of the Garden of Eden and his adventures became a major Irish maritime epic." The latter he directed at O'Donnell.

"All that," Bransfield agreed.

She tapped her mobi screen and spun the face of it in Bransfield's direction. "Does this look like something he'd have been interested in?"

Bransfield gave the photo of the stone from Castle Cluin a close look.

"Where did this come from?"

"We were told it was found in a field near Castle Cluin," Bullfinch said. "Do the markings mean anything to you?"

"There's a resemblance to Ogham of course, but that's not one of the recognized figures." He pronounced the word oh-wom or something close to that.

"We've had mentions of the early Irish alphabet? I didn't think it looked like one of the known characters."

"You're familiar with it?"

"It's not a specialty, but I've seen and heard of it, of course."

"Given the location of the find and the style of the characters, the angled slashes, it would seem to fit the pattern at least."

He tapped one complex marking that seemed to include almost a latticework of crossing lines. "That resembles at least one character from the Forfeda."

"Now what would that be?" O'Donnell asked.

"A set of extra letters you might say. Beyond the key twenty characters of Ogham."

"Isn't there one school that holds Ogham is code?" Bullfinch asked.

Bransfield gave a slight nod. "Secret language of the Druids, a cipher to thwart Romans."

"Any idea what this might say?" O'Donnell asked.

"Not unless it's about trees."

"Excuse me?"

"Another theory of Ogham is that it speaks of trees," Bullfinch said. "The twenty known symbols are said to each be the first letters of Celtic tree species and each has a calendar significance. Remember Druid means oak and their belief in the spiritual powers of trees is part of their story."

"Thought you were having me on for a minute," O'Donnell said.

Bransfield smiled and let his gaze linger on her eyes. "I'm an academic, but I'm not that arrogant. On top of the letter name conventions, it's said the Druids carved different Ogham symbols into wooden staffs for different purposes."

"Magic?"

"Well, ritual. We don't know all of the meanings."

"And we don't know all that what's called magic isn't tapping into something for which there's a rational explanation that we just don't understand yet," Bullfinch said.

"I know some of the professor's files have already been taken, but might we have another look at his office?" O'Donnell asked. "Professor Bullfinch might spot something of interest that others wouldn't have seen."

As crazy as it seemed, that was supposed to be part of *Aisteach*'s mission, and if a case had ever called for that perspective this was it.

"Certainly," Bransfield said. "Alison can help you with that."

He touched an intercom on his desk, and a few moments

later, Alison opened Burke's office door for them, admitting them to a room slightly smaller than Bransfield's. Shelves looked even more in danger of collapsing. Thick volumes on medieval history shared space with texts including an early edition of *The Golden Bough* and *Magic, Science and Religion and Other Essays* and other works that seemed to confirm Burke's interest in the influence of belief.

O'Donnell fingered a volume with a purple dust jacket, *Bullfinch's Mythology: The Age of Fable*. She cocked an eyebrow.

"Doubleday edition. Shame to see that gathering dust," Bullfinch said.

A small set of shelves beside Burke's heavy oak desk housed an array of science fiction and fantasy paperbacks. Lovecraft, Howard and lesser-known pulp-era writers such as Seabury Quinn and Rudolph Rottman crowded pristine editions of high fantasy and collectible editions of Stoker, Shelly and others. Bullfinch ran a finger across the spines as he passed the shelf and slid behind the desk.

Burke's blotter and note pads had been left behind, though his computer had been plucked away, an absence made obvious by a dust outline and abandoned power cords. O'Donnell pulled the desk chair back and gestured for Bullfinch to have a seat.

"Maybe you'll spot something if you look at things from his perspective," she said.

Bullfinch obliged, letting his fingers curl around the ends of the armrests and leaning back, taking in a breath as he scanned the real estate before him, doodles on the blotter, a note pad, unmarked, probably left behind as unimportant. An acrylic picture frame faced him. A dark-haired girl smiled, captured in a moment somewhere in a pub or restaurant.

"Did he have a daughter?"

Alison stepped to his side and looked at the photograph.

"Niece," she said. "Vita Burke. Brother's child. That had been knocked off. I came in after the police left and found it on the floor under the edge of one of the shelves. Assumed he brushed it off with his coat, so I didn't think it was anything that would matter to them so I just put it back."

"Anything else under there?" O'Donnell asked.

"I didn't dive too far."

Slipping a pen light from her coat, O'Donnell dropped to the floor on her knees and leaned down to look under the cherrywood unit behind the desk. It stood on short, thick legs that left about two inches of space beneath it. The chair creaked as Bullfinch twisted to look down on her.

"Anything?"

She stared into a narrow, shadowy space of dust bunnies and grit missed by the housecleaning department's vacuums

"Maybe."

She slipped a hand into the space with a little difficulty. Far back near the wall, a tiny black plastic figure lay on its side. Flattening her face on the carpet, she maximized her reach and felt her fingertips just brush it. With a breath, she stretched a little more, feeling tendons strain, but she found purchase and plucked out the little black shape.

"It's like the medical symbol," she said. "Interesting. It's a snake."

The small staff she held was entwined by a single serpent that stretched up its length and curved its head over the top.

"That's a Staff of Asclepius," Bullfinch said. "A little more traditional than the British Medical Association's that's gotten a graphic artist's logo treatment. Hmm, in the U.S. they gravitate more toward the caduceus. Two snakes vs. the one."

He took it and turned it over in his fingers. "Looks like the kind of plastic generated by a 3D printer."

"Probably given to him by someone over at CRANN," Alison said, stepping over to look for herself. "It's a research center. That's where all the 3D printers are around here, and Professor Burke lectured to them sometimes about the relationship between myth and science."

"Perhaps someone picked up on a detail and made it a gift,"

Bullfinch said, spinning the chair back toward the desk and passing the trinket over to Alison. "Maybe you should put it with his things. I presume eventually you'll have to clear his office."

"I'm not sure where his things will go," Alison said. "I don't know that he had a lot of family."

"Any idea what The Circle was?"

"The Circle?"

Bullfinch tapped a spot on the blotter. Amid other doodles and minor math calculations, the words "The Circle" were scribbled in ink that had smeared. They were barely legible any longer but they were there. As if to complement the words, Burke had drawn several circles amid other scribbles and doodles. One even looked as if he'd been approximating the familiar image of a snake swallowing its tale.

"I don't know that he's ever spoken of it to me."

"I'm not sure if he spoke of it to me either," Bullfinch said. "Not directly."

14

Sagging branches shrouded the lower portion of the stone wall at the lake's edge, and mists from the water swirled in ghostly twists around its base. It looked almost like an enchanted fairytale structure, except for the dead brush and craggy surface. And the fact that a portion of the upper walls had crumbled, leaving gaping openings exposing former rooms. Patches of green vegetation clung at intervals.

Freya felt her breath catch as she looked up at the edifice. What had it taken to construct it? Ropes and pulleys? And how beautiful had it been in its day?

Her awe was for more than the architectural feat, however. One of those crumbled walls had revealed the hidden chamber and the markings the old man had spoken of, something forgotten for perhaps a thousand years.

Jaager displayed less awe and more blind determination, marching past her as they emerged from the wooded area they'd traversed behind the old man's cottage. He headed in a straight line for a vaulted doorway.

She followed, tapping her phone's face to pull up the rough sketches they'd been provided based on the old man's sources, as well as satellite images. The jagged walls and open roof afforded a sense of what they needed to pass. More pieces had fallen since the photographs.

Her companion didn't seem concerned with the possibility that new chunks of stone might be coming down from the ruins. She followed with a little more caution, looking up at the overhanging remnants. It wasn't clear exactly what held up at least one jutting protrusion.

Spiral stone stairs began an upward climb just through another arched doorway once they'd stepped through the first. Slivers of light fell on green mossy coatings, but the steps appeared solid.

Jaager led the way upward, shoes crunching on grit and debris as he disappeared around the first bend. Freya hurried to keep up, feeling her chest tighten. Despite the openings, the air in the contained space seemed a little stale.

She almost ran into him at the next curve. He'd stopped abruptly as bits of stone dropped from one wall. Nothing too heavy. He gave it a casual glance then moved on.

She grabbed a breath of damp, outside air as they passed a vaulted window and continued the ascent, scanning the walls for anything about to drop. She'd devoted a good bit of her time to fitness and self-defense after her dismissal. She was in peak physical shape, but her heart banged the insides of her chest as they reached the top of their climb. The steps stopped a few feet below openings in the more complete portion of the structure that appeared to lead into intact chambers. Rock climbing would have to take them the rest of the way. Just a few steps.

With a ten-meter plunge.

A little surer of himself, Jaager reached up the wall, found a handhold and steadied himself. Then he slipped a toe into an indentation and pressed himself into the wall and started moving.

Freya slipped off her overcoat and her scarf. Then she drew in a breath, preparing herself, reminding herself not to look at the drop. The gains exceeded the risk, and she'd been told climbing equipment shouldn't be needed.

This from people who hadn't actually seen the structure.

She kept telling herself about the gains as she slipped shoes off as well in spite of the chill and tucked her toes into a deep indentation and went after the tall man.

Bits of grit and stone sifted off the wall and tumbled downward, and the breeze picked up as she slipped over the stone, working to keep herself steady. Fingernails cracked, and the stone cut into her palms while he rose without apparent effort. Perhaps she should have brought more equipment after all, but the task hadn't looked as complicated from the photos.

As punctuation for that thought, she misplaced a toe and felt her sole slip from what she'd thought was a secure placement, and then she dangled. Digging nails into what was at least a substantial outcropping. That almost forced a look down, and her lungs and throat constricted. The ground below looked like a satellite photo, and fallen stone seemed to wait for her to drop down onto jagged edges.

Jaager leaned out from the chamber he'd climbed into and found a hold on a sleeve, yanking her his way before she could draw another breath. The next time she breathed, it was a sigh of relief.

The opening could no longer be called a door. Too much wall had crumbled away. It was more like an open maw with jagged teeth all around. Freya followed Jaager into a narrow passage that narrowed again after a few paces, forcing a turn sideways to keep moving.

Sunlight slashed into the small room they found after the squeeze, allowed in by a pair of openings in the ceiling, possibly from decay or possibly designed as murder holes inside this secret chamber. In spite of the twin rays that pooled on the stone floor, shadows hung in the corners, cloaking the walls with black gloom.

Freya switched to a light on her phone and lifted it, casting a white glow, illuminating mossy green patches looking almost like splattered paint. She panned over two walls that were pocked but otherwise unmarked.

Her breath caught as the light hit the third wall, opposite them. Slash-mark characters like they'd seen before spread from floor to ceiling, a blanket of characters etched into the stonework.

They'd opened a treasure chest, or it felt that way. At a glance she could see markings they hadn't compiled from other sources, new symbols. She couldn't be sure if they formed a message or if they'd been stored here, placed somewhere out of sight in the day but preserved in stone. That didn't matter. Interpretation could come later. For now, they only needed to document them.

She switched over to camera mode on her mobi and took a step forward, beginning to snap photos as the flash flared—first broad shots for coverage. Then, as Jaager stood watching, she moved in closer, making sure she captured each character and distinct traits, providing a good view that would not be open to confusion.

When she'd finished, she moved to the big man's shoulder and held the face of the phone so that they could both see it. With a fingertip, she flicked through the captures quickly for his survey. When she'd finished, he gave a slow nod, and she stepped back while he picked up a heavy stone from their feet.

Holding it between his hands, he walked over to the wall and began striking the stone against the characters. He glanced up occasionally to make sure he wasn't jarring any dangerous bits of ceiling free, but he focused mostly on destroying the markings, making sure they were leaving nothing behind.

15

"The snake figurine can't be an accident can it?" O'Donnell asked. "Based on the other things we've seen?"

She and Bullfinch had left the offices behind and made their way back to her car, and an unsettling feeling wriggled into her abdomen. It was the kind of annoying gut spasm triggered when she sensed something dark and inevitable.

"No, it definitely has some kind of meaning. Too many coincidences otherwise."

"Plastic snakes, strange sketches and a man's been poisoned with viper venom? We're in agreement."

"Snake images are common enough in his area of research, even in Ireland where there are no snakes and certainly in the British Isles, but when all things start being tallied…"

"It suggests somehow he's stumbled into the path of some kind of crazy fanatics with a snake obsession and an interest in these Ogham markings."

"We need to gather more details, but that sums it up. We don't know enough about what's going on. I don't know if he's 'stumbled on' or is 'part of' something."

"This Circle that was mentioned?"

"Right. We need more details."

O'Donnell wedged their vehicle into a traffic stream and headed back toward *Aisteach* headquarters.

Letting Professor Bullfinch get a look at Burke's office hadn't been a bad idea, but it had unsettled her. A murky cloud seemed to lurk somewhere ahead. She didn't like not knowing its makeup or the sense that it gave her of something grim and inevitable.

As crazy as some of the ideas were and some of the things they seemed to be up to, she had to agree the purpose of *Aisteach* seemed reasonable in this instance. Indications of high strangeness—as she'd heard Bullfinch call it—and ancient lore wouldn't be scrutinized in the proper vein by traditional investigators. They'd be pragmatic and treat everything like craziness. She would have done it on a given Tuesday. Her father certainly would have had little patience for weird theories or anything that strayed from the concrete, but she was beginning to see there was more to it.

Someone like Bullfinch would look at things just as he was doing and pick up meaning in odd markings she and others would miss. But what did that say about what she'd been dragged into?

As the windshield wipers fought an onslaught of rain, her mind battled back insane thoughts. A lost alphabet, snake legends, shadowy needle men with syringes full of venom was the stuff of a Saturday night piped telly horror marathon and not a police investigation.

The killers she sought were killers, possibly spree killers the way things were shaping up and likely to strike again. But their motivation was stranger and more ominous than your usual brand of terrorist driven by political or twisted religious causes. They were going to need to understand what was driving these people and if there were more than the two that had struck at Castle Cluin.

Rees greeted them as they stepped back into *Aisteach* headquarters, slipping off coats and hats. His sleeves had been rolled to his elbows, his tie loosened, and he looked weary and beaten down.

O'Donnell didn't like that. "What's wrong?" she asked.

"Rumblings from pencil pushers. What have you got?"

"We'd have called ahead if it was really exciting, but Professor

Bullfinch picked up a few coils of data."

If Rees had been a teenage girl, he would have given her an eye roll, but his grim smirk said enough.

"It's something else to run through my friend Mack back at the O.C.L.T.," Bullfinch said. "Perhaps tied to what Professor Burke wanted to talk to me about years ago."

"If it puts us closer to naming whoever's running around killing people with snake poison to collect rocks, I'm all for it," Rees said. "Why don't you..."

He didn't finish. A shout from somewhere in the hallway cut off his suggestion.

"I'll not wait."

Deputy Commissioner Darce Sheehan followed the words into the room, flanked by solemn men in dark coats and suits. O'Donnell didn't recognize them. Homicide officers or bureaucrats? Probably bureaucrats.

His shoulders squared, his face looked redder than it had been on the street when he'd been blessing out O'Donnell.

"I knew she'd be in here."

The source of the rumblings seemed apparent. He stomped to Rees, stopping only millimeters from his face.

"I don't know what this operation you run here is supposed to be, but I don't want it interfering with official lines of inquiry, and you've got a hell of a nerve pulling in an officer I have on suspension."

"We have full sanction..."

"To impede a homicide inquiry?"

"We're in no way impeding. We're pursuing a line your officers wouldn't think about..."

Sheehan's gaze swept around the control room, where various paranormal website news feeds and videos were displayed, and someone in a white coat was leading a large black dog on a leash. O'Donnell's gaze was tugged to the fish tank and the huge blue hammer-headed fish again. It seemed impossible, but she detected a distinct distaste in the thing's eye.

"This malarkey? Hell no we wouldn't consider the bunkum you have people pouring over. What? Aliens, *taibhsí*? And you have a suspended officer…"

"You're not utilizing her skills, so I am. Take it up with the president if you don't like it."

"She's already at the heart of a serious and controversial matter and you're stumbling around an active case, interviewing the same witnesses. We don't need her…"

"The line of investigation she's involved in has nothing to do with anything you're pursuing. You go ahead and sniff for the killer. O'Donnell can benefit from what we're doing and that's a damn site better than having her sit around in her apartment while you stew and answer political questions."

"I thought your little cubby here was supposed to be low profile. She's already in the press…"

"Which makes any rumors about her work here secondary to what journalists want to report on. Any relevant information we turn up about the homicide inquiry will be shared."

Sheehan drew a breath, prepared to spew more, but he held it, his shoulders sagging. He'd finished venting.

"We'll be watching to make sure you don't interfere, that you're just tracking the spooky stuff."

"Fine," Rees said. "You go on with what you're doing. You solve the case, wonderful."

Sheehan didn't seem to have more to say. He gathered his bureaucrats and turned in a rustle of uniform fabric, his shoes tapping the tiles in a heavy path to the door.

"You have scenes like that often?" Bullfinch asked.

"Usually it's in budget meetings," Rees said. "Ignore it. Do what you need to do after you've filled me in. Tomorrow, though. It's late. It's been a hell of a long day and everyone needs some rest. Maybe tomorrow we'll figure out where Professor Burke went when he left his office."

"What if we get there ahead of the other investigation?"

"So be it. We'll deal with the shite as it comes."

16

A dark-haired man in a crisp black suit stood not far from the entrance in the hotel lobby. Though not particularly tall, his demeanor and expression made him intimidating. He nodded to Freya when she entered and he caught her gaze.

His arms were crossed in front of him, right hand gripping left wrist, and he wore an almost imperceptible ear and mouth-piece in the right ear. She saw but didn't hear him speak from the corner of his mouth. As she climbed a small flight of steps to the spot, he stood near a square pillar of a rich-looking wood.

"You're expected, Ms. Turnbull. Please step this way." Matter of fact but grim.

He thumbed a button next to an elevator, and the doors opened immediately. He then inserted a key into the panel, allowing the car to whisk them up to a suite where a couple more grim private security agents stood sentry.

The latest find had warranted immediate contact with the men bankrolling this operation even though the hour was growing late and Freya's lower spine throbbed while her temples threatened to implode.

She caught a whiff of liquor when she was ushered into the sitting room. Expensive stuff, it floated just over the sterile and generic scent of all hotel rooms that was tinged with just a hint of expensive male cologne.

The old man from the car, Malphas, The Shepherd, rested in a red armchair, his suit coat draped over the side. Balor stood near a window, features shadowed by his wide-brimmed hat, not partaking or engaging. Just listening as he stood with folded arms.

Across from Malphas sat two gray-haired men in dark suits, one at one end of a sofa, the other in a wheelchair parked near the sofa arm. The one on the sofa held a tumbler with amber liquid and ice. American preference, clearly.

The one in the wheelchair seemed to be the older version, wavy white hair, wire-rimmed glasses. The lenses had a slight tint. A woman in a long-sleeved black sheath dress, hair in a tight up-style, stood near him. If she was a nurse she was a damned elegant one.

Something that looked like vodka resided in his glass, and he swirled it with gnarled hands. That was really the only sign of life.

The man on the sofa proffered a smile that seemed alien by comparison.

"Welcome, Ms. Turnbull," he said, obviously the younger brother. "I'm Edward Groom. This is William. We're going to have to dispense with intrigue and trust your confidentiality."

"It's absolute."

The names rang a bell from the headlines. Made sense they'd be here. The big economic conference in town and all. She connected the dots and couldn't keep the realization off her face.

"Of course none of this is to be discussed and would be denied," Edward said. "I understand you've had a turbulent but successful day."

"Speaking of things to be denied, we've gathered new information, and we've brought a silence to some of the people who were of concern. And some others whose deaths could be of use."

"Every endeavor has some cost." Gruff, the first sound from the one in the wheelchair. The woman beside him remained stoic.

Feeling a little unpolished in the woman's presence, Freya looked at the scuffs and scratches on her hands and her skinned knuckles. They offered an account of the day's events.

"Unfortunately your activities have attracted some attention," Edward said. "People some of our friends keep an eye on have begun to sniff at your trail. We may be ahead of the game enough to maintain a lead on them."

"The markings from the keep?"

Edward looked toward the hooded man. "Excellent we're told. A real help. Invaluable."

"Will we be on deadline?" Freya asked.

"If we can keep up this pace, we should be able to complete the mission before the end of the conference."

"That's a goal?"

"One of them. The other's set by the analysts in our think tank who were able to connect us with friends here." He nodded toward the old man. "It's a little more cosmic. But we're on schedule to act while the planets are where they ought to be."

"What's our next location?"

Edward rose and leaned in front of Malphas for a moment, listening to quiet whispers. He nodded as the final sounds issued.

"Unfortunately, you've done excellent work, but he says there's a key piece with markings that's not documented anywhere. It has to be rooted out from among those who were part of what the scholars call the Old Conspiracy among themselves. We owe them a great deal, but they are not allies. For a while, you're going to be seeking people and not artifacts. People can be less cooperative than stones, but we're hopeful some of the warnings that have been issued are enough to get the ants moving a bit."

"Warnings?"

"Little messages planted here or there. Deaths of inconsequential individuals known to our subjects."

Freya swallowed. So that was why some people had had to die.

Edward titled his head toward the assistant. She slipped a slim laptop from a case at her side and walked over to display it, holding her hand under it like a waiter holding a tray. It offered a photo of a pleasant-looking gray-haired man with a mild smile. One hand had slipped casually into the pants pocket of his tweed suit, and he seemed to be chatting to someone outside the frame.

"This is Geoffrey Bullfinch. Watch out for him," Edward said.

"He gets in your way, Mr. Jaager can do what he needs to," William added, perhaps a little to Edward's dismay if the expression was accurate.

Freya gave a nod. "Also noted."

"The gentleman you met on the way in is our old friend Mike," William said.

Edward folded his arms. "We're in a bit of a debate about whether he should pay Mr. Bullfinch a visit. Perhaps we'll flip a coin."

17

Bullfinch positioned the computer tablet's case so that the screen stood almost upright on his hotel table. Then he touched its face to bring up the encrypted login. After typing in his code and a few flickers on screen, he peered into the face of an African-American man with close-cropped salt-and-pepper hair, almost a crew cut.

Reed Christopher Hayes, better known as R.C., looked tired. He was several time zones away, making it even later—or was that earlier?—than here. Bullfinch suspected his investigation wasn't the only thing keeping R.C. awake.

R.C. commanded the network of O.C.L.T. operatives, meaning at any given time he was privy to crisis situations around the globe. The pressure of that had to build up.

"Hello, Geoffrey," he said, managing a bit of a jovial tone in spite of it all. "Let's see…"

He gazed somewhere outside of the range of the webcam he was looking into and reached for something.

"Ogham-like symbols, venom and stones, right?"

"That about sums up our case," Bullfinch said, leaning back in his chair and sipping the drink he'd poured into a short hotel glass.

"We've had the word out on the network, and there are reports of some chatter about Ogham. Vague at the moment, but we've been looking back, trying to connect what you're seeing with other activity, especially given Professor Burke's tweet to you, or whatever he sent."

R.C. took in a slow breath and looked down at the information he'd reached for.

"In the early aughts some buzz went out about Ogham-like symbols and artifacts. We sent you a few details. We have a little more. The web wasn't what it is today, so we're talking about documents on paper and even old-style computer bulletin boards that were still breathing. You know Mack. He's on a couple of jobs for us, but he's even been scanning old gopher files and Telnet back channels. He hasn't sent me a full report. He thinks there's been a bit of effort to keep some things below radar, so he's on that."

Mack would be Wendell Macklemore, and if there was information to be ferreted out, he'd be the one to do it. Bullfinch had observed Mack's technical acumen first hand as a dire situation developed, so he had full confidence in his abilities. Perhaps it was even more than confidence. Mack's skills were beyond comprehension.

"The big question is how much of it's real and how much of it's hoopla," Bullfinch said. "We could be looking at a series of local murders by fanatics, which could be bad enough. What concerns me is that the belief has foundation, that they're onto something powerful that could wreak havoc in ways we're all too familiar with."

"If you keep scratching at the layers, you'll know soon…"

A burst of Italian from the hallway cut off the remainder of R.C.'s remark.

"Sorry," Bullfinch said. "You'll have to repeat that."

Bullfinch headed toward his door, leaning into the peephole. A man in a tight black jacket moved along the hallway outside, seeming to look for a room number.

"I was just saying something will become apparent soon," R.C. said.

The man outside staggered a bit, muttering something else in Italian, almost under his breath.

"You're right," Bullfinch said. "The pieces will…"

Without warning, the man left the center of the hallway, hurling himself toward Bullfinch's door. The professor had just enough time to react, pulling back from the peep hole before the door crashed inward.

He found time also for an exclamation and a partial spin before the man followed the door inward, the mass just missing the chance to slam into Bullfinch full force and pin him to the floor. A glancing clip came from the door's edge, but he was already on the move. His tablet flew from his hand and bounced between bed and wall with R.C.'s words continuing to flow from it, though they'd turned to inquiries about what the hell was going on.

Bullfinch let that go unanswered and concentrated on his cane leaning against a table by the window. Meanwhile, the intruder barked what sounded like warnings in Italian. *Congelare.* Freeze? Did Italians use "freeze" like Americans did? He seemed to want Bullfinch to stop.

Bullfinch ignored the order and grabbed a glass from the table, flinging it behind him in the man's general direction, sending liquid flying. The Italian had to raise an arm to deflect it, delaying the withdrawal of a sleek and compact black weapon his jacket had concealed.

But only by a few seconds.

O'Donnell dropped her handbag onto a small table beside her apartment door and surveyed the upheaval in her living room. She wished it was the product of a ransacking. That would make a nice excuse, but the damage was all her fault, the result of neglect and distraction. Opened mail and magazines cluttered her coffee table, newspapers and blankets the sofa. A couple of plates from recent meals complete with crusts and crumbs also decorated the coffee table. She didn't want to step into the kitchen and confront the sink's stockpile.

She just shrugged off her coat and scarf and headed for the bedroom. The bedclothes were a tangle, but otherwise the space was clear. She allowed herself to spill forward onto the mattress in a swan dive, burying her face in the pillow upon impact. She needed a shower and something to eat, but for the moment, resting the load of bricks her head had become superseded everything else.

She felt the weight not just of weariness but of the situation. Was this the inevitable she'd trained herself to accept? The commissioner's assault had been disturbing. The ire suggested she wouldn't be finding her way back into good graces and her normal position quickly.

She rolled onto her back, realizing the exhaustion was not going to drag her into the instant sleep she'd expected. What she'd been assigned seemed important. Lives had been taken, yet the gnawing feeling that she'd been thrown off course wouldn't relent, and she had to prepare herself for the worst outcome of this case.

All she'd worked for, the trajectory she'd achieved in spite of pessimism seemed suddenly tenuous. And what would her father, God rest his... think of her working on the strange squad? He'd been a pragmatic man. He'd have understood taking an assignment as a lifeline amid turmoil. If strange became the new normal, however, that would feel like an affront to his old school world view and belief in methodical and sober police work.

It would be an affront to her own as well, long term. She had to remind herself a rational explanation would emerge from this craziness. She needn't worry about a lasting threat to her perception. Time for a drink.

She pulled herself off the bed and was headed toward the cabinet where her scotch was stored when she felt something drawing her to the window. She didn't usually bend to compulsions, but the urgency seemed strong, stronger than the draw of scotch. Maybe she had she spent too long at weird central.

She padded across the carpet to draw back the curtain and spot something moving somewhere in the distance, somewhere over what ought to be the River Liffey. A bit of gray sky remained. She could glean only a hint of the shape, but it was large enough to disturb.

"Based on this venom, Irish artifacts and legends and my personal experience the last few of years coupled with my luck, I'd say a giant serpent."

Her heart fluttered as she recalled the professor's words. Had his fear already been fulfilled?

She rubbed her eyes and forehead, trying to shake any fatigue and make sure she wasn't drawing something out of rolling clouds. Then she looked again, and the movement continued, a convoluted twist of what looked like long, narrow appendages.

She felt mesmerized for a moment, and in the next she felt the need to open her window and move toward whatever was out there. Because it wanted her to, wanted her to come its way.

Her mobi sounded.

She reached for her forehead again and realized she was in bed, not standing at the window. She'd never risen to head for the scotch. Being at weird central was having an impact on her psyche.

She kicked the cover back now and headed to her discarded things to dig out the still-chirping phone.

"There's a disturbance reported from the professor's hotel at Parnell and…" came Rees' voice.

"I know where it is. Is the professor all right?"

"Not known. I'm heading that way."

"I'll be right there."

18

Bullfinch dodged to his left, dropping to his knees and wincing as they thudded into the carpet, which didn't offer as much padding as he would have liked. As the shock reverberated up his thighs, he willed himself not to be slowed. Bullets whizzed past, thudding into a chair near the window.

He saw little round holes in the upholstery, and bits of stuffing popped out, a preview for his blood and internal tissue. To be avoided.

He twisted the cane he'd managed to get a hand around, and with a whish he yanked the handle, extracting the blade that had been buried deep in the hollow shaft.

As the Italian panned his gun barrel to the professor's current location, Bullfinch gave a backhanded flip of that shaft, sending it spinning in the man's direction. That forced a raised forearm to deflect it, and before he could regain his aim, Bullfinch launched from his knees, plunging forward.

He slammed a forearm into the gun arm, and jabbed the blade into the assailant's abdomen, going just under the lower rib. He couldn't afford delicacy. He drove it in as far as he could manage then slid it out with a streak of blood along the steel. He gave the man a shove into the room's dresser before bolting for the door.

He stopped just short of the hallway and peeked out, checking each direction for backup before heading for the stairwell. A slug bit into the door facing just as he cleared the space. In spite of all, the man had held onto his weapon.

Cursing the pain still pulsing up his legs, Bullfinch hustled through the stair door and started the trip down. His heart had stepped up its rate, striving to meet the demands of his accelera-tion. Two at a time, down the stairs, around the first turn, then two at a time to the next level.

He exited into the hallway, pausing for breath as the door sighed closed, relishing the reprieve but knowing he couldn't hesitate. He scanned the corridor, and, sighting no accomplices, he exhaled and pushed off a second later, heading past room doors, letting the blade arm slide down to his side so that he didn't look like a marauding pirate. He thought about knocking, a quick rap on each door to generate some attention and chaos, but he didn't want to endanger other guests. His assailant might not care about acting in pubic or taking out other targets.

Should he risk the lift?

He calculated the odds. It seemed unlikely that it would ding open on just the right floor where another gunman waited, ready to fire, but he'd learned it was best to assign the good luck to the people chasing you while figuring yours would be bad.

He waited a few heartbeats.

Then he peeked back into the hall.

Empty.

He waited a few more heartbeats.

Waiting would be in his favor. The Italian's wound had been deep. The man might fight on for a while, keep pursuing his mis-sion, but the more blood lost, the weaker he'd grow.

Bullfinch wished he'd had the presence of mind to grab for a cell or the tablet. Hopefully R.C. had picked up enough of what had happened to call for local help.

He thought he heard the stair door open. Had the attacker decided to try this floor rather than pursuing him downward?

Time to risk the elevator.

He moved past the floor's vending area and walked on to the lift doors where he knuckled the *Down* button, keeping his sword pressed against his leg.

He had no ideal course here except away from the known attacker.

The lift arrived empty. One bit of luck. After a breath, he stepped in and pressed the ground floor button with his sword hand. He'd leave the building, find a way to contact the *Aisteach* and wait for backup.

Just had to ride down a few floors.

Ding.

The elevator stopped two floors below. He moved to the elevator's back corner and kept his hands at his sides, positioning his body to block the view of the sword. And the doors sighed open as he inhaled and held the breath.

A middle-aged couple in heavy coats and scarves stepped on after a second of observing him. American tourists ready to look for a spot for dinner, a heavy man and his thin, graying wife. He let the breath go and stared straight ahead as they entered and found spots to stand on the opposite side of the car.

He noticed the woman size him up. He must look disheveled.

He ignored her gaze. Let them wonder what he was up to. If anyone stepped on to further the attack, he'd put himself between the couple and the bad guys, and they'd be thankful he was on hand.

And the car's descent resumed with just a second of hesitation then came the smooth glide, and they watched the numbers on the small screen click their descent.

For two more floors.

Ding.

Wait.

The doors opened on a man in his twenties. He seemed German based on a few hints of fashion and overall style. Longish black hair spilled from under a knit cap, and he wore a body-hugging gray sweater over tight jeans. He could've been a skier who'd somehow been transported to the wrong hotel.

Whush.

Doors slid back into place.

Bullfinch studied the kid from the corner of his eye. He sensed something not quite right about him.

The descent continued.

Bullfinch stared straight ahead.

Then the German kid turned. He had a blade up the tight left sleeve of the sweater. He slipped it out.

19

Traffic near Parnell backed up on connecting streets, throngs of honking cars and vehicles stretching back along narrow arteries leading to the thoroughfare. From what she could pick up on the radio, O'Donnell surmised someone had slammed into a bus near Parnell Square.

She finally wheeled into a one-way the wrong way, steering up the narrow street with her foot light on the gas until headlights splashed through her windshield. She yanked the wheel left and bounced onto the sidewalk then, braked and shoved the gearshift into park.

Ignoring the horns and curses, she climbed out and started a jog in the direction of Bullfinch's hotel, which should have been only a couple of blocks. Her coat whipped around her, and the chilly night wind scraped at her cheeks, but it seemed the most expedient method. She pressed her mobi to her ear after thumbing Rees' recent call for a re-dial.

"Any word? I'm almost there?"

"Uniforms are in the building. They haven't picked up any sign yet of the professor."

He hesitated a moment, getting a message from somewhere else.

"Oh, God, there's blood in his room."

Her heart felt like it had been jabbed with a burst from a defibrillator. God, no, don't let the man be hurt. She'd started to respect the old guy in their time together and realized how deep his knowledge ran.

Aside from personal feelings, they needed him for whatever

insanity was up. Clearly someone else felt that too.

She jogged on along the narrow street, avoiding irregularities in the sidewalk and reaching almost a sprint as she approached the wide and clogged Parnell. She began to thread her way through the traffic snarl, sliding between bumpers and over one fender, weaving to the opposite sidewalk then pausing only long enough to get her bearings before bolting in the direction of the hotel.

She might wind up with another shooting on her record, but she'd be damned if any partner of hers was going to be harmed without someone facing consequences.

"*Sich nicht vom Fleck rühren,*" the young man said to the American couple. Then he lunged toward Bullfinch.

Bullfinch raised his blade and parried, putting himself between the attacker and the tourists.

The sword blade clanged against the knife and Bullfinch twisted his wrist, knocking the smaller blade aside and delivered a knee to the young man's groin. He absorbed it with an expression of pain but wasn't neutralized. He came back slashing.

Bullfinch drove an elbow into the man's cheekbone, buying a couple more seconds.

Then another ding sounded, and the doors sighed open.

"Get out of here!" he shouted.

But the couple couldn't move.

People stood facing the opening.

Behind those waiting for the car, a thick collection of bodies spread across the lobby. Conversations in various languages rose into a hubbub over the area. It was a peak hour, people on their way to dinner or evening events, people arriving, people headed for the hotel bar. That might be useful.

Bullfinch drove with his blade, an aggression that surprised the young man and made him step backward. As he jerked backward in retreat, Bullfinch was already moving in the other direction, splitting the wall of people in the elevator opening, ignoring their gasps, then weaving through the guests behind them, heading for the exit. Maybe that wasn't the best decision, but he might manage to lose himself if he could get outside.

"Call security," he said as he brushed past a young man in a dark suit who looked like hotel staff.

"Security," he repeated to a woman as he went zigging past a couple of American girls in brightly colored jackets. "Security, now!"

He dodged past men in suits, ducked past more couples and clusters of people, and then slid through the sliding doors at the mouth of the lobby and out into the chill wind.

A short, well-dressed man with dark hair stood on the sidewalk in the entry drive where cabs and vans could unload. Somehow—perhaps it was simply something in the way he presented himself, the display of confident authority in spite of his size—Bullfinch knew he was there for him.

He made a slash with the sword as the male approached. An arm rose in a reflexive defense. The blade raked across the thick fabric of the coat sleeve. The man gave a slight grunt, but the blade was deflected without doing harm.

Bullfinch looked into the man's cold dark eyes. If he'd read confidence before, he detected a disturbing indifference now, more determination than he'd seen in the Italian or the German. This was a man who'd act dispassionately and was prepared to kill. He didn't have time to study the expression further.

The man ducked under Bullfinch's outstretched blade and slammed a fist up into the older man's jaw, a smash that sent pain radiating all the way through his teeth and snapped his head back.

He grabbed for the lapel on the man's coat, hoping to slow him or deflect him, but he didn't find purchase. The man continued forward, intent on sending him to the ground with a re-distribution of weight.

"Hold it."

O'Donnell stood several paces down the hotel's semi-circular drive, a nasty-looking black handgun leveled in front of her between both hands, aiming their way.

"You'll blow your friend away," the man warned.

But Bullfinch dove to the side as the man was distracted.

O'Donnell's weapon blazed in the next second, and the sound echoed around them.

It was enough to make the man hesitate even though he wasn't hit.

Bullfinch straightened and launched himself in O'Donnell's direction.

In the next second, as he glanced backwards, tires screeched. A vehicle had arrived—one they'd hoped to shove him into no doubt. The short man dove into the back seat and the vehicle reversed down the driveway.

O'Donnell's gun blazed again, but the vehicle shot away from the curb and into the night.

"Sure. They get a clear roadway," O'Donnell said.

20

Bullfinch insisted he'd had enough rest at 8 a.m. when he joined O'Donnell for a meeting with Rees.

"Patrols weren't successful in finding the van," Rees said, as they settled in his office.

"The Italian?" Bullfinch asked.

"Checking hospitals and the like, but nothing so far. He crawled away to lick his wounds. We might have a decent image of the German on hotel security cameras, but you can bet they're hired hands. They won't know who they were really working for if we find them."

"The Americans would call it a clean getaway," Bullfinch said. "Clearly a lot of resources are on hand, at least to employ freelancers."

"They know you're here and want you off their trail," O'Donnell said. "What does that tell us?"

"Worried about what I might know or what I might recognize."

"We'll keep our eyes out," Rees said. "Meanwhile, I've got other news for you and the professor. Overnight, the analysts figured out Professor Burke's destination. He was bundled for the rain, made it hard."

"Where?" O'Donnell asked.

"A little shop near the Trinity campus actually. It belongs to a gentleman named Peter Redmond."

O'Donnell looked toward the professor. "Up for some browsing?"

Bullfinch flexed his arms a bit.

"Certainly. It'll work out the stiff muscles. I don't think we have any time to waste."

At the counter, a blonde girl was detailing an antique candelabrum with silver polish when they jangled the shop door bell. She looked up and offered a smile that faded slightly as she stared at guests who somehow didn't look like antiques collectors.

"We're looking for Peter Redmond," O'Donnell said, approaching the counter. "In yet?"

"He's in his office."

Before O'Donnell could flash a badge, Bullfinch flipped open his computer tablet.

"You work here every day, young lady?"

"Nelda. Most. When I'm not in class."

"You recognize this gentleman?"

He displayed a full-screen photo of Burke.

"Dr. Burke. He's a friend of Mr. Redmond's."

"He been in lately?"

"The other day. He was in a bit of a hurry."

O'Donnell tipped her head in respect for Bullfinch. If Redmond had any hesitancy, she'd removed his option for denial.

Now she showed her badge. "Could you find Mr. Redmond? It's very important."

In a few moments, they were seated around an antique table in a tight little room. They faced a small, round and silver-bearded gentleman wearing equally round spectacles. Nervous eyes were magnified by the lenses and looked mistrustful.

"He was just in briefly," Redmond said. "Hello, goodbye."

"Have you heard of his death?"

She watched for a reaction. She didn't get shock, but she detected a flash of sadness.

"Yes. I read of it."

"Did it occur to you to make contact with the police, since he was probably by here hours before his murder?"

"It occurred. It also occurred to flee to South America, but nowhere is really safe."

"What are you talking about?"

He rose, moved to a cabinet and pulled out a packet of information.

"The professor brought word that something he—I guess we, since I was filled in on it—were a part of had gotten out of hand again."

"He expressed concern of something like that to me a few years ago," Bullfinch said. "But we never re-connected about it. Until I got a text. From what we can tell it was around the time he visited you."

The old man nodded.

"He brought a packet, a collection of a few signs he'd received that a circle of believers had become active again."

"What do you mean, circle of believers?" O'Donnell asked.

"Professor Burke had a few students who decided to conduct an experiment a few years ago. A theoretical experiment, socio-logical, anthropological, choose your label."

"What were they trying to do?"

"Exactly what they seem to have accomplished. They gave birth to a new strand of mythology, or a fresh adherence to old ideas."

"What, they created their own Scientology?" O'Donnell asked.

"Not quite a religion," Redmond said. "They wanted to see, in an enlightened age, if they could spark belief if they dropped some old ideas into the stream with just a few revisions and new ideas to accommodate modernity."

"Did you memorize that from their brochure?" Bullfinch asked.

"I heard it stated quite a bit, when things were being dis-cussed a while back, once Inerney figured out what the students had done."

"What exactly did they do?" Bullfinch asked.

"It started when they were on an archaeological dig. Just a cataloging effort really. Then they stumbled on a fragment of information. They started to report it apparently, then decided it might be more interesting to try a different approach."

"This was a piece of a lost alphabet?"

Redmond's eyebrows wrinkled, but he nodded. "One night, when all this was just conversation among young intellectuals in training, the talk of ubiquitous themes emerged."

"The rabbit in the moon," Bullfinch said.

"What does that mean?" O'Donnell said.

"I've mentioned it though not by that name. It's a reference in folklore," Bullfinch said. "It's called a pareidolia. Think of it as a shared interpretation or misinterpretation of a natural phenomenon. There are patterns on the moon that many have seen as shaped like a rabbit. Particularly in Asian cultures there are stories of a rabbit that lives in the moon. They say he's preparing rice since that's an action that was part of their world. There are similar themes about the rabbit in Aztec myth. The specifics of the rabbit's task vary by country based on acts the cultures recognize, but it's widespread, all because of a vague natural formation."

"Dragons are even more common," Redmond said. "And more exciting. You can find a lot of world-origin theories rooted in dragons and serpents and giant things. That's what the young scholars decided to root their myth around."

"So they wanted to see if something deep in one of the old mythologies would resonate today with a little prompting?" O'Donnell asked. "Like the finding of a lost alphabet character."

Redmond nodded. "Some in academic circles might call it seeding."

"Putting rocks in obscure fields just as long as they're on a perceived ley line? I'd say 'seeding' was a good term." Bullfinch asked.

"They thought it out well. A few clues, a few symbols, a few planted whispers and voila, a new belief, a new story, a new myth of a doorway to old things like Crom Cruach." He pronounced it "crook."

"So, what happened?" O'Donnell asked. "Am I correct in suspecting nothing good?"

"The Circle of Ning was born."

"Ning?" O'Donnell asked.

Bullfinch seemed nonplused. "From Ningizzidda, I presume."

Redmond nodded again. "Son of Enki and Ereshkigal. They were behind the creation of the world in some stories. In Sumerian legend, he's a snake-like guardian of a deity's palace. There are suggestions in the information they put out that Ning and Crom Cruac are cousins."

"This crap I can't even pronounce is tied to a string of murders today?" O'Donnell asked.

"Calm, dear lady," Bullfinch said.

"You could see where it might fit with the murders including Inny's," Redmond said.

"Go on. What did they do?" Bullfinch asked.

"How does any good con game work?" Redmond asked. "With a story. As I said, they'd been working as volunteers with the Kilduff-Power Archaeological Trust. They found a character that didn't fit with known alphabets. It looked like Ogham, but it wasn't a standard character or part of the later forfeda, and being young and imaginative, they decided to use it as a way to drop bits of a story into the world's information stream. Not to spill a whole tale out in one place, but to make it a mystery that would pique the curiosity of people who ran across it. They were clever in where they buried it. Where gophers wouldn't go, they said."

"Rather astute thinking," Bullfinch said. "You have to dig for something versus being handed a dry thesis, you get excited."

"We like questions, we humans. Since we were all in Ireland, it made sense to tie the story around our legends and things like Crom Cruach and the Voyage of St. Brendan with hints that it went beyond, connected to other cultures like the rabbit. This is what Inny indicated later anyway."

"It sounds like an interesting discussion for a dorm room," Bullfinch said. "Even for an expansion of a role-playing game, but it seems to have really gotten out of hand."

"These were very bright students with possibly a couple of geniuses in the mix. Young, intuitive and unfortunately unseasoned. That can be a dangerous combination. They didn't really understand what can happen in the world. What people can want."

"Druids, Ogham, ancient history." Bullfinch said.

"Druids are mysterious, and real. A good hook."

"What did they promise?" Bullfinch asked.

"What any good legend promises. Power for those who find favor with the mythical beings."

"So it, uh, went viral?" O'Donnell asked.

"Before we knew what viral was."

21

"Once they'd sunk a few clues in remote places, they started dropping hints on the computer bulletin boards that were still around and on the various websites that allowed postings, and they made contributions to Usenet and the systems that were still vibrant," Redmond said. "Scanned documents and text files were easy enough to fabricate. This was the days before Twitter and Reddit. Dial-up days, so they used what they had. Sprinkling pieces onto the burgeoning Internet, seeding information as they had in the ground, leaking out mostly electronic documents or rumors of documents that had the appearance of scholarly works. Or pieces of scholarly works. Again, they tried to cloak it in a bit of mystery, like they were details that had slipped out from some secret network."

"They convinced the casual that there was something there."

"And tied it to rocks in the ground with their markings for anyone who got that far. Geocaching, if you will, before people were doing GPS searches for hidden trinkets with their mobis."

"How do we go from fake research papers to real venom and dead people?" O'Donnell asked.

"Bear in mind, I came to know of this once it was starting to spiral out of control as Professor Burke and a few others were trying to figure out how to deal with it. They wanted to contain it without destroying the future of the students. They'd done stupid things in a brilliant way. Inerney realized they'd be ruined as scholars and possibly in the job market as a whole if their actions were revealed."

O'Donnell cocked an eyebrow upward and gave a tilt of her

head. "Wouldn't have helped his reputation either, right? Or the trust's?"

Redmond lifted his shoulders. "What's the American businessman, Professor? Morgan? Went by initials."

"J.P. Morgan," Bullfinch said. "The quote is: 'A man always has two reasons for doing anything: a good reason and the real reason.'"

"Does anyone work without some self-interest?" Redmond asked.

"Just go on," Bullfinch said. "How did this shape up?"

"Before Professor Burke knew what was going on, the students began to notice activity—not long after the seeds were planted and a few nudges given," Redmond said. "People sharing messages, chatting about ideas even looking for stones and trying to assemble text from the markings. Burke and his friends would drop into chat room sessions and see conspiracy theories being discussed and expanding. They grew excited that things were taking hold."

He drew a breath.

"Some of them were so excited they decided to add fuel to the phenomenon, for the purpose of continuing their study. They dropped letters to individuals they identified as meeting a few criteria."

"Those who were expressing interest?" Bullfinch asked.

Redmond nodded. "They pinpointed individuals who seemed to exhibit a high degree of intelligence coupled with a predisposition to an interest in the strange and unusual and a degree of paranoia."

"Someone bright who'd buy into snake-oil stories and propagate them?" O'Donnell asked.

"That's precise, actually. One of those was a young man pursuing a PhD. Shawn Drury was his name. He read about Ogham and reptiles, and his paranoia percolated until he began to take his suspicions and fears to others. He became an evangelist for the message, and started to assemble the research papers and bits of data the scholars had sprinkled out there, joined some Internet theorists and crackpots as well."

"Really fulfilling their purpose," Bullfinch said.

"He collected the narrative, found a unified thread and began to talk to a few people around a table in a bar. Then a few more and a few more until Olina Lerma Quiñones heard his story."

"She doesn't sound like an Irish Catholic," O'Donnell said.

"She was from Spain, living in Dublin in poor quarters. She was the daughter of miners in the Asturias actually who came here looking for something better. Unfortunately, she wound up homeless. The stories Drury was telling seemed to resonate with her. She took up the cause of spreading the word, drawing in a few more adherents and a few more, operating underground for a while to gather knowledge, though the scholars detected her movements and made note."

"I take it this all went somewhere bad?"

"They gathered enough believers to become concerning, especially because they started to drag in homeless people to increase their ranks."

"Press gang proselytizing?" O'Donnell asked.

"Something like that. The scholars feared some who failed to become true believers might have been killed. When they attempted investigation, threats were made."

"That would have been around the time Professor Burke contacted me," Bullfinch said.

"He'd become fully aware at that time, I suspect. They were clutching at ways to deal with what looked like a growing problem. As they tried to investigate, Madam Quiñones started having people follow them."

"Were there threats?"

"Not outright, but there was what might be called a campaign of intimidation. That was tied to a belief that seemed to be accepted among the believers that the scholars had held things back, and that there was more information, and that...mentioned gateways were being concealed. Madam Quiñones had blended aspects from other sources, fomenting her ranks with promises that might be obtained."

"Had the scholars, as we're calling them, really stumbled on something?" Bullfinch asked.

"They'd mixed and matched pieces with real finds and scholarship. There was disagreement in the circle about how far they should let things go, especially with someone like Madam Quiñones, who may have been delusional but was also charismatic. Also they argued about what might be real. Some felt there should always be gaps in the narrative. Others felt the social experiment they were conducting superseded other scholarly considerations and if they'd stumbled onto something real, so be it."

"Not so much into things like peer review?"

"Among other protocols. Some of them began to sprinkle more details here or there to be found." Redmond said. "It wasn't hard to blend in their new pieces of data and extrapolations. Some of the scholars felt as long as they kept an accurate record, what laymen discovered and even what got reported in the press didn't matter. Especially if it furthered the experiment. Professor Burke, you should know, never approved of seeding."

"You've said they put more things out there that came from other archaeological excavations for believers to find?" Bullfinch asked.

"We're reaching the extent of my knowledge. I'm not sure what all went into the mix because I heard all this second hand from Inny. I think it included the Ogham-like symbols and other details."

"No one was harmed back in the day?" O'Donnell asked. "Among the scholars, I mean?"

"No. Followed. Telephoned. Watched. Not harmed. It appeared to come to an end when Madam Quiñones died. Six, seven years ago. We thought she was the glue and that when she was no longer around, the followers had drifted apart just as the scholars had."

"But we flash forward," Bullfinch said.

Redmond nodded. "To a few months ago. When the first of the now-former scholars died and hints that what Madam Quiñones started was still alive. That was a man named Thomas Kelly in Galway."

"If we check into that, will we learn it's an unexplained poisoning?"

22

"**H**ow many names can he give us?" Rees asked once they'd return to *Aisteach* headquarters and briefed him in a small conference room. "These people need to be protected."

Redmond had agreed to come with them for further interview and was nervous enough to let Rees put him in a bunker. He'd been taken to an *Aisteach* safe house, though Nelda, his assistant, had refused, saying she was outside the scope of the situation having only worked for the shop the past year. She had a test coming up and needed to study.

"He'll give us a list," O'Donnell said. "We'll need to find them before the snake handlers do. I think we need to try and look up Burke's niece also. We saw her picture in his office. Vita Burke."

"We'll look for her," Rees said.

"When we find any of these people, we need to see what more they can tell us about what they've done," Bullfinch said. "And what the disciples might be planning. If we can understand the story the scholars—as Redmond and apparently Burke called them—set up for people to find, that may help us anticipate moves, and in pinning down the killers' ambitions."

"Redmond doesn't know the whole created myth?" Rees asked.

"Something about unleashing great power tied to mythology," O'Donnell said. "Not the specifics."

"Will the people we track down talk? This an egregious maneuver for academics isn't it? If they've established careers…"

"They definitely abandoned the usual protocols in favor of a thought experiment," Bullfinch said. "I can't imagine Burke or serious colleagues were really happy with what they'd done, though they may have become intrigued by the repercussions. To a point. We'll have to hope their fear of death will overcome other concerns."

"Pressure can be applied," Rees said. "So where are we? "We've uncovered a secret history that was under all our noses. What's made these believers or whoever they are suddenly more dangerous? What's the trigger? Why are they killing?"

"It would appear they want to accomplish something, and at the same time they want to eliminate the information trail," O'Donnell said. "It's preparation for what we need to treat as a terrorist act. You silence anyone who might give you away or help your enemy. We've seen it time and again, and I think Professor Bullfinch's earlier assessment is true. We need to put our ear to the ground just like we would for bomb-making or…"

"There's something in secret history they don't want others to have," Bullfinch said. "Something they think is to their benefit, and they're killing anyone who can't help them."

"From what Redmond could tell us, these people have always been on the sketchy side," O'Donnell said.

"They've been so sketchy and insignificant over the years that even organizations like mine, that monitor these things, haven't given them much of a sniff," Bullfinch said. "Something's delivered them a bit of a push, perhaps even gotten them better organized."

"To what purpose?" Rees asked.

"We can't see that yet. We haven't turned that card over yet, but we'd better," Bullfinch said.

"You're harboring a deeper worry," O'Donnell said. "What is it?"

"I've seen things in the world you wouldn't accept from just my word, and the O.C.L.T. records are classified even to the *Aist-each*. There's enough out there to be worrisome. These people think there's something catastrophic they can lay their hands on in what they're trying to assemble. My deeper worry, as you put it, is that there's something to their twisted ideas and that they might be able to tap into it. They may be killing to keep anyone from being able to undo what they want to attempt."

"You heard it yourself," O'Donnell said. "Half of it's made up. Don't they just want to get their hashtags in order to honor their late madam or something?"

"The story was inspired by a few real findings and the accumulated knowledge of archaeologists and anthropologists. These people are trying to assemble all the pieces while keeping them out of our hands. They wanted to kill me to inhibit us from figuring everything out."

He stuffed a hand into the accordion file holding the information they'd put together and pulled out the small black serpent figurine.

"Patrick had to battle a snake god. Other Irish tales speak of a serpent so large the world rested on its back and of demons that could rain fire down on the world. I think that's what our friends want to awaken. They want to find it and they want to be the only ones who hold the knowledge about it. Letting it out, or closing the door on it."

23

Keon Bello stared for a long time at the image of slash marks on coarse paper that had been relayed to him via email. Reportedly it had been received by his old friend Nathan Finch a day before his death.

He walked over to the desk not far from the entryway of this hovel he'd been staying in. He'd been moving from cheap hotel to cheap hotel for some time, once ripples had reached him that the old circles seemed active again.

He enlarged the image for a better look. Someone had taken special care with the calligraphy. It was formed with careful precision, and of course he recognized it.

He felt a new stab of fear.

If they knew Nathan, they knew who he was.

What he had done had come back, had boomeranged. His throat tightened a bit.

The character was from a lifetime ago. The thought experiment had been fresh then, still in the discussion phase.

He experienced a quick flashback. The hours at old stone ruins, sectioning off areas of dirt and documenting findings layer by layer, then, later, the pub table, the old friends and the markings on napkins and drawn on the tabletop amid the moisture from water rings left by beer steins.

He dragged a hand down his face, as if the gesture might wipe away anxiety. Why had he thought it could be forgotten or that all might remain undetected? A fire burned that could not be put out.

He'd been so young then, excited to be in college, in a new

country, and to be part of the circle of brilliant friends he'd met here. Excited to wander Dublin's wonderful, noisy, bustling streets, encouraged to make the most of education by his father who'd come from poverty in Ghana.

Did this message mean he'd been somehow marked now? He'd read the papers. Seen the names of people dead, strangers and familiar names. People who'd hoisted beers with him once upon a time. Friends who'd drifted in different directions, buoyed away by time but impossible to forget. He'd wept for them when he learned of their untimely deaths.

Poor Professor Burke who'd just been an advisor had been the latest. Burke had been a bit shocked by what they'd done, but he'd always remained their friend and mentor.

With Nathan's death then the professor's, they hadn't bothered to make it look like an accident, which made Keon think there was more to the reports he'd read of the others. He tucked the paper into a pocket and rubbed his face again, both hands, palm heels pressing in on his forehead as if that would facilitate deeper thinking.

Pack a bag, find somewhere to land, wait. He could call the pharma company where he worked, buy himself a few days off and lie low. Then he could do what he'd been thinking about, contact the others. Who was left? He ticked off a mental list.

Kaity?

Hayden?

Liam? Where was Liam these days?

Would they want to hear from him? He had to at least reach out. Perhaps it was time to tell what they had done. Perhaps it was time to find them again, talk the situation over.

He stuffed the mailing into his pocket and hurried into his bedroom to grab an overnight bag, even though he suspected he might need to be gone more than a few nights.

24

Bullfinch had ridden with New York cabbies who were less aggressive than O'Donnell. He pressed his palms against the dash above the glove compartment to brace himself as she wove her car through Dublin traffic, making the most of every sliver of space to keep them moving forward, even when traffic slowed.

In the moments when she lost out on open spaces to other drivers, she held back on the gas but released strings of expletives, mixing English and Gaelic oaths.

They'd opted to look for the person on Redmond's list who was closest geographically while Rees coordinated efforts to find those further afield including Burke's niece, Vita, who attended boarding school in London. The sooner Mack and O.C.L.T. ferreted out a few more threads in the oddly woven conspiracy, the sooner they might find a pattern that would anticipate future moves by the disciples.

"Do I have a turn coming up?" O'Donnell asked.

"Three blocks and on the left."

He drew in a breath and held it as she swerved around a lorry and in front of a compact, getting into the proper lane as the turn approached. Tires screeched—theirs and the driver's behind them—as she reached the intersection and jerked the wheel for the turn.

"You seem to have a bit of disregard for caution," Bullfinch said.

"My mam died when I was a girl. My father did everything by the book as a cop. Bullet got past his tactical vest in spite of it. I tend to just get on with the task at hand. Things fall where they will."

"You've faced tragedy," Bullfinch said. "Have you ever been told…"

"That I have a fatalistic outlook and pessimistic perspective? It's come up. It's on a chart of mine somewhere."

"I've found even when something seems inevitable, there are often ways to turn the tide on the worst."

"Good for you, Professor. We should all be so sunny, though I recall you being a little grim a few minutes ago. I do my best to change things, but I can't help but expect the worst and deal with it. We find this lady and the others on the list, maybe we can be hopeful. We'll see."

The building they sought was a four-story brown-brick with gray accents at the roofline and windows. O'Donnell wedged their vehicle in front of a pair of others, not in a parking place, but it got the car out of the flow of traffic.

They climbed out, and she led the way into the lobby.

"Thousand euros a month easy, and it's not that grand," she said, scanning the pale walls.

They found an elevator and thumbed Katherine White's floor. Bullfinch felt his breath slow a bit as he stepped on. Being back in an elevator was a little disturbing.

He didn't have much time to think about it. O'Donnell was thumbing the *Close Door* button to hurry things up.

Then they were on the third floor and hurrying toward No. 305. O'Donnell rested a hand on her hip where her weapon was holstered as she knocked.

There was no answer.

O'Donnell slid her weapon out of its holster, and she tried the knob, which turned readily.

No one meant to leave a door unlocked, even in a desirable building. She pushed it open and then leveled her weapon.

"Garda," she called.

Bullfinch's heart began to pound. This wasn't just a flash-back. There were too many chances that something was wrong.

He twisted the shaft of his cane, slid the bladed handle free, and followed O'Donnell inside as she stooped her shoulders, weapon ready.

Then, in a flurry of rustling fabric, she lunged to her left. Then came the sound of weight hitting the carpet. The weight of two bodies.

A woman had slammed into O'Donnell with such speed Bullfinch hadn't fully registered what had happened in the split second they were in front of him.

On impact, O'Donnell's weapon bounced from her hand, and the woman was on top of her, clawing, trying to pin her.

He tried to offer assistance, but something grabbed his coat collar and yanked him back. Half in the air, he saw a tall gaunt man, and then he was flung backward. He felt drywall give in as he crashed into it, and pictures in gold frames were jarred off hooks. He winced at the pain and let out a small gasp.

Hands grabbed his lapels, and he felt himself yanked forward. When his eyelids rose he saw the gaunt man's face rushing toward him. Correction, he was rushing toward it. He found himself inches from two narrow slits of pupil.

Bullfinch had seen plenty of things in his time, things beyond the accepted parameters of reality. He looked into that now. The eyes were not traditionally human. They'd been shrouded by glasses before. Now, uncovered, he could see they were a dark brownish green, flecked with yellow. Reptilian.

As a rattling hiss escaped the man's throat, Bullfinch raised both hands, delivering twin karate chops to the sides of the man's—or whatever's—neck.

The hands released their hold and he went spilling downward. The carpet was happily soft enough to absorb some of the impact, and he reached back, patting for his cane.

He found the shaft, not the blade, but as he pushed backward with his heels, he grabbed it and swung it in an arc that clipped the figure's chin before he could make a move to regain his hold.

Bullfinch allowed himself just a second to check O'Donnell,

and he saw her rapidly blocking her opponent's quick blows, deflecting fists and forearms that came at her with blinding speed. Then she took a step back and lifted a foot, managing a kick that hit high on her opponent's chest.

Holding her own.

He had to do the same.

He scrambled back, slid his hands along the cane and got a baseball bat-style grip on it. He swung, connecting near his attacker's jaw, spinning the man's head to one side.

He moved then, rising and bringing the cane down on the top of his attacker's hooded head. Even with the fabric absorbing part of the blow, it landed well. Bullfinch felt the shockwaves in his palms and knew he'd made a good connection. He couldn't say it stunned his opponent, but it slowed him and clearly brought pain, accompanied by a hesitation.

Another blow dropped the figure to his knees.

"Ja!" the woman shouted.

She'd seen the move over O'Donnell's shoulder.

She reacted with a round of blows more furious than she'd tried earlier, fast, hard, overwhelming. O'Donnell stepped back, raising arms and crossing them at the wrists to protect herself, and the woman seized the moment, slamming into her, knocking her to the floor, then stepping past her.

Bullfinch readied the cane for a swing in case the woman went in the direction of O'Donnell's lost weapon, but she rushed toward her colleague. Her hands cupped the large figure's shoulders, and she pulled him to his feet.

Bullfinch prepared a swing for both of them, but the woman launched a kick of her own. He felt her foot slam into his abdomen, finding a soft patch that drove pain up through his chest. He staggered as inky blackness sought to flood his vision. Dragging in breaths, finally finding air, he managed to place a hand against the wall.

As he steadied himself, he heard a flurry of footsteps.

A retreat.

He tried to shout for O'Donnell but couldn't produce sound. He heard plenty, though.

A couple of rapid blasts, deafening and echoing through the small living room. Slugs slammed into dry wall, and the intruders pushed through the doorway, unharmed.

"Professor."

O'Donnell was at his side.

"OK," he said. "Find the woman."

O'Donnell's feet sounded like a muffled bombardment as she rushed through the apartment, in and out of rooms, kicking doors.

"I think she's back here," O'Donnell said after several seconds. "I think she's OK."

"Let's get her to safety. If they had freelancers at my hotel, they could be back quickly."

O'Donnell led the way into the apartment's narrow hall and tapped on a back bedroom door when they reached it.

"Miss, I'm with the Garda."

That produced no response.

"Kick it in and let's get out of here," Bullfinch said.

His focus was toward the living room. He worried they'd be facing reinforcements soon.

"Miss, we need to get you out of here," O'Donnell said, giving it one more try.

Bullfinch gestured toward the door. "Before she goes out a window."

"We're on the third floor."

"She's desperate. A female ninja and a serpent man just invaded her apartment."

"What did you say?"

"Later."

O'Donnell stepped back and used a stomping kick to splinter the door near the latch.

An auburn-haired woman in her late thirties wearing a black sweater and jeans had positioned herself between the bed and the wall. O'Donnell put her at around 170 centimeters, 11 or 12 stone, not a twig but not terribly formidable. She held a figurine of a dancer above her head, ready to strike with it if anyone came too close.

O'Donnell had her badge in front of her.

"We need to go," she said.

"You being Garda means nothing."

Gray-green eyes were opened wide. Head cocked with a look of caution.

"This gentleman is from an organization that investigates the strange and the weird. We're partnered. If that doesn't ease your fears I'm gonna punch you and knock you unconscious and take you into protective custody."

A few minutes later, the woman had donned a parka with a faux fur-lined hood, stowed her cat, which had been hiding under the bathroom sink, with a neighbor, and climbed into the back seat of O'Donnell's cruiser.

"You were part of the student group who conducted the thought experiment?" Bullfinch asked. "You helped launch the Circle."

O'Donnell focused on getting them back into traffic, slashing back from the parking spot and producing a concert of random car horns.

"Circle?"

"Or whoever's playing the game that's driving these nut jobs," O'Donnell said.

She cut off a small Ford, and an angry shout flew out its open window. American accent. Laced with expletives. Must be a rental.

"We didn't make anything up."

"We've been filled in on the little game," O'Donnell said. "People are getting killed over it. Your friends. That's why you had the knock at your door a few minutes ago."

"We didn't make anything up," Katherine said. "We just sort

of compiled it all and…packaged it."

"No time for splitting hairs," O'Donnell said. "We need to know what you did so we can figure out what we need to do to put a stop to it."

"Especially if something real's at the heart of it," Bullfinch added.

"Real? It was an experiment, based on what we'd been studying in school and some things we found helping on a dig. Then we might have intercepted some information."

O'Donnell zigged into a narrow space producing honks and tire screeches, back to the driving she'd been exhibiting on the way. Bullfinch ignored it and twisted in his seat. She hadn't failed them in traffic so far. His focus on her driving wouldn't make any difference.

"What'd you find?"

She hesitated.

"Come on, nobody's benefiting from secrets now."

"A few things. Some writing on a wall, the tip of a standing stone with markings. We thought what we had at first was just a few more lines of Ogham and decided to make it about psychology and anthropology, see what that, along with primitive beliefs, might do if injected into the modern world. A new bit of mystery. We decided to throw the stone in the water and see where the ripples went."

"You hid all this from your professors?"

"For a while we were able to."

"These markings, you think you found them all?" O'Donnell asked.

A long and persistent horn blast punctuated her statement. Bullfinch had to turn around, but O'Donnell had already corrected whatever course had produced the honk before he glanced through the rear windscreen.

"We felt we had an almost complete set of characters. Others were created with calculations, and we sort of slipped them out on fabricated, but realistic stones."

"How'd you do that?" O'Donnell asked.

"We had a friend who was a sculptor. He liked the challenge. We found stone of the right type and age, and he set to work."

"How'd you extrapolate the markings?" Bullfinch asked.

"One of our friends had been doing some research, and he'd found a guy who had some lost notebooks of this pulp writer."

"Rudolph Rottman," Bullfinch said, tilting his head back and wrinkling his features as if he wanted to slap himself. "I saw some of his books in Burke's office."

O'Donnell glanced his way.

"Eyes on the road," he said.

She righted the car's course. "Who's Rudolph Rottman?"

"A pulp writer like Miss White said. He died in the Thirties, but he left behind endless stacks of notes and bestiaries for a mythology that served as underpinning for his stories. His ideas or shadows of them bubble up in all sorts of conspiracy theories."

"That's the name," Kaity said.

"He wrote of secret alphabets and a grimoire his characters were always desperate to get their hands on," Bullfinch said. "There have always been urban myths that the grimoire was based on something real or at least that in the stories the information it was purported to contain had some basis in reality."

"We had a friend who got hold of some of his papers, and they seemed like just what we needed along with Keon's brain."

"This guy like, what's his name, Lovecraft?" O'Donnell asked.

"More like Seabury Quinn as far as recognition in the mainstream," Bullfinch said. "He didn't sell a lot of stories but he had as many notes and papers as Tolkien, and conspiracy theorists have loved him. Based on what we've been seeing it's almost like one of his stories has come to life."

"You need to talk to our friend Keon," Kaity said. "He was the real wizard in those days and the one who really put it all together and figured out the missing pieces between the ones from the notes and the ones we found in various ruins."

25

Keon stepped off a bus near Merrion Square not far from the National Museum. As he strolled to a corner, stopping near the square's black iron fence and a cluster of trees, he slipped the burner mobi from his satchel and dialed the memorized number, keeping his eyes wide, scanning his surroundings. He should see anyone threatening coming at several paces.

At the moment the area was clear, so he listened to the dial tone again and again until finally came the *click* of someone answering.

"Go ahead."

"It's your African friend," Keon said.

"You think I only know one African?"

"I think you know which you're talking to."

Shawn Drury had always been paranoid and cautious.

"The friend from the old days," he said. "The one you tracked down."

"Where the Irish coffee was always strong and the MiWadi was always necessary the next day."

They'd often joked about MiWadi, an Irish fruit drink used for hangovers, which they agreed almost sounded African.

"What did you want?"

"We need to talk."

"Are you in the clear?'

Keon gave a look around. Anyone nearby seemed mundane.

"I think I am. I'm near a spot once as dear to us as O'Broder's. I'll be strolling there in a while looking at the stuffed hares."

"Forty-five minutes," Drury said.

And forty-minutes later, Keon stood in front of a stuffed moose that towered over the first floor of the natural history museum while deer and goats' heads looked on from a second-floor gallery. It was easy to see why some called it the Dead Zoo. The showroom was so packed with preserved animals, it almost felt claustrophobic. With a little imagination, it felt like walking among a diverse herd of creatures from many continents.

When a man with long, graying hair stepped to his side and flipped up the brim on a floppy black hat for just a second, it was as if he had emerged from the African bush.

The glimpse of his face confirmed he was Drury.

"You're watching what's going on?" Keon asked, focusing his attention on the moose as if he had a deep fascination with its coat.

"I've seen activity," Drury said.

"Do you have a feel for what's happening?"

"Some remnant of Madam Quiñones' followers seem to be going for the pieces of your puzzle that the original disciples never found. I've been following news and chatter. From what I can tell they have the stone that was at Castle Cluin."

"The old man died up in County Fingal," Keon said. "The authorities haven't connected it, I believe, but I think it's safe to say they have the markings from there."

"Then there's the elephant in the room," Drury said, smirking only slightly since they'd strolled past a display of rhinos.

"They're killing anyone in their path," Keon said. "Or almost anyone connected who can't or won't do them any good."

"Professor Burke didn't know where the pieces were buried."

"He was just an advisor."

"Word has it players are getting messages using the new symbols."

"What else do you hear?" Keon asked.

"Soon after the symbols they seem to die."

"I think I can confirm that. If they refuse to help, or can't, they seem to die anyway."

"Have you picked up how they're dying?"

"Poisoned."

"I'm hearing it's venom the authorities can't identify."

"Sounds like we're getting into that territory," Keon said. "You were the one who actually believed it might be real."

"If the offshoot reptile race exists, it would be one more chip on the scale for the theories you thought were fabrications. If the reptiles are really there, then what you thought was just a story…"

"If the reptile race is real, then why would they need the characters?"

"Lost knowledge, needed to tap into whatever energy's under our feet or in the air."

Keon felt an eerie ripple along his spine. Hidden Knowledge. His message.

The message he'd helped shape, thinking it was just legend.

"If any of this is true…" he whispered.

"They'd just need to find the last piece," Drury said. "Your control piece. Is it impossible to find?"

"Not impossible. Clues were planted. I always kept the algorithm on a computer that wasn't networked, so that should be safe."

"Maybe you should go dig it up."

"That might lead them to it. Maybe it's safest in the ground."

"If they find you, they'll torture you until you talk and then they'll have it anyway. Won't matter to you, but the rest of the world will find out if Rudolph Rottman was talking out of his ass or if he really had secret meetings with snake men in nineteen twenty-seven and sprinkled bits of what they told him into his stories."

"It has to be just a story."

"I decided long ago, what might be true was enough to sever ties with the disciples I'd met."

"Can you help me? I need to get off the grid until I can figure something out."

"I can lend you a pad, but I won't be coming there. I don't need them torturing me."

"Give me a key and the coordinates," Keon said. "I'll take it from there. Now, do you happen to have access to a car?"

26

"It really started when we worked on a real archaeological dig one summer. We were supervised by some of our professors, but we found markings on a wall and on a bit of stone. We got kind of enraptured by what we were doing and decided to keep it to ourselves for different purposes. We started doing a little more research, and things got out of hand from there."

"I should be impressed by the enthusiasm," Bullfinch said. "I find it hard to engage contemporary students."

"When did you figure out this wall had a new set of characters?" O'Donnell asked.

She was pulling past one of Dublin's bendy buses, a two-sectioned bus with an accordion-like connection at the center for cornering. Bullfinch held his breath as they whisked past its rear bumper.

"Keon recorded the marking, became kind of the keeper of what we had, started looking it over, started checking a book then online sources. He realized he had something, so he showed it to us at the pub the next night. We started joking about what it'd be like to plant it in some farmer's field."

"Then we started realizing that if there was one unknown there must be more, and we started sniffing around."

"You found what a number of full-fledged archaeologists didn't?"

"Well, we suddenly knew to look, and we started tapping into what others might know. We even found this call that was passed on to the institute we were working with. It hadn't been checked out yet, but this kooky old man claimed he'd found forgotten chambers in a ruin on his property."

O'Donnell shot back into the lane in front of the bus just in time to make a hard turn at a corner, crossing an oncoming lane only a few seconds ahead of another bus. Bullfinch looked through O'Donnell's window and saw the driver's panicked eyes as they zipped on past his front bumper. He thought about giving a reassuring wave, but then they were past.

"And we started to extrapolate," Kaity said from the back seat.

"Extrapolate."

"Keon started to assemble the secret Ogham alphabet, and, he was a mathematical genius. We started to figure out what had been found where, and he started to run probabilities and make educated guesses about the markings we had. He did pattern recognition, you might say."

"Part of the second alphabet is made up?"

"No. No. Nothing that simple. He worked really hard to fill in characteristics of missing symbols, and in some of the perusals of old information, we started to realize things were floating around that aligned. We started tracing them back and..."

"Rottman's grimoire," Bullfinch said. "The random markings from the grimoire stories? I feel like I should be slapping my forehead."

"You want to go easy on yourself and just fill me in?" O'Donnell asked.

Horns echoed in what seemed to be stereo. Bullfinch just closed his eyes. Better not to see anything coming.

"Rottman built a world and a mythology for his stories as we've mentioned. It included snippets of artwork. In correspondence, he claimed he'd been given some of it by shadowy figures he encountered in secret meetings and one-on-one encounters."

"Things in his stories resembled the characters we'd found, but it wasn't quite right. Keon noticed that the pieces that matched had characteristics that had been altered. Rottman changed them in his stories, but Keon tweaked everything, figured it all out."

"It's said Rottman incorporated his secret knowledge into his stories," Bullfinch said. "But in letters that have surfaced he revealed he wondered if it was real, so he changed things to make it safe and withheld some information."

"Except you had enough to use his alphabet to fill in the blanks and fix the changes?" O'Donnell asked, looking at Kaity.

"Keon had computer lab time. He worked with a program he wrote and kept under wraps that would model the characters and speculate on the pattern of the changes Rottman made. Keon was able to make decisions about the way he modified."

"This is kind of like what you were telling me about the Dead Sea Scrolls, sort of, isn't it?" O'Donnell asked.

Bullfinch opened his eyes just a fraction. They seemed to be in their proper lane and proceeding fast but in a reasonable trajectory.

"That's about right."

"So you took Rottman's ideas, the forgotten alphabet, filled in the blanks on yours and fixed it."

"That's about the size of it as the Americans would say," Kaity said. "Whether it was created by a secret order of Druids or whatever, we felt it was fairly accurate."

"Then you decided to play the game," Bullfinch said.

"We started to think it could be more interesting to do an experiment than to just turn in a few more rocks to sit in museums or have old scholars speculate on their contribution to the story of early man."

An array of symbols on various types of paper were spread across the table. Malphas sat at the end, looking more ancient in the harsh fluorescent light of the hotel meeting room as Freya and Jaager strolled in.

The symbols she'd contributed were in the mix. A large piece of drawing paper had been placed at the end of the table for her to look at the almost complete array of characters. One wide space was left open between strings of slashes and whorls.

She looked across the room. Seated beside a slumped and weary William Groom in his wheelchair, Edward and a young female assistant seemed to wait patiently

William Groom looked almost like he'd aged more since he was last seen.

Edward remained as crisp as ever. Malphas peeled back the hood. He was more ancient than either of them, the skin on his cheeks a wrinkled parchment. His eyes were watery yet intense and wild.

"I understand the black man has eluded you."

"For the moment. Vacated his house a while back, took anything that mattered it seems, but we're working on it."

He rose and walked to the paper that featured the compiled list of characters. He tapped a spot left empty between other sets of hash marks.

"We need the final character."

He pulled over another piece of paper, a topological map with networks of lines and red dots arranged along the lines. He tapped one of the dots.

"An incomplete configuration won't serve us, and the celestial alignments are available for a limited time."

"In addition to helping with your needs, our friends here have generously provided us with assistance in the search," Freya said. "We have eyes on him. We'll let him lead us to the final piece."

"This is not a leisurely process. We're putting pieces in place as we speak. My associate is out now exploring options, but we don't want to miss opportunities. Is that clear? You were chosen for your tenacity. Trusted with this task. Are you up to it?"

"Yes. You don't need to worry."

"The Grooms are making resources available even though it might make them vulnerable. Go find the African and make him lead us to that last mark."

"I will, sir," Freya said, summoning all her confidence.

She'd make it work.

Bullfinch found that his heart rate actually slowed a bit once he was outside O'Donnell's vehicle, even after a climb up the stairs at Keon's small two-story house. Since the dwelling proved to be empty, he wondered if they'd needed O'Donnell's derring-do pace. Then he wondered for just a second if the term derring-do was archaic and that it made him old. Perhaps he was a bit old to be running around, chasing this kind of strangeness.

But the world kept needing to be saved.

The state of the house confirmed cause for concern for the man he sought. The place had been tossed. Cabinets had been emptied. Clothes had been yanked from the closet, and the mattress had been tumbled off the bed frame then ripped open so that stuffing spilled out.

"No stone unturned," O'Donnell said.

She stood at the center of the bedroom, scanning, but it just looked like any spot in the suburbs that had been upended.

"Is there a landline?" Bullfinch asked.

"Couldn't tell you," Kaity said. Her distraction was evident. Her gaze was trained on the devastation, eyes wide at the thoroughness.

A search failed to yield a phone, but Bullfinch's hopes hadn't been that high about a redial telling them anything. He followed O'Donnell crunching over strewn breakfast cereal through the kitchen to look out through a small window into Keon's narrow and fenced back yard. A tiny garden shed, pre-fab but made of cedar, stood under a squat little tree near his fence. The door flagged open in a gentle breeze.

They stepped out a back door and headed toward the structure for a look. Bullfinch noticed a twisted padlock in the grass on the way. Inside the small chamber, potting soil, shovels and gardening tools had all been disturbed, even the wooden floor of the shed pried up.

"He's not here and neither is anything useful," Bullfinch said.

O'Donnell turned to their charge. "Ms. White, any thoughts on where he'd go?"

She had approached quietly from behind them. She stood, seeming nervous and a bit vague as she looked around.

"Keon was always the brilliant one. He compiled the information, kept it all. He was always careful."

"Could they have taken him?"

"If he was here when they were, looks like he didn't give them anything."

Bullfinch let out a slow sigh.

"We need to find him. Why don't we take her back to your headquarters?" he said to O'Donnell in a low whisper. "We're going to need Garda analysts again and their facial recognition to try and figure out where Mr. Bello has gone. If he does hold the key to the kingdom and he took it, we're going to need him alive and so are they."

"What if the disciples took him?" O'Donnell said.

"I guess we'll find out soon enough and learn if it was a game or if Rudolph Rottman was onto something."

27

Freya approached Mike quietly, stepping near his left shoulder, not getting too close before she spoke. She'd learned that before he was the head of their security team, he'd served in the American military police, then been a cop before going private, so he had surveillance experience on his resume.

With his background and training, she didn't want to trigger any reflex responses she'd regret. If her nerves were tense, and her reflexes coiled, she could imagine his were even more likely to flare.

"I hear you," he said.

He'd picked up some subtle trace of her approach and sensed her caution. He turned with a quick, grim upward tick of one corner of his mouth to relieve her. Then it was gone and calm stoicism returned.

"Our man's in a coffee shop over there. Liking the free WiFi, I suspect."

Now that she was aware of it, she could almost feel his military confidence and read the underlying power in posture. Not terribly tall but solid.

"He looked nervous when he went in," Mike said. "Looking over his shoulder. Didn't see me."

"Alone?"

One quick tick of the head affirmed.

"My recommendation's follow for a while." He kept his gaze trained on the front of the shop. "We need a professional approach."

Freya felt her jaw lower in quiet shock, but she held back words and avoided turning his way. No need to give him a reaction or a personal defense. Nor to remind him of the assault at the hotel and that failure. She could tell he'd just grunt his response and disapproval or remind her that the hotel attackers had been free-lancers. *Help* wasn't always all it cracked up to be.

"I agree," she said. "Do you have the manpower in town to handle this?"

"Got a guy on the back door. Another at the corner. We'll find whatever rock this is the bosses are so sold on."

"You're gonna be surprised," Freya said. She let her accent go full force. She hoped that carried a subtext of contempt, though she mouthed a *focáil leat* only in her head. Why did it have to be an American?

She pushed back her annoyance as the African emerged from the shop door. He checked both directions, but didn't look their way. After a second of looking like he would head up the sidewalk, he stepped to the curb and lifted a hand.

A little silver car marked TAXI cruised to a stop. No one ever got a car that quickly. Freya felt panic start to rise, but as the silver compact pulled away, a small black sedan slid past after it, and in the same second a mobi chirped in Mike's pocket.

"Got 'em? Good."

He broke the connection and hit the phone face again with his thumb and waited just a second.

"Pick us up."

Freya swore silently again. A little black sedan was pulling to curbside in a few seconds. The son of a bitch really was efficient.

28

"**I**f you were Keon, where would you go?"

O'Donnell stood in front of a full-screen map in the *Aist-each* conference room. The predominant color was a muted beige for most of the geography, with thoroughfares contrasting in a bold mustard yellow. Reds and blues pinpointed various locations, while round blips indicated law enforcement and emergency vehicles.

Rees had had it pulled up and said it offered the latest geographic information system available along with smart mapping and interfaces with other systems including terrorist databases. That included a terrorist-tracking system and feeds related to strange phenomenon that other agencies wouldn't have found as exciting. Too bad they didn't have an undercover operative embedded with this Ning group.

Rees sat now beside Kaity while Bullfinch stood just behind them, looking toward the view screen. All of them were bathed in the screen's glow, blanketed in a distorted mirror of it.

"Maybe I'd go after the last puzzle pieces to keep them safe, but I don't know where the symbols and stones are buried. Like I said, after a point, he kept it to himself. Wouldn't tell anyone."

"How well do you know him?" O'Donnell asked. "What's he eat? What kind of coffee does he like? We'll track him like we would a terrorist and tie in with the cams around the city and facial recognition."

"Coffee?"

"Tea, juice, scotch, cigarettes?"

"He quit smoking. Uh, he likes his coffee."

"Starbucks?"

"Just regular coffee. Black."

"A favorite shop then? What's he buy?"

She closed her eyes, thinking.

Rees relayed the info through his Bluetooth as O'Donnell coaxed details from Kaity, softening her voice. A patience and gentleness Bullfinch hadn't seen before emerged from the officer. When she needed, the brusque manner could be submerged. She projected all the empathy and patience of a victim services counselor.

Bullfinch let the relay session continue and stepped from his place behind the others and approached the map screen's beige glow. He scanned street names, noted the highway numbers and occasional bursts of blue indicating water. Just about everything of the city's topography was represented.

"Can you show Ley lines on this system?" Bullfinch asked, raising his voice to interrupt the gentle quizzing. Given the proficiency of Rees and his team in matters of the paranormal, it seemed possible.

"Magic paths again, professor?" O'Donnell asked.

"Energy lines," he said. "They're relevant to the beliefs of those we're tracking and were noted by the conspirators. They'll be relevant to the task."

Rees touched the Bluetooth earpiece again and in a moment a new network of crisscrossing lines appeared in orange across the display. They stretched across the city in a couple of places.

"Can you zoom out?"

Rees spoke softly again.

Bullfinch observed the trajectory. They angled on up the coast and southward as well. He mentally calculated distances and spots on the lines, sacred locations, ancient sites.

He realized everyone stared at him. He looked back at the curious eyes. O'Donnell looked particularly quizzical and skeptical at the same time.

"Go on with your work," he said. "It's important to stay

practical. I'm just gathering my thoughts."

When the questioning began anew, he stepped toward the map and lifted a hand. The screen continued to reflect the map's topography onto his skin, but he stayed focused on the map's face, running a finger along one line and another, letting an index finger tip glide west then back to the city.

Ireland was dappled with sacred places. So many choices. Keon might go any direction, but perhaps some of the puzzle pieces had been planted close to Dublin.

His finger glided north and landed on Mellifont Abbey. County Louth. What was that, twelfth century? It was a beautiful collection of ruins, certainly a qualifying spot. He let his finger slide a little west, and it fell on the Hill of Tara, an important point for the Celtic high kings. Equally worthy.

He let out a quiet sigh. Needle in a haystack. Or a stone in rock pile. It was impossible to guess where the young scholars would have placed their little puzzle pieces.

But almost against his will, his hand slid west, farther west toward a point of myth and legend that had been in his thoughts for a while now as all the talk of serpents and legends had, well, coiled and writhed.

It was there all right, dissected by a Ley line.

Wherever the puzzle pieces were held, he had had a feeling they'd be going to the spot in front of his eyes now. Croagh Patrick. With all his time in the states, he had to remind himself it would be pronounced crow-guh. County Mayo, not that far from the North Atlantic Ocean. The spot was often called The Reek, and it held great significance in the annals of Irish faith, mystery and legend. It almost had to be the point they were all heading, if the little pieces told the story they seemed to.

It was a monument to what the people they pursued were about, what they wanted. In his gut it produced a deep and troubling fear.

He moved near its point on the screen and put a finger on its locator dot.

"Mr. Rees, do you have anyone near this location? It might become important if we don't locate our young man soon."

They were getting closer. Freya felt excitement building.

From the back seat, she watched the young African man step out of the Europcar rental outlet near City Centre where the hired car had deposited him. He was accompanied by a young woman in a green blazer and dress that almost matched the company's sign. He nodded frequently, hearing a spiel about the care of the vehicle, no doubt.

"Too much to hope he's got it in a storage locker in town," Mike said. He sat in front beside the stoic driver, and his tone was a blend of boredom and weariness.

"Guess I'm gonna get to see the lovely Irish countryside."

"You might enjoy the scenery," Freya said.

She'd tired of his grim attitude. She wouldn't let him kill her mood. She was the one who'd climbed around crumbling ruins and chased through half the country already. She was the one who'd killed more people for the cause than she cared to think about.

Mike was just a necessary evil because the disciples needed his people's bankroll. His commentary wasn't necessary.

The young man shook the Europcar representative's hand and tossed his satchel into the back seat, then climbed behind the wheel. Would he lead them all the way?

She closed her eyes just a second and drew in a breath, reminding herself that wherever this took them, they had to be getting closer. Closer to the goal, to realizing the possible. Closer to proving the truth of the past and realizing the glorious excitement of harnessing the power and energy so long forgotten, literally buried.

29

Keon had not traveled the highway in years, but suddenly it all seemed familiar again. As he headed through the countryside, looking across the still-familiar fields with occasional sprouts of stone—old walls and houses and vestiges of turrets and keeps—he remembered the old days, slinking through those structures. At first he'd been seeking more marks or more pieces of his little puzzle he could use. Later the purpose had shifted.

He'd cruised in another rental in those later days, a van, hurling toward adventure, excited by the game, wondering who'd find the clues they had been placing and how it would all come together. All of it had been coupled with the tantalizing notions and fragments they'd picked up. What if the symbols, the secrets tied to real legend?

The road signs and the names of the small towns had sounded quaint to his immigrant brain in those days. Kil- and -derry prefixes and suffixes seemed to be everywhere. They'd envisioned archaeologists of the future, what was then the future, puzzling over the artifacts and the beliefs they seemed to represent.

They'd had a celebration back in the day, when the last piece had been hidden. Kaity had poured wine when he'd met them after the placement, and they'd hoisted them high and toasted.

They'd never imagined the urgency or the real power of what they were playing with. They'd compiled the pieces just for authenticity. The real players today in their little scavenger hunt were more ominous than the quizzical scholars or the quirky amateurs they'd imagined.

The GPS map on the rental's dash unfurled before him,

clicking off the distance in small numbers at the lower corner. A turn was coming up, an angle off the main road that would lead him down the final leg.

Then what?

He'd find that last piece, dig it up, and then drive to the ocean and throw it in. That would do it. Sunken beneath the waves, that would be good enough. No one would ever find it there. It would rest with the things it might just possibly have the power to summon.

"He's turning," Mike growled. "Slow down a little."

The vehicle dropped speed almost too abruptly.

"Go past the turn. We'll catch up with him." He turned to Freya. "Get on the horn to your friend and tell him the same."

Freya felt a flutter in her stomach as she thumbed Jaager's number. It was amazing how close they were to finishing. They definitely didn't want to tip their hand now. Not with the rise so close, so possible. Everything might be realized now. Everything she'd dreamed since she first read hints of the Ning in the handouts from the little group she'd attended. She'd dreamed of the power and turning the tables on the world. Now it was in sight.

The driver slowed after passing the roadway and then made a U-turn on the narrow highway and backtracked. The African's rental was just disappearing around a curve ahead when they angled onto the road he'd taken, gravel and grit crunching under their tires.

She spoke softly into the cell, giving directions. She looked up at road signs as their vehicle moved along. First was a small highway number marker. Not far past it, another sign appeared, and she knew when she saw it that it had to mark their destination.

Blackton Priory.

A Celtic cross stood just inside the gray stone wall that stretched beside the roadway. Jagged and craggy, the wall still looked sturdy in spite of the centuries it had weathered.

Keon counted them in his head. Blackton was a thirteenth-century settlement, so eight hundred years? The awe of that hadn't struck him on the previous visit. He'd been too young.

He'd known when it was selected the marking would pre-date the settlement, but that was supposed to be part of the mystery for any searchers who came later. It would be unexplained, just as the disparate markings they'd discovered on sites they'd worked.

He had a few more years behind him now. He understood years and their passing just as he understood many things he hadn't on his last visit. He'd come to understand gravity and youthful indiscretion as well as the solemnity of the study of the past.

He took things seriously in a way he hadn't in the old days, in a way he'd never have listened to back then. Who could have anticipated how wrong a game could go all those years ago?

They'd joked the pieces might never be found, but even by the time of the last piece being placed, Keon had worried about the little hints of the truths behind the hidden alphabet.

As reports of findings from Roman graves and other digs plus new theories about the influence of comets had filtered to him through news accounts and reports in archaeology journals, he'd grown more concerned over what they'd stumbled upon. They'd been obfuscating more than they'd realized in their thought experiment.

In the day, he, Kaity, Hayden, Nathan, Liam, the others, had all laughed at old Professor Burke and his worries and concerns about integrity and ethics when he learned of the game. They'd told him they were breaking new ground, inventing a discipline, a blend of archaeology and sociology with a dash of psychology and anthropology, not to mention the metaphysical. They would shatter tired old protocols and invent their own new models with the world as their lab and the people their lab rats.

The giddiness had long faded. The time had come to pay the price for their arrogance and insurrection. The rats had turned.

He walked across the familiar expanse of lawn, resting the small collapsible shovel he'd brought with him over one shoulder, scanning the random, jagged stone blocks that jutted up at intervals that bore no discernable pattern.

They looked familiar, but the piece had been hidden somewhere beyond the first wall, or the remains of the wall, which had served the priory as a fence but also formed a portion of one building corner. All that remained of that dwelling now were a few bits of wall with window-shaped openings.

Green mossy growth coated much of the stone while sprigs of grass and brush popped up in various spots between stone. He moved past those as well. He'd wanted to place their prize so that it seemed it was something previous excavations of the site had missed. In those days, the excavations of this spot had been just a decade before.

As he moved around the first wall, heading toward the heart of the settlement where more complete structures remained, dark clouds began to roll in.

He should have brought a poncho as well as his little shovel. Live and learn. It was as if the world did not look fondly on his actions today, but things had been bright and sunny on the first visit. The plan had seemed blessed by the heavens. Maybe omens weren't reliable.

A crack of distant thunder rumbled. A challenge to his train of thought. He ignored it and stepped around stones and past the central wall with a series of vaulted openings. They looked familiar.

How many paces from the wall? He'd memorized it long ago. Now he wasn't quite certain. Had it been ten, a nice round number?

He'd start with that. If he had to dig a couple of holes, that wouldn't be the end of the world. Suddenly his head tilted back and a laugh he couldn't contain burst from his throat. A couple of holes wouldn't be the end of the world, but what rested at the bottom of one of them might be.

He looked down at his feet, and at the grassy patch just in front of his toes. Time to try and avoid finding out. He took the shovel from his shoulder and drove the blade into the ground.

"Let him do the work." Mike passed the small pair of binoculars to Freya. "Worst thing about waiting, you can't have a cigarette. He might see the smoke."

"Maybe it's not buried too deep," Freya said. "When we nab him, you can light up." She hoped the sarcasm just lightly coated her words and didn't drip down onto his shoes.

They turned as slight vibrations rippled their way across the ground. Jaager approached, flanked by the walking Groom brother.

"Gang's all here," Mike said under his breath. "Guy digs up the rock, we're ready to get the show on the road."

"OK, we've found him," Rees said. "Or at least we have a sighting."

"Quicker than before," O'Donnell said.

"He wasn't fighting rain and covering his features. And someone named Mack from Professor Bullfinch's side of the pond stepped in digitally to offer his help, I'm being told."

He spoke into his Bluetooth and jerky color imagery filled the screen in front of him. Angled from overhead, the video pointed down on a car, and a man working with the hose from a petrol pump.

He looked to be in a hurry.

Rees moved to Kaity's side and put a gentle hand on her shoulder.

"Is that your friend?"

The camera offered a view mostly of the top of the man's head. Her eyelids narrowed as she studied the form.

"The build is right."

"Anything else?"

O'Donnell focused on the woman rather than the screen. As the man returned the pump handle to its cradle she caught sight of something that brought a flicker of recognition.

"What is it?" O'Donnell asked.

"He's still wearing a dangling earring. I can see it. Maybe the same one he always wore. That's Keon."

"Where is this?" Bullfinch asked.

"Map point," Rees said softly for the Bluetooth.

An overlay appeared on the screen.

"That's almost into Country Cork," the director said.

"Can we see the Ley lines?" Bullfinch said.

The screen flickered again, offering a new network of lines over the highway view.

The professor stepped toward the screen, studying it for just a few seconds, his gaze moving from point to point.

"There," he said.

His finger angled toward a point high on the map.

"That has to be where he's headed. That's an old monastic settlement. When was this taken?"

"Two and a half hours ago."

"My god that's two hundred and fifty kilometers away," Bullfinch said. "He's had time to get there."

"You really think that's where he's headed?"

"It's a pretty good point for their little scavenger hunt. Kaity?"

She nodded.

"It makes sense to our thinking in those days. We wanted the pieces to turn up where they seemed to fit naturally with a little mystery at times."

"If they catch him there and obtain the last symbol, we don't know what could happen…"

"We can get you there fast," Rees said. "We'll call up Garda Air Support. They should lend us a chopper."

"You have a chopper? Not winged unicorns?" O'Donnell asked.

"Don't be absurd," Rees said. "If we were going to use anything like that we'd have winged humanoids, not mythical creatures that don't exist."

He paused just a moment, thinking.

"Since we don't quite know what we're up against, we do have an artifact that might be handy."

He tapped his Bluetooth again. "Bring up the sword," he said.

Bullfinch lifted an eyebrow.

"You may have noticed we have some unusual objects and other items around here."

"I saw the dog and that blue—" O'Donnell started.

"Not all odd finds come our way, obviously, but quite a few do," Rees said. "Some men found this weapon in a spot in County Sligo after a flood. We've been studying its markings and properties, and it's been in the vault a while for safekeeping."

"Age?" Bullfinch asked.

"Probably Bronze Age, older."

A worker in a white jumpsuit brought in a long item wrapped in a cloth.

"It features some kind of symbols on the blade, not quite like Ogham or the secret markings, but it seems to have some unusual properties and seems to store or channel energy," Rees explained. He folded back the cloth and gave the sword a bit of a shake. It seemed to produce a slight hum.

"Who knows, could be something we might need."

O'Donnell and Bullfinch moved in to look over the markings which lined the blade from top to bottom."

"We cleaned some rust away after a good bit of debate," Rees said.

"Can't hurt to have it on hand," Bullfinch agreed.

Rees tested its weight a bit. "We've jokingly said it might be the Celtic deity Lugh's sword of lightning."

"He was called Lugh *Lámhfhada*, Lugh of the Long Arm," Bullfinch said. "Recent study associates him with comets and their appearance, and some say the lines between Lugh and Patrick as mythic heroes blur a bit. Perhaps he was a man who found an alien sword."

Bullfinch had been focused again on the map until the sword

mention, studying the surrounding terrain. He turned his focus back to that now. Bring it along. "Looks like there's a field close enough by to set down."

"All right, let's move," Rees said.

30

When the shovel blade struck something a few inches down, Keon sighed with relief. After a few layers of dirt had been piled beside the hole, he'd begun to worry his memory had grown fuzzy, and at least the short man seemed to be armed.

Now, here it was, the old stone. He knelt and brushed dirt back and wedged fingers under the piece, working it side to side until he'd pulled it free. He turned it over in his hands then, feeling the cold and the damp as he searched for the marking. It was on the side that had faced down, so he had to scrape back a layer of dirt caked to it and then run a fingernail along the etched canals to clear more flakes away.

But then he was looking at it, and the angled lines and upticks were familiar again, and it was as if he'd been here yesterday, looking at the piece one last time before sinking it in the hole.

For a moment, he was the self he'd been all those years ago. With great clarity, he recalled how he'd wondered then what would become of it, when it would be found and what would be happening at the time. Suddenly, in a flash, he was here and he knew, and the time between seemed like mere seconds.

For one heartbeat, he felt a bit of elation. The experiment had generated more fervor than he could have ever imagined. It had worked. It had done what they'd thought it might, grown into a new tendril of belief.

Now he had to ask the same thing he'd read about one of the Americans who'd worked on the Manhattan Project. When the first bomb dropped he'd felt a sense of elation because it worked. In the next instant, he thought: "My God, what have we wrought."

What had they wrought?

Perhaps he'd crush the stone here and now. Better to never find out. Better to never know if they'd re-constructed an elaborate secret alphabet that bore real power or if they'd played a fun game with old legends. He'd decided long ago never to let the computer with his algorithm on a network. Back in the day, that hadn't been quite as hard as it would be now.

That isolation didn't mean someone couldn't re-create what he'd done, but until now, as far as he was aware, no one in the disparate circles had attempted it. It wasn't quite in the wheel house of many of those the whispers had attracted. Unfortunately, more sophisticated converts had arrived. The only good thing was that building and running an algorithm took time. Finding a rock was perhaps easier.

He looked around for a spot to put down the rock he held. He could pry loose another heavy stone from somewhere in the ruins and smash it. He could obliterate the last piece. Put an end to this. End it all.

He took a step toward a sloping central wall. Perhaps he could just bang it against that. For all its age, it appeared sturdy enough.

The sound of footfalls made him pause. He turned his head just enough to give him peripheral vision over his right shoulder. The figure that stood back, almost at a diagonal, was a blur. Tall, draped in a coat, head shrouded. He didn't see a weapon, and as his heart fluttered he prepared to run.

He didn't take a step.

Something coiled around his abdomen. Something that constricted and held him fast. Something not cold but moist. He felt the moisture through his shirt. Then he turned his head a little more and confirmed what he'd feared, what his brain had suddenly screamed at him.

The tentacle encircling him stretched from the figure he'd thought to be just a man.

31

"**H**ere's an empty hole," O'Donnell said.

"I think I found something," she added in a raised voice when she realized she hadn't been heard over the wind that swirled through the complex.

The blue, yellow and white Garda chopper, piloted by Jimmy Ahlstrom, a small and overly jovial man with a slight tick tic, had landed five minutes earlier. "I promise to wait on ya," he'd said. "For a while."

She'd given him a glare and they'd hiked from the nearby field and fanned out as they'd spotted the silhouette of the stone remains on the horizon. O'Donnell had had her weapon ready, keeping Kaity at her side to protect her, but as they moved through the various arches and around the ruined walls, the place proved pretty quickly to be deserted.

She cursed under her breath. Minutes short of the goal.

"Dirt's fresh. Been here and gone," she said, spinning as she spoke to look around and make sure "here and gone" was accurate.

"Maybe Keon got the stone and ran before the others got here," Kaity said.

"Let's hope for that, but, dammit, back to square one either way. We don't know where he went."

Rees had eyes out among traditional Garda forces, but they couldn't see and be everywhere. Bullfinch approached from off to the right, a hand on his hat to keep it from being lifted by the breeze. His coat sounded like a ship's sail as the wind assaulted.

"Any ideas?" she asked. "Because it's lookin' like we got nothin'."

He was about to speak when Rees came in from the direction he'd been searching, sidearm pressed at his side, finger on that bloody earpiece as usual.

"What's that? It's windy out here," he said in a raised voice.

He dropped his free hand to his side a second later.

"Couple of cars were just spotted near Cork Airport. Cluster of folks including a woman and a tall man. Black male in the mix."

"So we have efficient officers out there, but you're not the only one with air power? And they're literally in the wind."

"We're requesting flight plans so we can figure it out, but they're putting distance behind them. Air traffic control is saying they headed west."

"Leaving the country?"

Bullfinch mulled the directions for a moment.

"I have an idea where they might be headed," he said. "If we want to risk a goose chase."

"There's a storm coming," Rees said. "We're going to be grounded soon. Then we're just sitting."

"Based on the hints of Rottman themes and the way they're drawn to sacred places along with the interest in serpents, if they have the last piece they think they need, The Reek can't be ruled out and that's on your western shore."

"The Reek? Three hundred kilometers from here at least," O'Donnell said.

"But it fits. Croagh Patrick is the most sacred site in Ireland."

O'Donnell gave a hard nod. "I know, I know professor. You're thinking it's where St. Patrick is supposed to have faced off with Crom Cruach. It's where these people will bring Crom back. You think that's real?"

"I've seen enough in the world to believe that anything's possible. Have we heard anything from there, Mr. Rees?"

"I've asked people to be on alert. No reports yet."

"So they want to use these little squiggles and slashes to wake everything up like you've been dreading?" O'Donnell asked.

"Possibly."

"Clew Bay is filled with little islands an' pockets," Rees said. "Lots of places for an entity to hide."

"I can't say I believe that," O'Donnell said. "But maybe it'll get everyone involved in our murders into one place, and maybe we can stop a few more."

"Whatever they're up to, it's the *Aisteach*'s job to check it out," Rees said. "Let's get the bird in the air before the Jimmy gets itchy about the weather."

"If he's nervous, maybe that'll stop his goddamned jokes," O'Donnell said.

32

Freya's heart fluttered and her breath tightened. They were so close. So close to unleashing everything she'd read about, everything she'd heard whispered in her first encounter with a believer and the meetings that followed.

She leaned against the small plane's bulkhead, looking out her window at the country below as the engines droned. Soon it would be a different place, a re-shaped and re-imagined island.

As she'd listened in that first musty and cramped little room on a side street about what followers of the serpent and Madam Quiñones hoped to bring about, she'd contemplated a new world, a new form of empowerment.

A world born of chaos, reshaped, reimagined by the disciples once the Ning—many names were used, but that was the one she preferred—had been unleashed.

The Brothers Groom had their plans, their ideas, things they wanted out of this, but she would have her place, her own opportunities to carve a new existence and a new corner of the world. A new place for girls like her from poor families with no resources or protections.

"Would you like wine?"

Edward asking. The other brother was buckled into a seat and sat slumped and silent.

"No, thanks. I need to keep my wits sharp."

The people after them weren't idiots. They didn't understand what was about to happen, but they weren't idiots. The old man had eluded Mike and skilled gunmen. The woman was clearly formidable. They were dedicated and as tenacious as she and the others. By nature, they'd want to interfere.

She watched Mike lift a hand, declining a drink as well. She didn't care for him, but at least he'd be handy if they met opposition at the heart of the ritual.

Let them come.

A black car met them at the airport. The brothers were a bit long on style. They rode quietly, the Grooms and Malphas still sipping wine as they cruised to a rendezvous at a café a couple of miles from the airport.

They piled from the vehicle there, William helped into his chair, for a quick trip to the back of a lorry parked at the edge of the gravel parking lot. A couple of workmen with beards and heavy jackets waited.

"Everything's as you wanted," one of them said when the brothers approached.

The other worker, tall and less talkative, drew back a canvas flap that covered the back of the vehicle, and the brothers edged forward. Edward took a look inside, then nodded an assurance to William as Malphas approached.

The old man stepped between them and peered into the truck's shadowy depths. He stared in for just a second and seemed satisfied, then gestured for Freya to step forward.

She joined him along with Jaager, and they looked in at neatly piled rows of fresh, smooth timber stakes, small poles really, nicely rounded, sharpened at their ends. She could smell the rich, fresh aroma of the wood.

"Perfect," the old man said.

Jaager leaned forward and took one of the posts, sliding it toward them until the upper end emerged from shadow. One of the newly found symbols had been burned into a spot leaving shallow black indentations of about nine or ten millimeters. The lines and slashes looked precise and clean.

Another bearded workman in a plaid wool vest stepped to their sides and leaned into the lorry, searching just for a second for an unmarked post. When he found it, he nodded to another who helped him slide it out and lean the top of it on the bumper.

"Do you have the last marking?" he asked.

Freya produced her phone and offered a photo she'd snapped of the last image after they'd brought the stone out of the ground and dusted it off.

"Get the original," the old man said. "We don't want any mistakes."

Freya and Jaager headed back to the vehicle they'd arrived in. Mike had waited near it and popped the trunk now with an electronic key ring. Jaager, who'd followed, lifted the stone and the leather shammy they'd wrapped around it.

Before he could slam it, the car began to rock or at least bounce a bit.

Freya jerked her head toward the truck to send him on, then walked to the door and looked in at the African.

"What are you people doing?" he shouted through the glass.

They'd kept him seated in the back of the sedan, hands bound behind him.

"Shut up," Mike said, tossing a cigarette and returning from the spot where he'd dropped back to observe the activities.

"You'll see," Freya said, giving him a wry smile. "You'll see how right you were all along."

She followed Jaager to the truck again where he turned the stone so that the symbol was there for the workman.

"Don't you need to make a stencil?" she asked.

"Ideally," the bearded workman said. "But I've got this."

He slipped a small, cordless power tool, shaped almost like a power screwdriver, from his vest pocket. Instead of a screwdriver head it featured a small, cylindrical stone head. As he thumbed the power button, LED lights lit up around the nose.

Satisfied it was at full strength, he leaned into the post and, with the tool held almost like a pencil, he began to etch a new version of the marking from the stone.

"You gonna climb the mountain with those?" Keon shouted from his spot.

Mike stepped to the window and delivered a light backhand whack to the side of his face, designed to deliver a sting rather than a bruising blow, it appeared.

"We won't need to go that high," the old man said. "The power's in the earth, and we're looking to the sea."

The brothers had cell phones out, speaking as they watched, bending against the wind but eyes wide with excitement. Freya couldn't be sure who they were calling, but clearly they had people waiting to hear the outcome, people as anxious as they were. She had to admit they'd made the operation easier, especially this final component. It made the construction of the implements easy as well. Out-of-work craftsmen didn't ask many questions.

"The others can be put in place while he finishes," Malphas said. "There are some old walls near the edge of the bay. I'll show you the placement."

A few drops of cold rain stung Freya's cheeks, but she ignored them. A storm wouldn't matter now.

Too much was about to happen to be worried by a little rain.

Rain spattered the chopper's cockpit windshield and streaked across the curved surface as the cabin tilted from side to side, buffeted by wind blasts that seemed to slam them from beneath.

"ETA?" Rees asked.

"Better part of an hour in this wind and we'll be dippin' into the reserves at that," Ahlstrom said. "I might have to finish on a prayer unless your guest here has any conjurin' tricks up his sleeve."

"I'm not a magician," Bullfinch said. Silently, he wished Rebecca were with them. There were ways, of course, but without a proper talisman or object, it was beyond him. "How are the ground forces doing?"

Rees spoke briefly into his cell and came back to his headset mic.

"They just reminded me we're talking about a mountain," Rees said. "There's a lot of territory. No sightings of giant serpents yet. Nothing out of the ordinary. Just the usual pilgrims trying to keep dry."

"Some of those pilgrims are not there to worship the usual deity," Bullfinch said over the chopper's whirr and the wind. "They've got to spot them."

"Do you have any idea how these people are going to perpetrate this act?" Rees asked. "That might give us some direction."

"The literature is vague," Bullfinch said. "If they're inspired by Rottman's works they're going to want to peel back whatever barrier is in place or that they think is in place to unleash what he called *The Ancients* in his fiction. It'll involve some channel of energy."

"Energy."

"It's all about energy. Isn't everything? It's just how it's manipulated, what form they're using or hoping to harness. They could be looking to carve symbols directly into rock faces, but they're going to be looking to the sea in some way, I suspect."

"I'll suggest the officers on the ground need to be on the lookout," Rees said.

The burly man used a post hole digger to open up a patch of ground after kicking back rocks and pebbles at the point Freya indicated on an incline. Then, gripping the tool's twin handles with work-gloved hands, he began to shape a smooth, round, and cylindrical hole.

He ignored the bite of the cold rain and the wind that whipped at his poncho, and Freya watched the hole take shape from a few meters away, giving him room. She pressed the back of her hand down on top of head to keep a rain hat in place.

"Won't the point let you drive it in without all that?" She tried not to sound impatient, but she wanted to keep things moving.

"'S nearly five meters high. Hold your horses. We just need to go a little ways," the man said. "The point'll let me stick it a little deeper and we can get it stable."

The Shepherd had given coordinates for the placement of the stakes to her, Jaager, Mike and a few other minions, charging them with the overseeing of the laborers who seemed to view this as a way to make a few bucks off eccentric tourists, even if it meant working in a brewing storm. It meant putting up with being under a woman's direction in the case of this one, Freya observed.

Once he'd sunk the post into place, she held it as he used a separate spade to move displaced earth back into the hole. Before it was completely stable, she adjusted the post's face, making sure the symbol burned there was aimed toward the bay at the correct angle. She realized it was one of the marks they'd found in the old keep. It was good to see the perilous effort come to fruition even though she supervised this post only as a luck of the draw.

After a few seconds, the post was sturdy and in position.

"What's next?" the burly man asked.

"A little farther up the rise," she said, checking coordinates on her phone.

It wouldn't be much longer.

33

"**A** caretaker just reported someone sinking a post in the ground near the mountain," Rees said.

"What the fuck does that mean?" O'Donnell asked. "Putting up a fence?"

"That's all you've got?" Bullfinch asked.

"We have people hustling that way," Rees said. "No eyes-on yet."

"That won't be the only one," Bullfinch said. "If we get a look I think we'll see the symbols they've been collecting are etched into the posts."

"Druids and trees?" O'Donnell asked.

"Something like that. There's a history of the Druids using staffs with Ogham markings. If this knowledge traces back to some secret order of Druids, it makes sense they'd mimic other rituals and practices. These cultists, or whoever they are, are probably looking to tap into the energy of the Ley lines and their tributaries. If they think the serpent is under the sea, they'll aim toward the bay and try to unlock whatever barrier's been put in place."

"How do you know this?" O'Donnell asked.

"Supposedly Rottman, the pulp writer, died in the Thirties trying to perform a ritual based on the research he used in his stories."

"True?"

"He had a bad heart," Bullfinch said, raising his voice. "Most of it's been dismissed as a rumor that grew out of a story by a Rottman acolyte named Samuel Motes. It was written a short time before Rottman's death and had a fictionalized Rottman figure utilizing sticks and energy to try and awaken some earth elemental or something like that in the Rottman universe of Ancients. Supposedly Rottman gave his blessings to the tale even though it killed him off."

"So Motes wasn't just making it up?" O'Donnell asked.

"They were longtime correspondents. Motes would never tell more, but people have searched Motes' archives and files since he died, trying to locate letters from Rottman indicating what he was attempting or other details."

"So these people are on the side of Croag Patrick trying to re-create something out of *Weird Tales*."

"Technically something older than that," Bullfinch said. "But not that different from the fiction. Evacuating this area might not be a bad idea. Whatever people you can get there at the moment."

"We'll see if the Coast Guard boats and more air support are handy," Rees said. "And worry about looking insane later."

"And those posts need to come down, Mr. Rees. Or some of them at least. The power stream needs to be interrupted."

"I'll relay the message."

"Why would someone want this? If it's real?" O'Donnell asked.

"There may be some excitement just in seeing if it will work," Bullfinch said. "Or there may be some other desire for chaos."

"Some kids build things with their Lego sets just to knock them down," Rees said.

"We'll know more when we get there," Bullfinch said. "Hopefully before the Legos start to fall."

"We might need to think about an exit plan," Mike said into his cell. "And you guys might want to stay a little more under wraps since there's going to be a wide audience out here. Things don't work out, you might need a little distance."

He stood on a stony path, watching a man in a blue uniform with a bright yellow jacket making his way toward him. He put the phone away and slid his hand to the small of his back, gripping his weapon there.

His charge, one of the younger laborers with a ruddy face and swept-back hair, was just getting his post into place. In spite of the wind, he could pick up the sounds of his exertion.

"Hello," the uniformed man said. "Getting a bit blustery isn't it?"

"Getting used to it out here on the coast," Mike said.

The uniform stopped a few paces away from him and looked past at the workman. His lips tightened just a little, conveying disapproval.

"American?"

"Is it my haircut or my fashion sense?" Mike asked, letting his lips peel back in a broad smile.

"More the accent."

He gave a nod toward the workman.

"Is that some kind of propaganda you're putting up there?"

"It's a religious symbol," Mike said. "We're pilgrims."

"I've never seen a marking like that in a Catholic church," the man said. "Reek Sunday we see a few flags, but they usually have crosses or angels on them."

"We're from an order that goes back to the older trappings," Mike said, trying to improvise something that sounded reasonable. Should've paid more attention in Sunday School. Would've helped if it had been Catholic and not Methodist.

"Everybody's got issues with one pope or another, but I can't let you be digging here, religious reasons or not. Don't suppose you're going to surprise me with a permit. Have you got your identification with you?"

"Passport do?" Mike asked, glancing back toward the workman who'd hesitated with the officer's approach. He gave a twitch of his cheek, not quite a wink, to keep the guy going. Then he slipped the small blue binder from a left coat pocket and passed it over with a smile.

The officer gave a polite nod of acknowledgement and flipped the binder open, cupping a hand over it against the rain and wind, trying to focus on the grim thumbnail photo that made Mike look like a corpse.

"So where are you from in the stat—"

The question didn't get past his lips. The butt of Mike's weapon froze his words as it connected with the man's skull just between the line of his cap and his ear. His eyes widened with the stun and shock, and then he slumped sideways.

Mike lowered himself and hit again as the man crumpled, and he readied his weapon in case the blow wasn't enough. But the officer went to the ground, his face sagging against the stones, and his eyes glazed.

"Keep going," Mike said to the workman.

When that didn't produce any action, he gave the guy a look that got him moving again.

Then he took the hat that had spilled off the man's head and rolled him slightly to get a grip on the edge of his yellow jacket. Keeping things moving might actually have just gotten a little easier.

He pulled out his cell and thumbed a contact. "Can I get my special package over here?" he asked.

Malphas climbed into the back of the Hummer they had brought to the visitor center parking lot. The brothers waited there. They had decided after Mike's call to stay out of sight, not be visible until the moment arrived.

"The placement is moving forward," he said. "It will take a little while. The authorities are here but not in force yet."

"Our security chief reported to us," Edward said. "He has the situation in hand at the moment and will keep people from bothering you. When will we know?"

"If it works? Almost immediately. The symbols are almost in place. With those, and the earth, celestial alignment isn't as important. It'll probably be wise to…"

Edward nodded. "Much as it pains me, we'll need to start

back to Dublin. There's work we can do there if you're successful, things we can get rolling."

"Perhaps it is time for you to move then. Moving will get difficult if things work as we expect," Malphas, the Shepherd, said. "Roads could close. I know you wanted to be on hand for the beginning, but…" he paused and drew in a deep breath. "I might not survive."

"Understood. We have statements ready for the press. We'll have our plan ready to roll out. There'll be no reason to hold back."

"Go now, back to the air strip. We don't know if planes will be taking off after, either."

"We can order our pilot to defy any instructions."

"I'm sure you can, but there may be disruptions in fields we don't even understand."

They looked at each other and nodded.

"We'll get out of here and wait for word."

Edward extended a hand. "Good luck."

A rare smile curled onto The Shepherd's features. "I could not do this without you. We've come this far. Here's hoping all our goals are met."

"How are we doing?" Mike asked, cell pressed tight to his ear. He picked his way along the stony path having donned the uniform hat and coat which he'd closed over his suit. He looked official enough with the weather distracting from scrutiny.

"Mine's in place," Freya reported.

He clicked to another connection.

"Done," came Jaager's raspy voice, barely audible.

He clicked again and collected a similar response then another. He responded with an order to send the laborers away.

After the last check, he thumbed a disconnect, then the contact number for Malphas. The answer was almost less of a word than Jaager's.

"I'll get hunkered down then," Mike said, looking around for a stable spot.

"No, please meet me at the coordinates I'm sending you. Five minutes."

Mike's first impulse was to remind Malphas that he worked for the Groom brothers and not him, but it was the brothers who'd told him to give the old man what he needed.

He'd been with them through other eccentric pursuits that stretched far outside their more traditional endeavors like running their company and funding think tanks. Their involvement with this Ning snake-chunking group had come out of some obscure paper on the nature of belief generated at one of those egghead enclaves.

It had been aimed at illustrating how the Groom's political agenda and ideas could be furthered among the masses, but the notion of a grand experiment had arisen as a joke that had gained traction. Then the brothers had grown almost delusional, in Mike's opinion, based on what he'd heard about closed door meetings. He'd been outside, guarding the doors, but things trickled out.

The idea was about to play itself out, probably with negative results the way their most outlandish moves did, though he had to give them credit for some of the professorships they'd endowed and things they'd funded that had fueled public debate. He just had to give this all a little more time and manage to get out without winding up in custody.

He'd managed that before. Just had to do it again.

Then it'd be time for a vacation in Tahiti.

34

"You seeing anything?"

O'Donnell stretched against her seat harness to look past Bullfinch out his side of the chopper.

"Not on the inland side," Bullfinch said into his mic. "Can we get a little lower?"

"Wind's building and being a real bitch," Ahlstrom said, but the craft dipped as he spoke. As the altitude dropped a little more, blasts pitched them more, giving O'Donnell's stomach a flip.

She choked down bile and tried to focus.

"OK, on the bay side, look." Bullfinch tapped the glass. "Northeast."

O'Donnell spotted them, posts, not huge but definitely out of the ordinary. They were not in a straight line but scattered across a small area beginning near the base of the mountain and dappling the rugged landscape. They weren't particularly close to each other. On the ground each probably looked like an isolated stick some pilgrim had put up.

In an area always filled with pilgrims, one post would just look like some believer's personal flourish. Above, things looked more strategic. They were a series of relays.

"Look like anything from the rumors you created?" Bullfinch asked, looking toward Kaity, who was holding tight to her seat's arms.

"Maybe. In what I was aware of, we kept some things vague."

"What's going on in those ruins?" O'Donnell said. "Not far from the visitor's center."

"Take us that way," Bullfinch said.

"Your wish is my suicide mission," Ahlstrom said.

Rees gave him a grim look, but the craft curved slightly and dropped even lower, the rotor's buzz almost seeming to protest against a new crack of thunder.

"Is that a Garda officer?" O'Donnell asked.

"Helping the old man? Looks it, but he's helping him onto that wall, not evacuating him."

Indeed, it did. The uniformed man held the older man's elbow, and the old man braced against a gnarled staff that had to be better than a meter in length, maybe a meter and a half.

A new wave of rain splashed the chopper's windshield, and more wind picked up, rocking the craft even as it slashed the men below and drew Gaelic curses from Ahlstrom, whipping the old man's long jacket like a sail.

"Set us down," Rees said. "That's gotta be who we're looking for."

As Bullfinch leaned down for the wrapped sword at his feet, Rees slid a hand beneath his coat for his sidearm.

O'Donnell did the same without taking her eyes off the scene below. Despite the weather, the decrease in altitude improved the view. The old man was headed toward a peak on the wall, the highest point of what must have been a chapel once. Perhaps it was supposed to be a point of concentrated energy.

The uniform stayed with him, just a few paces behind, arms raised with the palms out, not touching the old man but ready to catch or steady him as he found his spot and his footing. A lightning bolt split the charcoal clouds then, looking like the sky above him was ripping open. He wasn't fazed.

He didn't hesitate as the rain intensified in the next few seconds. He adjusted his footing, rotating slightly, positioning himself facing toward the bay, almost parallel to the sticks.

O'Donnell held her seat arms as the chopper dropped lower and she was jostled again.

"You OK?" she asked Kaity.

"Little woozy."

"Hold tight and try to keep your breakfast down."

Kaity nodded and closed her eyes, lips moving. Silent prayer. The seat seemed ready to tear loose from its connections to the floorboard. Even with the storm O'Donnell would be glad to get outside and moving. Whatever the old bastard down there had planned, they'd put a stop to it, and conveniently, she saw another pair of figures ducking into the wind and moving in the direction of the wall—a woman and a tall man. Had to be the two they'd been pursuing. Time to answer for killing the soccer mom and their other damage.

The chopper banked farther with more Gaelic curses spewing, then it dipped near an open patch of grass, dropping lower and lower. Even as the jostling continued, O'Donnell unhooked her harness, grabbing what she could find for stability until they'd dropped to a bumpy touch of the earth.

"Thank you for flying Jimmy's Miracle Airlines," Ahlstrom said. "Keep us in mind for your next hurricane or monsoon."

O'Donnell had to grip a chair arm to avoid being pitched against the door, but she managed to hold on as did Bullfinch. Then they were stable and Rees was grabbing the chopper's hatch handle.

The hatch burst open, letting in the wind's howl along with an onslaught of rain, but they squinted against it and started moving, stepping out onto the ground, ducking though the rotor couldn't reach them.

"Kaity, stay with the pilot," O'Donnell ordered. Then, she looked toward the ruins and realized that was a bad idea. The man in the Garda uniform had stepped away from the ruins. He had a weapon in his hands, something with a large cylinder at its center.

"Out! Now!" O'Donnell shouted, leaning back into the chopper and snatching at Kaity's harness buckle. She failed to unlatch it on the first try, and Kaity clawed at it as well, desperate to get it open as she strained against the harness straps.

Something outside roared louder than the wind, and a tuft of ground several meters away exploded. The chopper rattled and thrashed for a second, threatening to tilt over.

"That's a grenade launcher," O'Donnell said. "He'll adjust the next one. Even with the wind, if he's got the worst fragmentation rounds, he just has to get a little closer."

Rees moved to the pilot's door and jerked it wide, grabbing Ahlstrom's arm. He pulled him free and away from the chopper.

"Go!" O'Donnell shouted at a hesitating Bullfinch. After a heartbeat, he grabbed the sword and ran. She slapped Kaity's hand aside and levered the buckle open, flinging straps back and grabbing Kaity's coat lapel.

Dragging her from the seat, she took her arm and jogged with her, putting as much distance between them and the aircraft as possible. As the uniformed man's weapon roared again, she pulled Kaity to the ground, throwing a protective arm over her.

A second later, something soared in an arc toward the chopper, almost defying the wind.

In another few seconds, that something exploded, and bits of debris were hurled in all directions. He'd corrected well for the wind. What felt like a heavy breath of hot air swept over them.

The bastard was well prepared and lucky too. With an arm over Kaity's shoulders, she stayed down, giving it a few tense seconds. A piece of metal landed with a swish half a meter away. A piece of twisted gear, stabbed deep into the earth. It would have impaled one of them with just a little variance in its landing.

Squinting against the rain, O'Donnell looked up. Nothing else seemed to be coming. She got on her knees and helped Kaity up. The chopper behind them was a smoking mess.

They wouldn't be going home that way. No time to think about that now. She gave Kaity a nudge toward the pilot, who looked on in a bit of shock and at a loss for a remark.

"Stay with him. Stay close to Jimmy," she said.

She gave the woman a nudge then turned and headed toward

the ruins, sidearm in hand, squinting, her eyes almost closed against the stinging rain. She was halfway to the wall, hearing some kind of shouted chants from the old man, though she couldn't make out the words when what felt like a sandbag slammed into her side. Pain shot through her ribs, and she tumbled to the ground, stones digging into her side. One elbow landed hard on a piece of rock, bringing tears, yet she somehow held onto her weapon and started to swing it in the direction of the assault.

Another forearm collided with hers, sweeping the weapon aside and then a fist smashed her face, flattening her nose and delivering the hard-pressure pain back through her head.

Just before that forced her to blink, she caught sight of the woman silhouetted against the rainy sky. The woman they'd been looking for. Even as O'Donnell's brain clouded, something reminded her, a little pulse deep in her thoughts, that the woman carried the deadly venom. She couldn't afford to black out, couldn't lie unconscious. An injection might be administered.

Fighting the waves that seemed to converge on her brain, she raised her arms, got them in front of her, as punches came her way. Somehow, though she felt numb and as if her limbs weighed tons, she deflected.

Then she found herself pushing into the ground with her heels, not quick scrambling but getting out of the way of the onslaught. Struggling upward. More blows came as she got into a crouch, and she kept her arms up.

The cold bite of the slashing rain helped.

Like a splash of water to the face.

She straightened, took a step back and leveled her forearm in front of her, then moved forward, reflexive basic self-defense training kicking in. The woman was a little taller than she was. She could work with that.

She put her weight into it, got the arm past the woman's ready hands, slamming the forearm into the throat.

Her side kick came next. She aimed for the head, the goal: unconsciousness.

That didn't work out. Her foot landed somewhere near the shoulder, staggering the woman off balance but not stopping her. In an instant, she'd regrouped, and she charged forward with a new rain of blows.

Where the hell was Bullfinch?

And, what the hell was going on on the wall while they played?

Bullfinch had the sword at his side at that moment, ready but not poised in a defensive posture. His route to the ruins had been interrupted by the tall man stepping into his path just a short distance ahead, blocking the arched doorway on a ruined outer wall a few meters from the abbey where the old man stood.

Behind the figure, Bullfinch could see the old man on the taller wall. He raised his staff as thunder off the bay beyond him rose in an escalating barrage. A sea storm was not out of the ordinary, but the deafening roar seemed louder than a typical event, and the electric feel to the air was powerful. As if to punctuate that, the charcoal clouds on the horizon were ripped by jagged lines of lightning.

The professor planted his feet and sloughed off his coat and hat in spite of the wind and cold. He'd have to get past the tall figure. If the indications that the man was more than human were correct, perhaps this sword would prove helpful. It had been forged in a different age when knowledge of fantastic things remained at the forefront of men's minds.

He tilted the blade at a defensive angle in front of him and moved forward, summoning calm as the winds whipped at the figure's coat. A gust caught the hood and pulled it back from his bald skull, but the round-lenses of the glasses stayed in place, masking part of his features, contributing to the quality of oddness that tightened Bullfinch's throat. He'd sensed it on the video footage, and it was stronger still here. The pulp writer Rottman's work had spoken of beings, emissaries crossed between men and the ancient figures legends had sought to describe. Perhaps they still walked.

He advanced, reminding himself not to let his gaze lock on the smooth, dark lenses. He needed to keep the whole figure in sight, watch the limbs, to be ready to deflect any attack. He thought about issuing a warning, but that seemed fruitless.

Careful with the placement of his feet, avoiding jagged stones and dips in the terrain, he moved forward. His progress didn't seem to trouble the figure. The posture didn't change, nor the breathing. No signs of tenseness affected the muscles.

Not until the tight lips parted slightly.

Then wider.

And wider.

And a tentacle-like appendage shot from the cavern the opening created, coming from somewhere deep in the throat.

Bullfinch fought the shock of the contradiction. He'd seen all manner of strangeness, but the appearance of something outside the usual bounds of natural couldn't help but disturb, triggering some racial memory of warning and danger.

He'd read of aquatic snakes with vestigial tentacles, but those appendages were small, useless. The man-thing before him was incredible.

As one of the writhing appendages stretched toward Bull-finch, the man's coat was shrugged off. His body shuddered for a moment, and then more tentacles burst from behind him, stretching over his shoulders and around his abdomen.

Long, dark red, slimy, writhing.

Each ready to battle, not looking like it would succumb easily even to the bite of the sword.

Behind the figure, as the old man continued his flailing shouts, a line of blue energy shot past him. Bullfinch could imagine it extending from one of the symbol-marked posts somewhere behind, stretching for the next stick, channeling energy toward the bay.

Ready to rip open whatever lay beneath the water, whatever

membrane long ago had sealed away something of legend more horrible than mythmakers had chosen to record.

The voice came as a shout. Loud but barely rising above the tempest swirling around them.

"I'm gonna have to ask you to hold it."

Rees spun to find himself facing the uniformed officer who had a new weapon leveled at him. As his gaze moved from the nasty-looking semi-automatic to focus on the man, he saw he wasn't really in uniform at all, just wearing a few Garda accessories.

"You've got to let us stop this."

"Sorry. My job's to let it go on."

"Do you see that energy? Do ya think this is a normal afternoon shower?"

"I've seen my bosses get into some weird territory. This one's a little offbeat, I'll give you that."

Something rumbled from beyond the abbey, deep in the bay.

"We've found things where I work. Seen things," Rees said. "Things you'd know at a glance didn't belong in our world. Some are benign little orbs with funny feet. Some are like whatever's beneath those waves out there. You've got to let us stop this."

"Sorry," the man said, though he did give a second glance toward a waterspout becoming visible amid the haze and slashing rain over the bay.

"You see that?" Rees asked.

"Damnedest thing my bosses have come up with," the man said. "I'll give you that."

Fangs flared at the end of an appendage that stretched from the figure's mouth.

Bullfinch stepped to the side of its attempted strike and slashed downward with the sword. Ripples of blue, like electrical impulses, crackled around the steel as it sliced through the writhing coil. The symbols on the sword summoned some kind of energy not unlike the sticks were doing. Perhaps it was made stronger in this area. Or maybe it was the proximity to the post, and the symbol—some unknown tie.

At any rate, he'd struck it a quarter of the way up its length. The fanged tip dropped to the ground, and the professor swung the blade quickly upward, letting the blade point dip over his right shoulder. The blade stopped another appendage from the thing's back. This one didn't seem to have teeth, but it would have wrapped around him.

He didn't manage a blow that cut this time, but he used the blade to shove the grasping thing away. He jerked backwards then, several steps, out of range. He held the blade in a defensive diagonal, watching the various tendrils and the distorted face.

The figure was definitely a hybrid of some type. Bullfinch recalled one of Rottman's stories had been centered around a mysterious and almost-forgotten coastal town north of Black-pool, supposedly populated by hybrids.

As he looked on, the figure's most human-like arms stretched and extended, ripples pulsing beneath the muscles as long, blade-like nails inched out from the fingertips.

Bullfinch drew in a breath and readied himself.

On the wall, the old man's machinations continued, and the energy flow through the visible posts seemed to grow stronger, or at least it glowed a brighter blue and the waterspout over the bay swirled and throbbed harder, the central column blossoming at the top into a massive black cloud, almost covering the water below.

O'Donnell took that in while deflecting flailing blows from the woman, designed to tire and soften her. Her cheek was clipped. A hammer blow connected with her collar bone explod-ing agony through her shoulder and into her neck. Almost enough to topple her.

She delivered another kick, aiming for the solar plexus.

She connected, driving the woman back, providing a respite,

time for her to shut out the pain. Time for her to look past the ruins again. The spout's roiling black shroud cast a darkness over the bay and the land this side of it. Some odd middle ground, not quite night but far from day.

An odd gray-black hour.

And in the shrouded haze above the turbulent bay where waves pitched into high curls, something moved, something independent of the wind and water. She didn't have time for a good look at it. She had to deflect blows from her attacker. A left arm up, then a right.

Time to stop this.

She raised a forearm as the next blow came and simultaneously drove a fist at the woman's jaw. It connected hard with all the weight she could put behind it. Then she took a step back and delivered a snap kick. It connected to a hip.

That jarred the woman a bit, and O'Donnell seized the moment and crashed a forearm into her neck, following that with a combo of punches, doing what the woman had been trying to do to her.

When she went down, O'Donnell delivered another kick, this one to the chin. It snapped the head back and sent the woman spilling backward. Sweeping a hand back to her waistband, O'Donnell found handcuffs and after she'd flipped the woman over, she slapped them on.

"Kaity?" she turned and shouted. "Jimmy? Kaity? Where are you?"

"Here, here," Kaity called. She and Ahlstrom jogged to her side.

She pointed to the downed woman. "Keep an eye on her. Sit on her if you have to."

"Got ya. Where are you going?"

"It's time to upset the apple cart."

Rees held his hands up and extended from his body, letting the gunman see them well, then he complied with the fellow's motion to move toward the outer wall of the abbey, then through a small arch.

Rows of gravestones and stone crosses stretched along the narrow expanse there, between the small wall and the building ruins. The old man had moved up to the top-most point of the ruins now.

His staff was raised as high as he could reach, and he shouted at the blackened heavens, facing toward the massive waterspout.

"Insanity," Rees said. "What do you think's going to happen if we're here and he really accomplishes something? That spout's not natural. Not something that big in these waters. Hair-brained or not on your friends' parts."

"We'll find a place to hunker down," Mike said. "Or I'll go down with the mission."

"What were you? Special forces?"

"Ranger. Military police. 'Till I was drummed out. Shit happened in Afghanistan. You shoot one rapist…"

"That's why you were so comfortable with a grenade launcher."

"I'm comfortable with a lot of things."

He glanced around, eyes cocked slightly upward.

"Not a lot of shelter. Let's just have you stand over there."

He gestured toward a small tree not far from a Celtic cross and another pocked gravestone. The spot must've been serving as a mini-base of operations for him. A tarp covered a couple of boxes over in a corner of the graveyard, but it wasn't big enough to be sequestering the sticks.

Those had been wheeled in from another area, and there was no telling how far they stretched along the invisible lines Bull-finch had been talking about. Perhaps miles and miles, tapping into energy from the heart of the country, channeling it all here, to the old man and the bay and whatever had started to rise up out there, whatever that waterspout was sucking back a path for.

Rees let his arms drop just a little. His muscles needed a bit of a rest, and a couple of inches shouldn't make his captor that nervous.

Bullfinch took several paces back from the man-thing and felt his shoe sole slip on the ground. He dropped to one knee and felt pain shoot though his thigh as the kneecap made impact.

He was getting too old for this.

He pressed his fingers into the wet ground and pushed himself up, sword ready as new tentacles reached around the man's form from somewhere in the back. An endless supply seemed to be available. He drew in a breath. If each was equipped with fangs, this might be problematic.

"Step back, Professor?"

He jerked a glance over his left shoulder. O'Donnell's voice.

He did as she suggested even as he kept the sword at a defensive angle.

She stood a few paces behind him. Her sidearm was raised. She braced it under a cupping left hand.

"Stop right there," she said.

If the figure comprehended there was no sign of it.

Muzzle fire erupted from O'Donnell's weapon, and the report, louder than the thunder, made Bullfinch jump.

Blam.

The figure jerked back at one shoulder which still held a human shape.

Blam.

Jerked again.

Blam.

Again.

Blam.

Then the throat opened up in an explosion of blood and tissue.

It toppled then, thudding backward onto the ground. The long appendages continued to jerk, but the twitches seemed involuntary.

O'Donnell stepped to his shoulder, ejecting a clip from the weapon. She produced another from her coat, slipped it into the weapon's handle then fired again. This shell blew the figure's head apart in another explosion of blood and gray matter. The twitching didn't end, but it didn't get back up.

"You OK?" O'Donnell asked.

"OK," Bullfinch said above the wind.

"Let's move."

She set off toward the wall at a jog as a new bolt of lightning cut a jagged pattern across the sky.

From their position, Rees watched the bay. The dancing, writhing thing that began to emerge from the abyss beneath the waterspout was almost lost amid the water and the darkness, but he could make out an outline, something almost shaped like a head with distinct eyes.

That seemed balanced atop a column like that of the water-spout—narrow, abnormal, serpent-like but with…arms? Arms with claws as long as blades. If he was seeing it right. A cold deeper than the bite of the outside elements gripped him, coming from somewhere inside. And from behind what he could make out of the thing…more coiling shapes? He wanted to look away, but he couldn't, even as mist and waves obscured it.

It was the same for the man beside him. He was almost mesmerized, as if charmed the way legends always held serpents had the power to do, in awe of a dread he'd never believed.

Rees entertained a notion of asking. The combination of shock and horror almost seemed powerful enough to melt the man's resolve, but his loyalty suggested he wouldn't give in easily.

Rees jammed an elbow into his throat instead, trying to put the point into the Adam's apple. It stunned the man. He gagged and air caught in his throat, and even as he started a swing with his sidearm, Rees jammed a fist into his head near the temple. Unconscious would be good. He'd settle for unconscious.

That didn't quite work. The man's weapon raised, ready to angle in toward Rees' chest despite the stunning blows. Rees grabbed the wrist and tried to keep the weapon pointed at the sky.

A blast exploded from the barrel with a flash of orange muzzle fire and smoke, and a rattling sound jarred both of them. Pulling the trigger again wasn't the most rational move, but another explosion followed in an instant.

A slug bit into stone near the top of a wall. Rees grabbed for the yellow coat's collar, dragging the man toward him. He wanted to get him in a clinch then spin and force him back against the stone.

He didn't have to.

The butt of a handgun came down on the back of the man's skull, seemingly disembodied at first in the slashing rain, but then he saw O'Donnell behind it.

He let her take the stunned man who'd slumped into him. She caught him under the arms and slung him to the ground, kicking the weapon away as it dropped.

"Do *Aisteach* officers carry cuffs?" she asked.

"Got it," Rees said, dipping to his knees.

"We've got to interrupt the energy. Are there operatives out there who can break the posts somewhere along the line?" Bullfinch asked.

"I'll get on the radio. In the meantime, check under that tarp over there," Rees said. "I think that's where he put our surprise."

He rolled the man onto his stomach and found a wrist for the first bracelet.

"That grenade launcher's got to be somewhere."

"If it's got anything left in it, I'll blow as many of them out of the ground as I can," O'Donnell said. "Professor, do you want to try for the old man?"

"I'm afraid it's gone far enough that that won't stop things, but yes."

Bullfinch readied the sword and stepped through an arched opening, looking for a way up while O'Donnell scrambled toward the tarp.

A set of shots rang out, pinging into the stone beside her. She ducked and lowered herself into a crouch but kept moving.

"That's where his backup went," Rees said. He finished cuffing his charge then scrambled forward to grab the handgun.

Keeping low, he returned fire to the men he could see crouching behind gravestones and other debris. Three that he could see.

"Keep moving," he shouted.

His shots ricocheted off the stones as well, but at least that kept them a little busy.

"On it," O'Donnell said.

From the bay, a loud hissing roar rose above the tempest and all else.

Kaity saw the dropped mobi as the pilot ushered her away from the abbey. There was no shelter close, but he wanted her out of range of the conflict. They'd heard gunshots, and he didn't want her in their path if he could help it.

She curved an ankle just slightly, allowing herself to dip. She cried out in a low imitation of pain. While she was on the ground, she scooped up the phone and snagged it, getting it into a pocket before it had a chance to get any wetter. She couldn't tell at a glance if it was already waterlogged, but at least in her pocket, it would be out of the elements.

"Over there," the pilot said. "We'll stand under those trees. We can hold onto them if we have to, if this wind gets any stronger."

She followed. Someone would be interested in the phone later.

Bullfinch edged along the wall top, placing his feet carefully on the craggy path it afforded. If he was too old to be fighting, he was definitely too old to fall off a wall. He didn't want to consider the bones that would snap or the agony and time of recovery. If he survived.

Better to just focus on getting the man on the wall taken care of. If they both fell, maybe it would interrupt the summoning of the serpent thing out there in waves.

With the sword leveled in front of him, helping with balance, he moved on to the spot near the peak where the man stood, what sounded like gibberish coming from his mouth.

Bullfinch took a few more paces, squinted against the wind and shouted.

"Stop!"

One word should carry the message. Little else would make sense in raging wind and rain.

Indeed, the man heard it and spun, fiery anger showing in his eyes, which glowed a blue-white. He'd been in some kind of trance, probably taking in energy of his own from the process.

That meant the staff was probably charged and that he had more strength than a man of his age and stature might usually possess. Both of them might have to go off this wall.

Bullfinch tried to recall his fencing days and the time he'd had to face an attacker wielding a Japanese *naginata* while he'd been armed only with an umbrella. He willed the oft-used reflexes to awaken.

The old man swung at him.

No time for thinking.

Action required.

He blocked the blow with the blade and found his push back deflected better than he'd hoped. It was as if the staff bounced back from the sword. Something to do with the markings, those symbols etched deep in the steel. Rees had been right to hold on to it. Maybe it had belonged to the old Irish warrior Lugh himself. He raised it and forced himself forward. If it could parry, perhaps an aggressive move would be equally charged.

The old man got the staff in front of him in a lightning-fast move, blocking the sword, and something seemed to hum between them as Bullfinch pressed in with his weapon. The old man clutched the staff in both hands and shoved it back the professor's way with a resistance that didn't look possible given his slight form.

Nothing ever came as easy it should.

The rain had become blinding as O'Donnell yanked back the tarpaulin. She dragged a sleeve across her forehead and looked at the black case it covered. She began flicking catches. Six lined the lid.

She flipped it open to find the launcher the man had used secured in form-fitting foam. A round magazine seemed to have six slots. If it had been fully loaded when the man had started, that should leave her four. She searched her memory. Had she been taught the range on one of these, a hand-held? The blasts this had delivered so far didn't seem to offer the most powerful loads available, but they'd knock sticks off kilter if she could get close enough and allow for the storm.

She tugged the weapon from the foam and started to move. Shots dug into the wall near her but nothing hit. God, let Rees keep them pinned down.

She jogged along the wall and past a corner of the ruined building, heading quickly across the rugged ground beyond the abbey.

The posts were placed at intervals across the grassy expanse that stretched toward the mountain, disappearing into the haze. The blue energy linked them, like a thick fiber stretched from post to post, and the closest seemed to blast a line past the ruins. Another must be very near the sea.

She ran a few steps, working to calculate the safest distance, then dropped to one knee and lifted the launcher to her shoulder. Aiming upward for an arc amid all this bluster that might put a round in the ground near the first post, she ignored the continuing onslaught of rain and noise. She prayed no bullets would slam into her spine.

From the bay, what seemed like an abnormal cry rose. The watery tomb was holding its occupant no more. The waterspout fueled by the blue captured lightning was working, and her imagination conjured images of what must exist beneath the shimmering outline she'd glimpsed. A coiling, horrible thing capable of unimaginable chaos.

This had to work.

She held her breath.

She squeezed the trigger then lowered the weapon and squinted through the continuing onrush of rain and wind.

The cylinder she'd unleashed thudded into the ground near the first post.

Then the explosion roared, tossing up a burst of orange flame and dirt. The reverberations rattled the ground under her.

The post where the explosion had hit toppled to the right.

Hit the ground on top of disturbed clouds and debris created by the explosion and remained at perhaps a 40-degree angle.

And the blue line was not broken.

Disturbed but not interrupted.

It continued at a new slant to the sea.

The roar behind her continued.

She hadn't really managed to affect the flow.

Picking herself up, grabbing the launcher, she started toward the next post. Maybe one more blast would do it.

Echoes of gunshots sounded behind her.

Had one gotten past Rees? She couldn't tell if a shot whizzed past her or not in this storm. Damn!

Getting just a few paces closer to the next post, she dropped again.

Another drifting echo of a gunshot sounded behind her.

Then blood burst from her left shoulder.

Bullfinch blocked a swing from the old man's staff. The sword held as did his balance, but shockwaves reverberated back along the blade, rattling his joints again and sending new ripples of pain through his trapezius muscles.

The old man might have weakened, but he remained power-ful. If he toppled Bullfinch off the wall, he'd just turn back to whatever chants or hand motions were needed to keep calling the unspeakable thing in the bay.

Bullfinch mentally roused his will and adjusted his footing, readying for another slam. He'd been in tougher battles, hadn't he?

Then the cudgel struck the blade again.

Muscle had torn in the area near O'Donnell's neck, but she didn't think a bullet had lodged. She'd patch it in a moment. She needed at least to get one more round off before another bullet slammed into her in a more damaging spot.

Gritting teeth against the pain, she raised the launcher, pointed, couldn't aim. The barrel was in the general direction of the next post. She squeezed the trigger, hesitated a second and dropped.

She came down on top of the launcher. That kept her face out of the dirt. She braced both for the explosion and another shot.

The explosion came. A shot didn't.

The blast's thunder sounded over the noises around her. Dirt and flame again, followed by the stake's tumble to its side. She watched, letting rain just pour down her forehead into her eyes, ignoring the sting.

The blue line was broken.

She looked past the mound she'd created to the next post which seemed to channel its blue stream directly into the ground.

Good enough.

It would have to be.

She shoved herself up, swung, and aimed the grenade launcher behind her.

A man was running toward her.

His handgun was cradled against his chest as he rushed for a better position to fire on her.

She fired first.

The grenade cylinder slammed into his chest, lodging some-where near his sternum, striking bone.

In the next instant he disappeared.

The staff raised high over the old man's head, clutched in both hands. He would swing it down in a second, like a hammer aimed at Bullfinch's blade. The professor worried he might not absorb this one as easily.

Then the old man froze.

His eyes instantly lost their blue glow, and in the same second, sound, a rippling *ka-blam*, reached Bullfinch from behind.

He watched the old man freeze.

Saw shock in the eyes.

Then watched him tumble off the wall, letting go of the staff as he plunged over into the recess that had once been the heart of the abbey.

He crumpled onto stone at the bottom and lay still.

Only after looking at the twisted form did Bullfinch turn to see Rees jogging his way, handgun still extended in front of him.

"One got past me," he said. "I've got to check on O'Donnell."

Without speaking, Bullfinch jerked toward the bay.

It was as if the roiling black cloud had been suddenly cut free of the waterspout. It continued to swirl in the air above the water, but its spout had been cut off.

The serpent form continued to twist and flail, but seemed not to extend quite as far above the waves now, and if he could read anything from the posture, it seemed less confident.

The arm-like appendages stretched upward, waving, grasping for something that wasn't there. It was being sucked back down into whatever vortex held it beneath the bay, probably beneath the floor of the bay.

Some dark, murky abyss.

35

"There's going to be a bit of a dust-up about explosions near landmarks the entire world holds sacred," Rees said.

He pressed his rolled wool scarf against O'Donnell's shoulder as she sat on a huge stone at the edge of the abbey grounds, waiting for a paramedic to take over. A couple of local medical crews had arrived in ambulances a few minutes earlier, focusing first on the more seriously wounded.

"I prefer to look at it as keeping the sacred spot from going away entirely, but my old boss will have some choice words," O'Donnell said. "No one's going to believe what we saw and what might have happened. No one outside of the *Aisteach*."

"Our report will go in *Aisteach* records at least. There'll be some documentation of what went on, and we're going to have staff swarming the area and diving in the bay for information. I just wish there'd been more opportunity to capture video."

"Maybe some tourists or pilgrims had time for that."

"I can take it from here," one of the paramedics said.

Rees let go and stepped back. The rain had slowed again and the waterspout had disappeared. A couple of fresh Garda choppers had arrived and dispatched officers on foot to start tracing the line on which the stakes had been leveled, dismantling and collecting the posts as evidence. From what Rees was hearing through his earpiece, now that people knew what to look for, some posts stretched back for miles and must have been in place for days just looking like oddities, perhaps advertisements for Irish tourist sites. It would take a while for the uprooting.

"We're trying to contain everyone here to see about that and ferret out anyone else connected with the ritual," Rees said. "News teams are going to be asking questions. Gonna be some work containing panic."

"We need to figure out who was behind this," O'Donnell said. "This handful wasn't working alone. The grenade guy worked for somebody."

"The workmen they've found were just doing a job and paid in cash. I don't think the lead gunman's going to help much," Rees said. "Maybe the woman?"

"Because women are easier to break?" O'Donnell asked, wincing as a swab was applied to her wound.

"Easy," Rees said. "Not trying to be sexist. Just hopeful."

"I'll have a go at interrogation when we get back to Dublin," O'Donnell said. "Maybe my gentle feminine touch will bring something out."

The final remark dripped with a heavy coat of sarcasm. Rees only chuckled as Bullfinch approached. A white adhesive strip had been applied above his left eye, but in spite of looking tired, he seemed to be all right.

"You OK?" O'Donnell asked.

"Heart rate's a little elevated but I'm not bad."

"Are we out of the woods?"

"I'd like to know who wanted this. It won't be as easy to try this again here, now that Mr. Rees' people are alerted to the issue, but if there are people tinkering with the Ning-Rottman theories, who knows what else might be in store?"

"We've got to get back to Dublin," O'Donnell said.

The paramedic had cut her blouse open along the seam at the shoulder and had started to apply a bandage.

"You need to get this looked at, at a hospital."

"Is there a slug in there?"

"No."

"Just bandage it. We have work to do."

Bullfinch sat on a stone with his tablet on his knees, communicating with R.C. via a text window even though the face of the O.C.L.T. leader appeared on his screen. He didn't want things overheard.

"Can you tell anything about the prints?"

"They come back as a Michael Jaco. Last post was riding a desk. Looks like there was a bit of an issue in Afghanistan that got him sidelined. I can identify with hating the deskbound status. Profiles I'm seeing suggest he took a slightly different path in his departure."

R.C. had walked away from what had been increasing boredom in Military Intelligence desk jobs for a post with the FBI, before moving full time to the O.C.L.T.

"Looks like this guy worked private security for a while, then a stint with The Institute, you know, the PMC?"

"You're going to have to help me with the alphabet soup," Bullfinch said.

"Private military company. Contract soldiers. He went freelance after new corporate masters there implemented a board of directors and some restraints. Remember The Institute had some high-profile embarrassments?"

"Do any of The Institute's clients have anarchistic tendencies?"

R.C. let a half-laugh escape at that question. "Try all of 'em. Regulation tends to be anathema to people who hire private armies."

"Any sign our friend here peeled off any of The Institute's clients because The Institute was getting soft?"

"I can try to get that cross-referenced. We can see."

"Anarchist or not, someone bankrolled this and marshaled disparate strands of Ning disciples to assemble the pieces and get this all rolling. If we can determine that, it might come in handy."

"I'll get back to you. You going to get some rest?"

"I'm going back to Dublin for the interrogations," Bullfinch said. "*Aisteach* holds the offenders for a while, until counter terrorism — and really this was an act of terrorism — steps in."

"Hope you find some answers."

"I do as well, my friend. I do as well."

36

O'Donnell walked into the interrogation room wearing a pull over sweater with a cowl neck she'd grabbed in a store on the drive from the helipad to *Aisteach* headquarters. The loose wool allowed a little room for the shoulder wound.

She found Freya Turnbull, as they'd determined her identity, sitting at the table with a paper coffee cup between her palms. Her hands were cuffed at the wrists. Her hair was disheveled. She had a bandage on her cheek similar to Bullfinch's, and her eyes were as glazed by madness as they were filled with defiance.

"You ever see any photographs from the U.S. of the Manson girls walking along the hallway to trial?" O'Donnell asked as she slid a chair out and sat down. She let her voice drop low and disengaged formality.

"Can't recall," the woman said.

"They're walking along in Sunday dresses laughing and singing, all defiant of the system and thinking Charlie's gonna make everything all right."

She adjusted the chair so that she sat directly across from Freya. Then she looked straight into her eyes.

"That was a long time ago. Those girls were all devoted to the cause, defiant like you are, sure of themselves. Know where they are now? Still locked up. Every so often they have to go before the parole board and beg to be let out, but it gets them nowhere. All except Susan Atkins. She got out. You know how? By dying. She begged them to let her go die in peace, all swollen from cancer treatment, little skull cap on her head. Couldn't get up, barely could lift her head. Had to wheel her in to beg on a gurney.

Authorities just said 'sorrrrry.'"

She slammed her hands down, palms flat, rattling the table.

"That what you want? It's what's gonna happen."

Freya chuckled.

O'Donnell pushed her chair back and stood, leaning across the table to stare. "Like I said they laughed. Until they weren't laughin' anymore. We can find a hole to put you down somewhere. Forever."

She wheeled and headed for the door.

"That might not last for as long as you think," Freya called behind her. "Forever. Don't get too comfortable as a jailer, detective. Don't get too happy with yourself. Or your world." She let her voice take on almost a lilt of song. "'Cause it may not last."

O'Donnell walked on to the door and let it slam behind her.

"What's that supposed to mean?" O'Donnell asked once she'd entered the observation room.

"Other operatives must be out there," Bullfinch said. "We may not be dealing with just finding out what's just happened. She's talking like there's more to come."

"Any insights? Can we get ahead of this one with your knowledge of mythology?"

"Croag Patrick isn't the only spot where the snakes or dragons were battled…"

"Or whatever the hell that was in the bay?" Rees asked, stepping over to form a small circle with them.

"Right," Bullfinch said. "Whatever it was. The legends hold that there was another location where serpents were banished. If we want to marshal our forces that's probably the one to gamble on. Mr. Rees, I'm sure you know where Skellig Michael is."

"As far South as you can get in this country."

"There are a few legends that hold that St. Patrick worked there as well in the driving out of serpents or dragons," Bullfinch said. "Since we've seen there may be some kind of truth to it, maybe things were driven into the water in both places and locked down for a better word."

O'Donnell drew in a breath. "There are more like that thing?"

"We've seen that there's at least a bit of lore to that effect," Bullfinch said. "Not as many sources claim Skellig Michael as Croag Patrick, but clearly we're seeing precedent for the folklore, so I don't know that we need to split hairs if we want to go all in on that spot. Legend holds Patrick needed the assistance of St. Michael the Archangel for what he faced in the South."

"Oh, *that* St. Michael," O'Donnell said.

Bullfinch nodded.

"O.C.L.T. have any choirs of angels on speed dial?"

"Sorry. We haven't really managed to tap into that line of communication," Bullfinch said.

37

Kaity scrolled through the pictures on the phone, photo after photo of symbols in odd places.

They'd given her a blanket and hot coffee and put her in a waiting room upon reaching headquarters. She sipped her bitter brew and studied the old markings. Some were familiar from her student days, and the locations were apparent, even though the images were cropped tight. It brought back memories again of the grand game in the day.

She closed her eyes and felt a bit of elation. The information they'd assembled to beat as the heart of their little thought experiment all those years ago had proven true. Just as she'd begun to suspect even then. Keon had suspected it as well. As had some of the others.

Keon's anxiety had led to the concealment of the characters so that no one group member possessed them all. Except him. Though some had felt it absurd, there was just that outside notion that it might be true.

And it was. She'd felt heart palpitations as the waterspout had swirled. Even some in the old group would have said it was just a weather incident that coincided with the attempted ritual. She knew better. She'd see the thing dancing in the haze and darkness.

And she held all of the pieces now, even the last one only Keon had known and kept to himself as the check on the process.

Freya had put on a good show when the *Aisteach* team had come to her apartment, making the abduction attempt look real, choosing to protect her when they'd stepped in.

No need to tie her to Professor Burke's unfortunate death or hinder her viability in carrying on. She'd be safe and available now to keep going, to keep the work alive, to pursue the second possibility. That had been an instinctive decision on Freya's part, but it had proved to be wise.

Kaity felt a bit of satisfaction in that. She'd drifted into the gatherings that had formed around their secret symbols, first as an observer, just seeing what had taken off. Then more gradually she had become a believer in the invention she'd helped launch. She'd been part of the small group that had welcomed Freya the first time she'd wandered in, looking lost and frightened and seeking something. She hadn't appeared to be someone who'd become a key lieutenant, but her inner strength had emerged as she'd embraced the vision of the Ning and then found the confidence that came with the power, and she'd set out to perfect her physical prowess for service to the group.

Freya had brought the mission a long way. There had been little opportunity to warn any of the others since they'd taken her into protective custody, but now, with the threat perceived to be reduced, perhaps she could step outside that shepherding arm.

"Can I get a bit o' fresh air?" she asked, leaning into a hallway and catching the eye of a uniformed officer.

"Should be fine," he said. "Would you like me to go with you?"

"I'll be OK," she said. "I won't go far."

He ushered her along the hall to a doorway and pushed it open, letting her step into a brisk, calmer evening.

"Thank you," she said, waiting until she was several paces from the building before she slipped out Freya's phone and began to flip through recent calls.

When she found the one that looked right, she hit the number and waited until she got a cautious: "Yes."

"The coppers here have suspicions about a backup plan, but things can still happen. We just need to work fast."

"Understood. We're ready."

"We won't be able to establish the kind of configuration we had at The Reek, but the other approach should be effective. What do you need?"

"Transportation for me and a few others."

"Arrangements will be made."

"See you soon. The African?"

"Bring him. He may still be helpful."

She rang off then dialed another number. "Get ready to travel," she said. "I'm about to send you a photo from Freya's phone. It'll have to do."

38

O'Donnell splashed water on her face then watched the cascade stream from her cheeks in the little mirror over the basin in the small toilet area near the conference room.

With this moment to reflect, she remembered the dream she'd had the night before Rees had turned up at her door. It had almost been a prophecy.

Her gaze found her eyes in the reflection, and she stared, studying, looking for signs of madness or some indication that she might wake up...

"We're combing through Rottman stories for banishments," R.C. said as Bullfinch sat looking into his features on his tablet. "Whatever research or knowledge he stumbled on, seems to have had some accuracy. That may be closer to unearth than an archaeological dig."

"I'll take a pulp solution over no solution," Bullfinch said. "A lot of the stories have come back to me, but I haven't read them all and some are fuzzy."

He sat in a van with O'Donnell and Rees again, heading toward a Garda helipad, massaging his temple with his free hand, wishing he had his younger brain again.

"Have you ever heard of a story called 'The Provocation from Below?'" R.C. asked.

"No."

"Rebecca York seemed to remember mention of it, but it's possibly the most obscure. It wasn't collected in any of the early hardbound resurrections of Rottman's work, and it's rarely been seen."

"Even on the web?"

"Alluded to but not really distributed. She's in Chicago, so she's going to head to the special collections at the Chicago Public Library. We understand the original pulp magazine that featured the story is there. This was Rottman so it was pretty obscure."

"Worth a try," Bullfinch said. "Worth a try."

"At this point, anything is."

Meanwhile, R.C. had the Coast Guard on the line again, delivering an alert that ships might be needed in the area around Skellig Michael and that having the Brits on alert might not be a bad idea. They had subs with nukes. He added tumultuous seas just like those in Clew Bay might be expected.

"I'm going to send you something else we ran across," R.C. said.

An email alert popped up then faded on Bullfinch's screen. He opened his in-box to find the bold subject line: "Chaos Infinitum."

Opening revealed a long, narrow column of text in the email body.

"In final days as my despair climbed to new heights, I came to cherish the notion of a grand and infinite chaos..."

"What is this?"

"Rebecca said it's an obscure Rottman prose poem. It basically champions the idea that chaos is needed to shatter the world's complacency. It's like a philosophical outline. We thought it might be at the heart of what you're dealing with. To quote that sage The Joker: 'Some men just want to watch the world burn.'"

"Alfred said that," Bullfinch said. "Some people say I look a little like the previous Alfred so I keep up with these things."

"Gandalf came to my mind, first time I saw you," O'Donnell said from the seat beside him. "Gandalf with a haircut and a natty suit."

"So we're looking at a grand plan for chaos," Bullfinch said. "Someone seizing on the same ideas in this poem."

"You let your snake demons loose on an island nation," R.C. said, "there's a pretty good chance that's what you'll achieve."

"Does the lost Rottman story offer a closing ritual?"

"That may be asking a bit much."

A sedan pulled to a stop at the curb where Kaity waited with two young women at her side.

"I get The Brothers Groom in person?"

"It's supposed to be a secret," Edward Groom said. "But we're here and looking forward to a new economic canvass."

His brother beside him wore shades in spite of the dark interior along with an expensive black Burberry with hood up and toggles buttoned.

Kaity gave him a nod then gestured for the young women to slide in first before she followed.

"Can you deliver?" a voice croaked.

Kaity stared back at him.

"As we told you, we're relying on variables we didn't have at The Reek, but we should be able to make something work in the South. The cosmic moment is close enough that ripples should be flowing through the ether, so to speak."

She nodded toward a pair of young women who looked to be in their early twenties. "Alison and Nelda here will fill you in on the technical points. They've been working carefully for us for a while on a couple of fronts, not just as monitors. We can go over what we need to make things work."

"I've sketched out a rough schematic of the second configuration," Alison said, slipping a paper with a rough pencil drawing from her coat pocket. "Now if we could transfer just a bit of equipment that we have access to."

39

"**A**mazing view," O'Donnell said.

Her voice carried just a hint of rancor as she stood near a low stone wall looking across a misty expanse of water at Small Skellig, a kilometer and a half away.

They were a while past dawn. She'd grabbed fitful sleep only in snippets during travel time, but she'd managed enough of a doze to dream of writhing serpents that produced a grim aftereffect in waking.

Usually the island was occupied by birds from what she understood. Through the haze, she saw more than feathered friends. A black-garbed tactical squad, drawn from a Garda regional support unit stood facing the water, weapons held at-ease but ready. They were usually scrambled to deal with hostage situations or riots. This was a little different for them.

She and Bullfinch had followed a narrow trail once a chopper had deposited them on Great Skellig. Somehow they'd drawn Jimmy Ahlstrom again. He'd showered and rested while they were interrogating, so he'd asked for the assignment, chipper and un-rattled by what they'd seen at the bay.

"The monastic settlement is a UNESCO World Heritage Site now, so let's be careful."

"I know they used it in *Star Wars*, too," O'Donnell said. "Don't want to mess up Luke's refuge. I heard he wound up dangling from one of these cliffs or something."

"I believe that was apocryphal," Rees said. "Whatever keeps it from getting blown up."

"That's entirely up to the snake handlers," O'Donnell said. "I believe they're 'it' in this little game of whack-a-mole. Isn't that what the Americans call it, Professor?"

Bullfinch had been scanning the horizon, eyes in a squint as much for focus as to shut out the wind sweeping in from the water.

"It is," Bullfinch said. "Another metaphor comes to mind. Want to deal with a snake, you cut off its head. That may be the challenge, once we complete the task at hand."

O'Donnell tilted her head toward the water below them. Waves and ripples tossed about, but it was calm compared to what they'd seen at the bay.

"What's down there? Another?"

"Maybe nothing. Maybe another. Maybe the queen of the thing we saw at County Mayo. Maybe they're somewhere else we don't know about. Maybe they're regrouping and they'll try after we're gone. Or maybe there's something compelling them to act faster like an alignment of the stars we don't know about."

"Saving the world's a tough business. You're kind of confirming what I've always felt. It's all random."

"We're making an educated guess," Bullfinch said. "Against high strangeness. It's always a bit daunting."

Keon had thought himself too tense to sleep, but in the stuffy air of the van where they'd locked him away, he'd felt his eyes grow heavy and the center of his brain had dulled. That had spread outward until his head had slumped down onto soft canvass bags stacked next to him.

When he dreamed, he heard the call, the distant rumbling something that had come to his sleep in the old days. That *something* wanted and waited, and in the dream he seeped into its thinking and felt the longing mixed with malevolent desire.

He'd thought back in the old days when the dream came that it arrived because he'd spent so much time pouring over the old lore and the faded printouts of almost-lost pulp stories and fanzine articles and theories, but he had worried also. What if the dream represented more than imagination? What if it was a clarion call? A summoning?

The apprehension from long ago returned and permeated a detached portion of his brain in the dream, the nagging worry of a truth almost too horrible intertwining with the sense of hunger for awakening and...fury...in the mind of the *something*.

It didn't crave destruction, but it longed to be set free, and in that freedom brewed a frenzy he could sense would mean collateral carnage. Yet its desire almost cancelled the apprehension he felt. The want, the calling to be aided in release was powerful and mesmerizing.

His mind's eye peered through shadow and mist, upward through a covering of water and waves. He sensed massive size around him in the cold dark, could feel appendages and power along with hope and...rage. Rage at some lost enemy and at newer enemies who'd shut a dimensional doorway...

Ka-thunk!

When the sound stirred him, drew him out of the odd and extraordinary consciousness, Keon wasn't sure how long he'd been out of things or how far the van had traveled. He shook his head a bit and took a moment in remembering where he was. Just a heartbeat later, the dread exploded near his sternum. What had he felt? What had been wrought while he slept?

Light splashed in from outside as the van door swung open and chill quickened Keon's awakening. He blinked, then focused, first on the familiar. Kaity stood at the van doors. He didn't recognize the men beside her, stoic operatives looking like U.S. Secret Service men.

"What the hell's going on?"

He didn't like the look in her eyes. They betrayed something. He could read a fervor that hinted some deep conviction. He could imagine what that meant.

"It was incredible," she said.

"My God, Kaity. What have you done?"

"It's real, Keon. All of it. There was a frantic nightmare in the bay. They stopped it…"

And Keon's heart beat again at that announcement.

"…but it was wondrous. It had to be Crom Cruach. So powerful. Everthin' we ever talked about was true. They broke the chain that channeled earth energy and sealed the crypt again there, but we're gonna try while the stars are still right. We're gonna try the Song of the Air."

"What do you mean?"

"We're in County Kerry. If waking the thing at The Reek almost worked, we can try again for what's said to be off the Iveragh. We don't know which was parent and which was child, but if the one at Clew Bay was the infant, we could be looking at something incredible. I heard news the other day talking about comets in the old days. That was them, them comin' down."

"Something wants to be set free," he said in a low whisper. "I sensed it in the dream."

He shouldn't have said that. He saw the wonder spread across her features. She almost babbled in her excitement.

"You felt the dream? Then something's close. Others'll feel it too. They'll be coming here to join those we've rallied. Madam Quiñones said she had visions of that."

"Kaity, listen to yourself. Do you know what this means? It's not a joke, not a game. Proving the theory is…"

"A breakthrough. A revelation."

"It's destruction."

"It's fire so that something new can be created. Something our little minds can't even comprehend."

"Or maybe it's just chaos, Kaity. The old orders hid things for a reason."

"And someone even back then tried to preserve them, wrote things on walls so they wouldn't be lost. Some knew the knowledge would be needed again. They looked forward to new millennium."

The corner of her mouth curled up just slightly, and that

flicker along with the deep mania he detected somewhere behind her eyes chilled him. She'd sensed the hunger in the *something* just as he had. She had not been chilled, but elated.

"Who are those men you're working with, Kaity? What do they want? Why are they helping?"

"Just like with us. It's an experiment. They want to see a place that can start fresh."

"It won't be starting fresh. It'll be a waking nightmare."

Her teeth clenched.

"It'll be an illumination. Get out of there, Keon. Get ready to look into a new and golden dawn."

The Hummer's rear gate had been folded up, and a tarp extended from the back door, tied into place on two aluminum poles staked into the ground.

A young man lugged the black case around to a table set up there as Kaity trailed him with Nelda at one shoulder and Alison at the other. Keon followed behind them with the stoic men flanking him. They'd keep him in line. Kaity hoped his eyes would open and he'd join in soon.

"Careful with it," she said, knowing the man would take care but feeling compelled to give some kind of instruction.

He only grunted as he placed the case and stood aside for her. She stepped in and flipped the catches on the case's front then folded back the lid.

"Les, it's ready for your magic," she said.

Leslie Innes, a kid of about twenty-one, kept his head slightly bowed as he moved in to the device. He had long, dark hair that hung in oily strings around a long face mitigated slightly by the dark horn-rimmed glasses he wore.

He stepped over to the black plastic case without speaking and flipped up the lid. That revealed a metal framework within that stretched up vertically around a smooth flat panel housed inside the case's bottom. From foam pockets within the case, he slipped out small components and began fitting them into place on vertical side bars.

From a duffle stuffed into the back of the hummer beside the case, he slipped out a battery pack and several black cartridges.

"The last symbol you gave me is the last you need?" he asked, chin pointed in to his throat so far he was almost directing his voice down his collar.

"That's it."

"We're going to produce interlocking pieces," he said. "It's a multi-piece assembly for the obelisk. Then we'll switch over for your smaller staffs. Several small pieces interlocking for those also. We have enough filament cartridges to give you a large quantity."

"Time frame?"

"It'll go quick enough since we're keeping them small."

"Let's get started."

"We and the Coast Guard have choppers in the air again with eyes open," Rees said. "Nothing so far. IRCG is coordinating with the Naval Service too. We'll get an OPV in the vicinity soon. The *LÉ Clíodhna* was headed home toward Haulbowline, but it's being re-routed. It's still equipped from an operation in the Mediterranean."

O'Donnell only gave one tick of her head in acknowledgement. An offshore patrol vessel might be handy, and it would be good to have another set of observers at work along with the firepower it offered. Cannons might come in handy against a repeat of the thing from the bay. She had to keep in mind *soon* with a sailing vessel was a qualified term.

She kept her eyes focused on the distant shore beyond Small Skellig, almost lost in gray mist, and the swirl of gray nothing forced her to ask herself again what she'd seen. She had to wonder if in the fury of the moment she'd projected something, imagined the great and profane thing in the bay. Maybe all of this was still a bad dream? She kept wanting that but knew she couldn't rest on a bromide. No matter how much she doubted in retrospect what had seemed certain in the moment, deep down she knew the threat was real. Even if anything they could do was futile, they had to keep alert.

"Lot of spots for them to try from," she said, forcing herself to focus on the ridges and rises outlined in the mist.

She continued along a rugged path they'd followed on the island's edge for a while, Rees and Bullfinch behind. Small stone huts dappled the shoreline, still firm and intact and looking like huddled sentinels facing the ocean.

Rees noticed where she was staring. "It's said monks came here to allow the solitude to help them get closer to God."

"Maybe they were also serving as lookouts," Bullfinch said.

40

Keon watched the shaft on the 3-D printer bed take shape as the extruder zipped in a pattern of repetition. Long strokes alternated with concentrated shimmers. In the longer moves, it kept making a turn at one end that left a small open loop while layers of dark filament built on layers and nothing became something.

Earlier, three small blocks had been finished for the obelisk with intricate markings and etches along its edges, duplicating the lost alphabet symbols. Someone had carried that off to sink it in the sand on the beach.

These new items seemed to be the tops of staffs.

"How many members do you have?" he asked.

Kaity smiled. "Don't worry. There'll be enough."

"The dream…"

"Yes, you felt it." Her eyes flared with excitement, cutting him off, and chilling him because he saw madness and detachment becoming more pronounced.

"Is that what you're counting on? Dreams to…"

He looked at the small group of people who'd gathered and were busy at various tasks around them while the printer worked.

"The dream is the call, Keon. We have a contingent, but it will summon more."

"I only dreamed because my thoughts were concentrated on all this again. It was a game, Kaity. We were a bunch of nerds who wanted to get the old guard excited over our ideas and tricks so we could snicker about it."

"But we were right, weren't we? You should have seen what

was out there in the bay. It was just like the hints in Rottman's stories. He worked from research and secret meetings and from dreams, and he knew what was there, waiting, sleeping. He got closer than anyone and recorded the glimpses he caught in his nightmares."

"Was there really something out there? In the water?"

She laughed. "You made it all possible, and you want it to be wrong. It was huge, incredible, everything you could have expected, and if the dreams are touching you, that means the twins are there and others will come."

"Wait a minute, what? Twins?"

"Think about it. The one in Clew Bay was the mother. The ones dispersed here were the children, and there were rumors of the two, a pattern foretold in the Greek myths, too. The Rod of Asclepius showed one serpent wrapped around a staff. It's the symbol of medicine here in Ireland. Hermes carried the staff with twin serpents, the caduceus, but there were twins on the staffs that hailed Ningishzida, the Sumerian god as well. Those were rumblings from one land, and they were part of the reality here as well. Crom is Ning. Ning is Crom."

It was almost a song. He stared into her eyes again, into the lost country there, a place of delusion. If she was not wrong about the legends, it was clear she didn't fully appreciate what could happen.

"They will bring healing when they destroy and blaze the way for the new, and if they are guardians of the gates they'll be followed."

"If there was really something in the bay, if there's something out there under the waves, we need to study it. It's incredible if what we were playing is real and if we managed to really fill in the gaps with the symbols and my algorithm, but the study needs to be conducted under controlled circumstances, not in the midst of chaos. Dear God, Kaity. Think!"

"It's a dimensional door. Nothing can be studied without opening it."

"What then? The land overrun? Destruction?"

"The Americans want to create a great laboratory for their theories, a new economic model, a new political reality, rid of president and *taoiseach*. Maybe they'll get what they want. Certainly we'll have the chance to rein in whatever world is created. The dreams you're feeling, I've been feeling them, too. We're talking about a new level of consciousness. An opening of the mind's third eye. The ajna. We'll be on the cusp of it all. You can join me."

"Kaity, if so many ancient people feared and sought to seal the passage, what can that mean? Turn the printer off. If people come to join you, turn them away and let's stop this."

She shook her head. "The Druids knew 'about the powers and authority of the immortal gods.' It's all been suppressed, but they were overrun and outvoted by Patrick and his disciples and the little order that betrayed other Druids. It's time to turn things around, reverse and rediscover."

"There were some suggestions they worked with Patrick because they saw what was about to befall this land. They decided a different age needed to be instituted."

"The time has come. The time for a new birth of healing. Think of the turmoil in the world. It just perpetuates. It just keeps cycling over and over. Unrest, pain, poverty. The institutions and politicians fail us. The twins can be set free and what will follow will destroy all that's not worked and a cycle of healing will follow the turmoil."

The printer head completed its motion. Resting on the printer bed now was a shiny, firm loop, looking like a shepherd's hook though closed at one end, and a conclave notch had formed at the other end. Embedded just below the loop, he could make out lines of one of the lost characters. In a few seconds the loop was added to other pieces, assembling a staff two meters long.

Kaity lifted it and tested it to see if it was dry enough to hold. Satisfied that it was, she lifted it with one hand and dragged it about in the air. As wind moved through the opening, which

Keon decided really looked like the loop at the top of an ankh, a whistling sound issued from it.

"A musical note?"

"Ogham symbols were always sounds. The lost symbols are too. We've had a small group working secretly among the students at Trinity," Kaity said. "Interpreting the symbols mathematically and planning, re-inventing what you did. Wind whistling through the loops will create an arrangement that channels energy."

"That's what Rottman was hinting about in 'The Provocation from Below,' what he called 'The Song of the Air'?"

"The way people have tried to bury the story suggests it may be more powerful than channeling the energy of the Ley lines."

As she continued to sweep the piece in the air, the long-haired man returned to the printer, made adjustments to calibration and then flipped a switch to set it to work again.

"Portable prototype?" Keon asked. "That printer?"

"Latest thing from CRANN apparently. Some of the interchangeable pieces we pre-made, but Leslie here's prepped the loops with the values of the symbols. If it holds up, we'll have an array that duplicates what was probably accomplished with iron horns once upon a time."

"How many do you have? Here?"

"Enough, but others will come."

"You're going to wait for dreamers to hold them up for the wind and wake the caduceus pieces?"

"Don't sound so hopeful that it will fail. We have some players that may help regardless of the dreamers."

"What?"

"You didn't see him but Freya and the order had found some people who were also referred to in Rottman's texts and the old writings."

Keon had not noticed a small cluster of figures huddled together at the perimeter near the Hummer.

"The one that grabbed me at the priory. That was a tentacle? I thought…"

"You dreamed it? No, he wasn't one of a kind. They'll be serving as guardians of our effort, or they can hold up staffs as well, but the dreams will bring people. Wait and see."

41

A message popped up on Bullfinch's tablet which he shielded with his body, keeping a forearm wrapped around it. Text was probably the best he could hope for out here. Mack had explained to him once how typed words might travel even if signals weren't strong enough for other data.

"Found it," read the little bubble under the name Rebecca.

"Rottman story?" he typed.

"Yes. Chicago Public. Rottman writes of cult channeling the 'The Song of the Wind.'"

"That's different than what we saw before," Bullfinch said under his breath.

"What's it mean?" he typed, glad his numb fingers managed without mistake.

"A chant in the story," Rebecca responded. "Not sure beyond that, but it's not the ritual of oak and mistletoe that we know of the Druids. I'm going to get a scan out to Mack to see if it helps with his research."

Bullfinch strolled up a jagged set of steps then over a rugged patch to a vantage where O'Donnell stood, squinting toward distant land through a pair of high-powered binoculars.

"The chants and the wind seem to be about different approaches to channeling energy through the elements. In this story it's the wind. Supposedly Rottman's acolytes were scared of it when they collected his known stories."

"I'm back to thinking it's all hopeless, Professor," O'Donnell said. "We launch an incredible effort; they regroup down here. Possibly. We're not even sure, and we don't know how many they are or what they'll try or even what's below us. If it's as bad as before and you can't spot an angle, what'll it take to stop it? That ship that's coming's got antiaircraft guns, big cannons but not really equipped for a sea serpent the size of New Jersey. Maybe we need to call in a British sub with nukes and end it all."

"That's the fatalism creeping back in," Bullfinch said. "With a sprinkling of pessimism. You can never afford to give yourself over to despair, dear lady. Not in this line of work. The times since I've been with O.C.L.T. that I've thought all was lost couldn't be counted on Kali's fingers."

"Fan of Pollyanna are you, Professor? I'll go with my own gut."

"Suit yourself and keep your eyes open," Bullfinch said, and turned to stare toward the ocean, looking for signs of stirring other than the waves.

He didn't want to give up, and he didn't want to fuel O'Donnell's despair, but he didn't feel like Pollyanna. What had the story's optimistic lead said? Find something in everything to be glad about? As the bitter chill and the wind's ragged edge sprinkled with icy sea moisture bit into him, a notion arose.

What if they waited here and nothing happened? What if his educated guess was wrong? What if the cult sprang up somewhere else to perpetrate its dark ritual?

Or what if this was the time he didn't figure things out? What if Rebecca and R.C. or Mack couldn't channel something to him that would save the day this time? Maybe this was the day he'd go down fighting. At least he'd do it with one of the bravest women he'd ever known at his side. He put a hand on her shoulder, accepting the solace of that thought for the moment at least. She'd lifted the binoculars again, determined to keep looking, even if she had only a field of gray flannel spread before her.

He sought something else to say, but Rees trotted up to their side, alleviating the need. It would only have been a platitude anyway.

"Choppers are seeing movement of people along one side of the peninsula," he said.

"What kind of movement?"

"It's like a march they're saying. All along the Iveragh. Looks like they're headed toward the sea." He listened for a moment. "Eastern side."

"Lemmings?" O'Donnell asked.

"Doesn't sound right," Bullfinch said.

"Maybe they're luring people somehow, food for the thing we're looking for," O'Donnell said.

"Everywhere around here's sacred somehow," Rees said. "Maybe it's an annual pilgrimage we've just forgotten. They think they're seeing farmers and tourists and everything."

"It's on the Ring of Kerry, isn't it?" O'Donnell said. "Tons of guests traveling that route."

"I don't think it's a coincidence," Bullfinch said. "They're congregating. They've heard some kind of call."

"A trumpet?"

"Rottman wrote of things that came to men in dreams. If something's imminent, perhaps anything that's waiting below the water has reached out telepathically."

Rees put one finger in his left ear to block the sound of the wind and waves and listened again to the earpiece.

"There's something going on near the end of the peninsula," Rees said, listening then relaying. "A bit of an encampment near Ballinskelligs Castle."

"Can we see that from here?" Bullfinch asked.

"Don't think so," O'Donnell said. "It'll be up the east side of the peninsula. It overlooks its own bay. Not that different from our other site."

"Let's head to other side of the island," Bullfinch said. "See what we can catch a glimpse of."

O'Donnell set off along the craggy ledge, placing each foot carefully. From the way she positioned herself, Bullfinch suspected she was prepared to reach back and offer him support if she thought he was slipping. Thoughtful, but he placed his steps with care as well. They didn't have time for foolish mishaps.

"They don't allow climbing out here this time of year, usually," O'Donnell said. "I can see why. It's treacherous."

"There's a lot of haze out there, too," Bullfinch said. "Can I see those binoculars?"

They travelled a bit farther and she handed them over. Bullfinch squinted into the lenses. After a bit of shifting them about, he got them comfortable, then scanned until he spotted the outline of shore.

"You really think there's something in this bay?"

"I don't know. Could be there's something in the water between here and that shore. There's a lot of shoreline. Can we get a look from a chopper?"

"Let's head back," Rees said. "Jimmy ought to be able to take us up. It's not nearly as bad as it was at The Reek."

"Not yet," Bullfinch said.

But he didn't have a good feeling. Pollyanna was gone. He had a very bad feeling. Very bad indeed.

42

"What are they handing out?" O'Donnell asked.

"They look like giant licorice twists," Ahlstrom said.

"Get us a little lower," Rees said into his mouthpiece. "But not so close they take notice just yet."

"Staffs of some kind," Bullfinch said.

They'd been in the air more than an hour, watching random people trekking about and tourists leaving cars and beginning to hike in the direction of a small congregation of people near Ballinskelligs Castle.

"Are they going to stick them in the ground again?"

"They aren't as big as those we saw before," Bullfinch said. "An individual can carry it alone. What is that, about six and a half feet?"

"You've been in America too long, Professor," O'Donnell said. "That's just shy of two meters if I'm judging the perspective."

"So we've got the hand-held variety," Rees said.

"Why don't we round 'em up?" O'Donnell said. "Get the regional team over there. Take 'em to a barn somewhere for questioning?"

"At the moment they're peacefully assembled," Rees said. "I'm betting there are Americans down there. Botherin' them alone's an international incident, and we've got other nationals down there as well, you can be sure. Do you want to tell Sky and CNN we've arrested people on suspicion of conjuring a giant serpent? After you explain setting off grenades near the most popular pilgrimage site in the country?"

"I'm surprised nothing from Clew Bay's trending on YouTube,"

O'Donnell said. "No one recorded anything?"

"It's trending as a really impressive waterspout," Rees said. "Since it's serpents we're dealing with, interestingly there's plenty of what the Americans call wiggle room."

"Will a closer look get us called before a world tribunal?"

"Not if we use discretion."

"Soul of," O'Donnell said. "Right, Professor?"

"Certainly."

"Set 'er down," Rees said into his mouthpiece.

Kaity had not seen Liam Hennigan in some time, but he was as striking as ever with a few years on him. Standing shoulders above those around him with shoulder-length hair and a beard, he looked like some kind of sage. She went to him when he stepped out of his vehicle and gave him a hug.

"It's been too long," she said.

He took off his round-brimmed hat and gave her a kiss on the cheek. "Too long indeed. How are things shaping up?"

"For having to improvise with plan B? Not bad. We've got nearly enough equipped for an attempt based on the theories. A few more and we'll have a firm contingent."

She found a completed staff and offered it to him.

"Not bad," he said, turning it over in his hands, testing its heft, fingers checking the indentation of the markings.

"How do you want them aligned?"

"Get them down to the beach. Shoulder to shoulder. Where are our friends?"

"Already down there. A shame your father won't be here to see it."

"Least he got a glimpse out there from what I heard, confirmed it all for him. He knew we'd carry on. It's my grandfather I'm sorry for. Died long before it was all realized."

He turned back toward land and lifted a palm into the wind, testing the strength.

"Not bad he said, and it'll pick up."

"It did out at Clew Bay. Once everything began."

"I'll take that on at water's edge. I've heard my dad Malphas do it enough times. Time for me to be Balor."

Long ago, embarking on his father's mission, he'd drawn the name from Irish myth as his persona in mystical proceedings. He shrugged off his toggle coat to reveal a silky black robe with markings embroidered into the folds that hung down his body. A girl who'd climbed out of his rover with him brought up a burnished wooden staff with a textured and curved top. It didn't show the signs of wear the old man's had, but he held it up, confident with its balance.

"Let's get to it," he said.

"Who's this fellow?" Bullfinch asked.

He and O'Donnell had made their way to the ruined gray stone tower that had come to be called the castle, and they stood on opposite sides of what had been a window, peering out while keeping themselves hidden.

"He's dressed like their messiah, and it looks like Kaity knows him."

"He's going to take some kind of position, I believe," Bullfinch said.

O'Donnell clicked her mobi.

"If I were still in counterterrorism, we'd invoke national security about now," she said.

"Let's move forward cautiously," Rees said in her ear. "We'd better interrupt this. I'll get the regional team over. We'll deal with the diplomats later."

As he turned where he stood a few feet over and lowered his head to speak into his mouthpiece, O'Donnell climbed to the window bottom and prepared for a hop to the ground beyond as she drew her sidearm.

"Can you keep up, Professor?"

"Don't worry, I'm with you."

He slipped the sword from the folds of his coat, but she took only a few steps before pausing.

The tall one had stepped to the beach, and as he reached a spot where the waves lapped against the shore and slid up around his feet and lower folds of his robe, dark, heads began to rise from the water, just the tops of rounded, slick domes at first. Then large round eyes, black at their core, emerged.

Five.

Eight.

Ten.

All of them had to be like the figure the professor had battled at Clew Bay.

"I'm afraid one sword's not going to do it," Bullfinch said from her side.

"How do we get caught with our pants down even when we're ahead of them?" O'Donnell. "The fates hate us."

"This has been planned for a long time," Bullfinch said. "Snake gods are not exactly the kind of chatter our analysts listen for. We're going to need the regional team and their guns."

"Coming," Rees said. "I've been trying to convince some people we need an air strike and help from the Brits."

He jogged to their side and watched.

The dark figures turned and faced the waters of the bay, parting slightly to allow the tall man to walk to the center of their formation, to take point.

O'Donnell fought the cold feeling at her core that coupled with a tension in her innards. "We didn't get around to discussing what the fuck those are, Professor. I have my theories, but I'm just a copper."

"Hybrids," he said. "I'm not sure how they were formed, but they must contain the DNA from whatever beings are sequestered down there. There are legends of hybrid priests from as far back as Lemuria, cross-breeds."

"Where's Lemuria again?"

"Atlantis. Irish myth also references some unpleasant figures called Fomorians…"

"Got the idea," O'Donnell said.

The tall man had stepped farther into the waves as the figures moved forward, ahead of him as they were washed in the bay's waters. As they moved forward, their heads bobbed, and they became his protectors, a phalanx.

When the water had reached his waist, he raised the staff, and appeared to begin shouting.

"Just like the old man," O'Donnell said.

As an arm shot skyward with the shaft perpendicular to his body, a cadre of the people holding the issued staffs stepped in the water behind the man, shoulder to shoulder, moving toward his back and lifting the hooped ends high. As wind whistled through the openings, a ripple stretched across the water's surface beyond the leader, becoming a furrow, as if opening a channel within the water.

More figures stepped toward the beach edge, aligning on the sand and also lifting hooped staffs, a small battalion of tourists and villagers, women in casual dresses and raincoats, men in parkas, hikers, farmers in anoraks and sheepskin jackets, shopkeepers...

"How'd this happen?"

"A summoning," Bullfinch said. "Brewing for a while in the backs of their minds. Planted by dreams."

"My god, I had a dream," O'Donnell said. "I thought it was..."

Bullfinch pointed. "Look back from shore a few meters."

A shiny black obelisk about a meter and a half tall stood near the Hummer. Had to be made from the same plastic as the staffs.

"That channeling something?" she asked.

"Focusing," Bullfinch said. "In some way."

Pointing her sidearm into the air, O'Donnell paced forward and fired, hoping to gather attention. The wind deprived the blast of its roar, and the people continued falling into place, aligning along the shoreline, raising staffs, aiming the ring mouths to the water. Meanwhile more were filing under the tent near the Hummer while more were emerging from the other side with staffs.

"We've got to interrupt this," O'Donnell said.

"Dear God, they're so focused it'd take a bloody massacre, wouldn't it?" Rees said.

"Then if what's down there's like before, we'd better get that patrol ship and a few more headed our way."

Bullfinch raised the camera eye in the back of the tablet toward the shore and snapped pictures then tapped a few keys to send the snaps on to his colleagues, at least wanting to alert them to what unfolded before him. If he failed, they'd need to prepare.

Then he stood observing the line and the movement between camps.

"Each addition must make the signal stronger."

"Turning our guy there into Charlton Heston."

Water in the bay indeed seemed to be moving in an odd pattern, as if a furrow or trench was forming.

"The sound is doing it," Bullfinch said. "Those staffs are forming notes with the wind."

"With the regional response team, maybe we disrupt it, slow it down. I can work with them," O'Donnell said. "Do it as politely as possible."

"I think we're going to have to try it," Rees agreed.

Bullfinch's tablet vibrated. A message had come in.

"Looks like The Song of the Air Rottman wrote of," came Rebecca's response. "No easy answers in the text. Event in story only thwarted at a distance while others look on."

"Like Lovecraft's 'Dunwich Horror,'" Bullfinch said. "Avoiding detail."

O'Donnell moved beside him and looked past his sleeve at his screen.

"Looks like we're gonna have to improvise," she said. "How about I join the regional team, you head out to the ship, Professor? That's where you're likely to offer the most advice or spot vulnerabilities. Keeps us from all being in one place in the worst case scenario."

"I've never rammed a sea monster with a ship," he said.

"No, but you've got more judgment related to that than I do," O'Donnell said.

He slipped the sword from the folds of his coat.

"You might need this more than I do."

"Sure, I'll have it on hand. I'll act like it's not a lost cause. All we can do is give it our best shot, isn't it? When we fail, somebody's gonna have to make the call on the nuke. Someone who doesn't want the world conquered by a snake-thing."

43

As Ahlstrom settled in at the controls, Bullfinch crawled into a seat in the chopper that had brought them to Ballinskelligs Beach. He buckled his harness in a seat beside a response team member who'd been sent with them. As the rotor turned, soon he felt the craft rise. When he'd plugged his headset in, he tapped the tablet face, activating the app connection Mack had preloaded for him.

After a few seconds, a jagged version of Rebecca's face came onto his screen. Lucky he had that much, he thought. He felt a comfort in seeing even a distorted version of her features. It was almost like channeling a bit of her calm.

"What are you up to, Professor?"

"Heading out to sea," he said. "To find a ship that's allegedly headed this way but without the firepower to stop what we're likely to face."

"So, Tuesday," Rebecca said.

He couldn't fight the smile. If O'Donnell's dark sense of the inevitable was rubbing off, the levity pushed his own sense of futility aside, just for a moment.

"Air support?"

"Working on that too," he said. "Hoping we can avoid a massacre or worse."

"You don't actually have serpents above wa-aa-ater yet, do you?" The signal had skipped and her face froze then moved again.

"No."

The chopper climbed and he could look down at waves,

swirling back, seeming ready to part.

"Any ideas?" he asked.

"Stop The Song of the Air.'"

"On it," he said.

"A-a-a-nd k-k-eeeep your h-heaaaaad d-d-doooown."

He thumbed his screen again and brought up Mack.

"I'm headed out to an OPV," Bullfinch said.

"I've been listening to the chatter. I'm up to speed, professor."

"Any gains? Any answers."

"They've kept a lot of this off the grid but I've been assembling data. Reading Rebecca's story on my Kindle now. Keep me posted when you're on the ship."

"Talk soon," Bullfinch said.

O'Donnell and Rees stayed near the tower wall, looking past at the stream of new figures moving toward the beach. Girls with backpacks filed behind old men and women, an array of nylon and wool attire, snap-brimmed caps, scarves, tams and knit hats.

When she saw the chopper with the regional team descending, O'Donnell pulled away from the stone and ran toward the transport as it set down and men in black armor and helmets shuffled out, looking a little like spacemen with their dark helmets and visors. Rees stayed just a few paces behind her, his badge and ID raised.

"You're the one from SDU in Dublin?" the unit commander asked as he stepped forward.

"Used to be. Eileen O'Donnell. Special assignment."

"What is *Ais...*"

"Long story. You are?"

"David Quinn."

Rees added his fist to the bumps.

"Zach Rees."

"So what the hell is going on over there?" Quinn asked as his team assembled behind him, assault rifles cradled.

"It's hard to explain, but we need to disperse them before

something bad happens," Rees said.

Quinn looked past him to the shoreline, surveyed a moment and gave a nod. "We can give a dispersal order from the airship."

"They're probably in some kind of thrall, but we can try it," O'Donnell said.

"Your show. You want the mic?"

"I can give it a try."

They jogged to the aircraft flanked by a couple of Quinn's officers. A young woman grabbed the craft door, yanked the levered handle, and then leaned in.

In under a minute, a circular black speaker had been positioned on a tripod, and a gray case opened and connected. The young woman stood behind the speaker, tapping buttons and producing a quick whine before offering a mic to O'Donnell.

With the mic in her palm, O'Donnell took just a second to think then raised it to her lips.

"This is the Garda," she said. "The *Garda Síochána*. I'm Special Operative Aileen O'Donnell. You are ordered to cease your current activity and disperse this assembly. Immediately. Put down any weapons and step back from the shoreline."

Her words thundered from the small black circle, rising over the ongoing trill of the channeled wind. She let a finger off the mic and looked toward the beach. Then her stomach clenched. No one had even turned a head toward the sound.

"Can they hear me over the frickin' noise they're generating?" she asked.

"They should, ma'am," the officer at the controls said. "It's capable of clear communication at three thousand meters in all weather."

"I've read the brochures," O'Donnell said. "Personal opinion."

"Even with the noise, they heard us."

O'Donnell gave a nod then repeated a version of her message into the mic. Still no reaction from the group.

She let out a long breath and looked toward Quinn.

"We need to try a non-lethal physical dispersal."

Quinn raised a hand and offered a round-up hand signal to his team, bringing everyone into a huddle.

"Sling your rifles. Shotguns and beanbags ready," he said.

He took a step forward, looking at the line along the shore and the staffs they held.

"What are those? Spears?"

"Consider them religious objects initially. Not pointed," O'Donnell said. "Not gonna be fun if we're whacked with 'em, though."

"Bullet catchers," Quinn shouted to his team. "We're gonna treat it just like we would a riot in Grafton Street with cameras pointed at us."

Team members shuffled back to the chopper and began pulling out equipment cases and large black nylon bags, removing orange-handled shotguns and unsheathing tactical shields, black rectangles with twin headlights positioned just below narrow ballistic viewports. Small signs on the front read "Garda Armed Support Unit" in shiny gold letters.

"If I can get to the man in the bay, that may help," O'Donnell said.

"We'll do what we can," Quinn said.

The shields were hoisted, the guns readied, and the team formed a line, shoulder to shoulder for an approach of the beach.

Rees and O'Donnell began the walk toward shore behind them, their sidearms holstered but ready. O'Donnell kept the sword close at her left side, using the arm that hadn't been injured and wondering if she'd fare as well as the professor had against those sons of Fomoire surrounding the man in the water if her sidearm failed.

As they moved, she thought the rift in the water was starting to look more and more like the parting of the Red Sea from *The Ten Commandments*.

44

The patrol ship came into view, tossed on heavy waves while more white blankets of water burst up in front of it, the striped bow almost lifting out of the ocean before crashing down again for the cycle to start anew.

"The sea's got an upset stomach," Ahlstrom said.

Bullfinch watched from his window, studying the deep black-gray water's movement, rising and assaulting the ship again. He couldn't disagree, and the troubled sea concerned him. That had to be more of a tempest than usual, and it had to stem from the events they'd left behind. He prayed the judgment had been right.

"Can you set down on it in this?" Bullfinch asked.

The pilot gazed out at the sea as the rain pitched against the wind screen.

"I might if that was one of the OPVs with a helipad. Hate to say it, but the best bet's to set you down with a harness. Even if we could land we'd go right over the side unless they could run out and tie us down immediately. That'd be, what's the official term for it at sea? Iffy."

Bullfinch looked down at the ship and the harsh gray waves.

"So I'm going...That's why you asked for..."

The response team member beside him looked over and gave a nod.

"I'd better get bundled up."

Ahlstrom chuckled. "Guess you're gonna see why the Garda puts up with me. Captain's gonna think I'm crazy, but I can hold it pretty steady. If you'd give a wink and a request to St. Christopher, wouldn't hurt us just now."

"Let's give it a try," Bullfinch said.

The ship below dipped and rose again.

"Let me radio and tell them we've arrived. Cinch your buckles tight."

Bullfinch moved into position.

"They're wanting us to give it up until they get to calmer seas," Ahlstrom said in a few seconds.

"There won't be any calmer seas," Bullfinch said. He bit his lip. "Let's do it."

In a few moments, Bullfinch gave the flagging end of his harness a tug in compliance, then curled his fingers around the edges of the chopper door and closed his eyes. He'd wrapped his tablet carefully and secured it to his body under a life vest.

A team was coming out on deck, secured with their own lifelines.

"I guess this is going to be hairy for a while," Bullfinch said.

"Actually you should go down pretty fast," the team member said. "Gravity's on your side."

He didn't smile.

In a few seconds, Bullfinch felt the descent begin and he left his throat and stomach at the altitude where they'd started. He was almost deafened as the wind tore into him.

He'd caught words like insane from the ship's communications officer as Ahlstrom had conferred on the drop, and with his head bowed, Bullfinch reminded himself of the things he'd survived so far. If giant winged things and other monsters hadn't done him in, would fate be content to batter him against the deck of a ship? There was O'Donnell-think creeping into his head again.

Surely fate would wait for a more spectacular way to bring his demise.

As the descent continued, he felt the aircraft buffeted and churned above, flinging him about. He held tightly to the line and kept moving downward.

His head bounced side to side, needles of pain shooting

through the base of his neck. If he survived this, he'd need muscle relaxants if not a cervical collar. He entertained then dismissed the idea of opening his eyes. Nothing he could see would help.

Good or bad, he'd deal with the outcome when he reached the deck or the cold North Atlantic waves rushed in on him. Dashing off a farewell to Mack and R.C. and Rebecca might have been a nice touch, but there wasn't time now.

Finally, he opened his eyes to see crewmen just below, waiting, ready to grab him. He wasn't quite in reach. He gritted his teeth and tried to stretch his toes, but he was pulled in the wrong direction by a gust.

He swallowed and held tight as Ahlstrom adjusted somewhere above him. He felt himself moving. Moving. Almost over the deck.

Then he slid into the arms of the crewmen. Hands closed around him, grabbing him tightly. A thumb pressed his throat.

"Was afraid your heart had stopped," someone shouted.

"That was a good test for it, my boy. It's still ticking."

It was still holding when they were ushered onto the bridge a few minutes later after he'd been shoved into a tight little room to change into dry clothes including a heavy blue sweater.

"Have some tea."

A mug was thrust into Bullfinch's hand by a young dark-haired female officer in a white shirt with epaulets. Bullfinch accepted and took a gulp. It felt better than he could have imagined burning down his throat. In all the excitement he'd failed to notice he was chilled to the bone.

"Haven't seen much like this in a while," the woman said. "Lt. Kieran Darcy."

Bullfinch introduced himself and looked toward the narrow windshield that faced the front of the ship. A man of about fifty-five in another dark blue sweater with a captain's insignia stood there, thin and blond-haired with equally blond eyebrows.

"I don't think it's a normal storm," Bullfinch said.

"We didn't have anything on the radar or in the weather

forecast," Darcy said. "Thought the situation must not be quite normal, taking a risk like that. Helluva pilot you've got there. He's headed to the nearest shore to set down. Come meet the captain."

"Geoffrey Bullfinch," Bullfinch said extending a hand as he was ushered over.

"Lt. Commander Leonard Curl," the man said, taking his hand. "What is this occult service they're telling me you work for?"

"Orphic Crisis Logistical Taskforce, O.C.L.T., not actually "occult," but it often gets pronounced that way. How far out are we?" Bullfinch asked.

"From Ballinskelligs? We're not fast, but you caught us at a good time. At this point, forty-five minutes. That quick enough?"

"I honestly don't know. Can you fill me in on your firepower?"

"We got outfitted with a bit of new equipment for the Mediterranean mission," Curl said with a jerk of his head toward the bow. "But that's still the centerpiece."

The pitch of the ship continued, and water sloshed against the wind screen, but Bullfinch could make out a small cupola on the deck not far outside the window.

"It's called an OTO Melara 76 millimeter. The Italians made it, and they called it *super rapido*. We can take planes or missiles out of the sky. One hundred twenty rounds a minute, and with the special operations we've got lots of shells on board including some guided rounds and incendiaries."

"Fiery bullets sound good in this case," Bullfinch said with a hoist of his mug. He wished it sounded better, but he kept that to himself. "We'll see what they'll do, Captain Curl."

The corner of his mouth ticked up. He hadn't noticed the alliteration until it rolled off his lips.

45

A short, heavy gray-haired man in a red slicker stood at the edge of the tarp, solemn and patient.

Kaity watched another bottom section come off the printer and watched Alison Syn hold it up for inspection, checking especially for irregularities around the end that would need to interlock with the top section. When it got a nod, she turned and moved to the man, expecting speech.

He took her arm instead, tugging lightly and gesturing toward the shoreline.

"Liam's ready?"

The solemn expression didn't falter.

She nodded, and the man led her from the tent's edge across to another vehicle where Nelda and Alison waited. Kaity gave a nod, and they opened the door. Alison leaned in and took the arm of someone seated in the back, guiding her out against mild resistance.

The lithe girl was about sixteen, wearing a long white dress under a heavy coat. Long hair spilled down over her collar and shoulders. She blinked in the gray light outside the car, lifting a sluggish hand to shield her eyes. Vita Burke, Professor Burke's niece, had been drugged for a while. Some of the effects were wearing off, but she remained compliant.

"Let's take her down to the waterline," Kaity said.

"There are Garda up the shore," Alison said. "We need to pass through the line and move quickly."

Nelda slipped off the girl's coat, and then they each took an arm and guided her behind Kaity.

The cacophony of notes played by the swirling winds from inland had risen and turned into a discordant tonal pattern like nothing Kaity had ever heard aloud. When they'd discussed it, it had always been theoretical. Now the buzz-tinged shriek funneled through the row of open loops on the staffs, drifting in the direction where Liam stood, still flanked by the slick gray figures who protected him. As the water had begun to pull back, they were no longer submerged. They crouched, all scale, tentacles and menace.

Kept busy by the production line, Kaity had not looked toward the water for a while. The part in the waves had widened, forming twin, towering walls that shimmered like two great foam-topped parentheses.

Her gasp was sudden and involuntary, and the air stayed in her lungs until she almost felt dizzy and faint. There was no bay floor before them, but a parted opening that looked somehow like a night sky, or a vast beyond of stars, or an abyss of negativity. What did a black hole look like?

The dark figures around Liam parted, and he turned back to her and extended a hand, inviting her.

Her lungs snapped back to activity, and after a second, she walked across the sand and took his offered hand and stood at his side, and they gazed together as wind pounded and those walls of water throbbed and something moved down in that other place that was revealed before them.

The throng of supplicants stretching along the beach showed little reaction as the Garda team moved behind the line, shields raised, shotguns poised. The participants were too mesmerized by what occurred before them and by the odd sounds playing through the one-note instruments to notice the team.

"These people are dazed," Quinn said. "I don't think they even know what's happening."

"Can't disagree there," O'Donnell said. Behind the team, her focus had moved from the line-up to the water and the huge swirling opening.

"What the hell's going on out there?" Quinn asked. "Are we dreaming?"

"Afraid it's real." O'Donnell looked toward the tunnel of water. "If we break the line does that close the waves up again?"

"I don't know."

Rees spoke absently because he was staring at the new dance that had begun at the heart of the channel, slippery, slithering, profane appendages crept upward beyond the line.

"We've got to try breaking their concentration," O'Donnell said. "Push forward."

"Hold the line," Quinn said as a command. "Let's interrupt our friends there."

Keon had been working a while, flexing fingers, concentrating on folding his thumb under just right, and at last, though excruciating, he slipped his hand through the loop that had secured his wrist and soon he had himself free. Then he turned his attention to the van's back doors, which popped open, having been left unsecured.

Wind and moisture hit him instantly. He needed to adjust to these abrupt changes. He flinched and raised an arm at the blast, hesitating before moving out, picking up the cicada-edged sound borne on the wind.

He turned, determining the direction, and ran across rugged, dead grass that gave way to sand, and at the beach edge he could see the line with more people falling into place with staffs while what looked like police advanced from the other end.

Then he looked to the black-armored police. Thank the heavens.

Maybe he could get to them.

But what help could he offer against…?

His gaze moved to the bay and the opened waves.

He saw Kaity and, god, it was Liam tugging a girl in a white gown forward, and his heart froze or felt like it had.

Before his old friends were rising figures, a pair of things starting to appear from nothingness, foul amalgamations of gnashing...what were they to be called? He had to get to the coppers.

Sprinting across the beach, moving parallel to the line-up at the shore, he angled toward the black shields inching toward the crowd, hands raised to try and look non-threatening even with his speed.

He'd shout when he drew closer, let them know he was on their side and had something to share.

"It's a bloody wall of water," Darcy said looking through binoculars out the bridge window. "It's frozen straight vertical."

Bullfinch took the glasses and stared at the horizon, moving them until he'd trained on what she was seeing.

"That's different from what we saw before," he said. "Probably accomplishing the same effect, ripping an opening."

"In what?" Curl asked. "The sea floor?"

"Probably the fabric of the universe."

"Do we keep forging toward that?"

"Best we can do for now. Can you load up your incendiaries?"

"I'll give the order."

"What's beyond that?" Darcy asked, unable to take her gaze from it.

"If it's like we saw before, it's a... It's hard to describe," he said finally. "But you'll wish you'd never set eyes on it."

"Dear God. The thing behind the curtain of water," she said. "Right out of my nightmares. And we thought this was a routine mission."

"Possible hostile approaching," an officer from the end of the team line shouted.

They'd been inching into the crowd, using the shields to nudge people out of place and knock the staffs aside. So far it had had little effect on the overall screech.

O'Donnell spun to see the man charging them, hands raised.

She kept her hand on her sidearm but waited. He looked more terrified than like someone who wanted to attack.

She couldn't blame him on the terrified front.

She stepped from the ranks and put up a hand, wanting to slow him and...

And then one of the shotguns blasted somewhere beside her. The charging man's forward motion was interrupted. A bean-bag packet struck him in the shoulder. As agony flared on his features, he was spun partially sideways before he crashed back onto the sand.

"Easy," she shouted. "I don't think he was attacking."

She moved forward and dropped to his side, touching his cheek slightly and moving his face toward her. He was stunned, but his eyes moved in their sockets a bit and focused.

"You're Keon Bello."

His fear and confusion turned to an expression of surprise, a frown wrinkling his brow.

"Eileen O'Donnell," she said. "Special Garda operations. We were looking for you to try to protect you. Are you behind this?"

He blinked. "What?"

"Is this your party?"

He struggled to sit up.

"No. No. They've done a terrible thing." He lost it for a moment, shuddering. Under better conditions, O'Donnell would've called in a medic. Now, she helped him into a seated position, and began to massage his shoulder.

"My old friends are deluded," he said. "That's Liam Henni-gan out there, and Kaity White. They're going to upset..."

"I know what they're gonna do. I got a preview. What can we do to stop it?"

"There's a pulp writer..."

"I know. What...can...we...do...to...stop...it?" She spoke slowly and emphatically over the screech and wind roar.

"Break the line?"

"We're working on that. Not having much effect. If you move anyone, more fall into place."

"They're playing what's called 'The Song of the Air,' channeling these lost sounds that harness…"

"I'm getting the picture. How…do…we…stop…it?"

"If you could, I don't know, blow the sound back? It might interrupt it. With the chopper over there?"

"The chopper against this wind at this point? Lost cause. You need to talk to the professor."

"Who?"

"Our secret-agent-of-the-strange friend who's on a ship at sea now and ready to direct a ramming of those things. If we're lucky."

She dragged him to the chopper and pulled him inside, sitting by the door to block some of the noise.

46

Bullfinch watched the thing rise above the wall of water, just not a shimmering coil like before, but what looked like the tips of leathery wings and a form more horrible than they'd seen before stretching above it, the worst of it lost and indistinct in the pall from mist and cloud that hung above everything.

"Oh my God." Darcy's jaw dropped almost to her chin. "It's the gates of hell."

"I'm not sure we're seeing daemons," Bullfinch said. "Whatever the Fomoire and Crom Cruach and their cousins were, and wherever they came from, they probably inspired the legends of a few, though."

At the moment, it looked considerably worse than a rabbit in the moon.

"Ready weapon," Curl said into a mic. "Don't fire until my command."

The canopy spun a quarter turn, and the barrel tilted upward, targeting the shape in the storm. Bullfinch leaned against the bridge, gripping the unit's casing until his joints ached.

"It's going to move toward shore," Darcy said.

"It is starting to move," Curl agreed. "Prepare to fire."

The cannon barrel ticked upward almost imperceptibly amid the waves crashing across the bow.

"Let the birds fly," Curl said.

The barrel made quick, short jerks.

Ka-boom.

Ka-boom.

Ka-boom.

Huge casings belched from its side to clatter into the wash on deck. Shells flew and eventually arched into the mist above the waves revealing themselves as little bursts of orange that ignited for seconds then faded as quickly as the gun had roared.

"If it was a plane or tank it'd be gone now," Curl said.

"I don't think it even felt it," Darcy said.

"Let's try for the heart," Curl said. "We'll guide one in."

"Sir, we have someone on the horn looking for Mr. Bullfinch. Saying urgent."

The captain gave a nod for the communications officer who'd spoken, who turned toward the professor. "I can get you into a headset here," he said.

Bullfinch moved to the console.

On the deck, a small hatch opened in the canopy that housed the cannon, and a small dish with a narrow cone at its center emerged to call on satellite systems.

"Bullfinch here."

"Don't know if it will help, but we have the man who compiled the symbols," O'Donnell said. "He just turned up, and I thought it might be good to get him on the horn with you. This is Keon. Keon, Professor Bullfinch."

"Sir."

"Greetings. What have you got?"

"The staffs are playing a song based on the lost markings. There's an order to them. I'd begun to figure that out once, but someone's done deeper study. It's mentioned in some pulp the stories, but someone's figured out even more specifics…"

"Ideas? If I didn't make it clear, anti-tank and aircraft shells are bouncing off whatever's out there. They ought to cut a snake in half, I'm told."

"You're on the other side of the waves. Maybe if the song were played over there it would reverse the effect."

"There's a legend that Patrick dispersed demons with a bell. Maybe the noise was something like we're experiencing. Maybe he dispersed whatever he faced in a similar way, but we don't have the staffs over here."

"The sounds could possibly be re-created."

"Do you have all of the symbols in your head?"

"Well, I might be able…"

A message icon popped in on Bullfinch's tablet. Mack. Perfect timing as always, as if by magic.

"I have another call on my other line," Bullfinch said. He thumbed the message icon.

"Mack, my boy. Do you have a miracle for me?"

"Looking grim? I've been monitoring your situation."

As if to confirm that, an operator shouted off to Bullfinch's right. "We're getting the shape of two things on the scans."

Bullfinch spun toward Curl, who was in turn looking at the tracking screen in front of the man who'd spoken. Two blue rectangles represented the huge figures on the screen.

"They're almost as tall as those waves."

Red lines indicated the course of the guided shells that the deck's cannon had belched. They moved in small fractions toward the rectangles.

Bullfinch looked out the wind screen feeling a stab of fear he'd rarely encountered at the heart of his carefully disciplined resolve. He'd looked at winged Aztec deities and writhing minions of nightmares around the globe without losing optimism. "Those waves" were as tall as a mountain, and he wasn't sure they'd find an answer.

"Grim it is," Bullfinch said, looking at Mack's image on his tablet. "I've been conferring with the—"

"I was listening. Let me see if I can pull us all together into a circle," Mack said.

He looked away from his cam lens a moment, fingers no doubt dancing on a half-a-dozen keyboards.

"Can everyone hear me?" he asked a moment later.

"Who is this?" O'Donnell asked.

"My friend and co-worker Mack," Bullfinch said. "Miracle worker we hope."

"Aileen O'Donnell here, Garda SDU."

"Keon Bello. I'm afraid I…"

"No time for blame," Bullfinch said. "Solutions."

On the radar screen, the red line curved downward, angling toward the center of one of the rectangles. The rectangles advanced by small increments, a far from adequate representation of the horror beyond the waves.

Bullfinch held his breath. Another second, two at most.

The red line connected with the blue shape, and a loud sound echoed beyond the waves. Then, the rectangles kept moving. Tiny increment by tiny increment on the screen.

"Our round just went directly into the center of one of them. Still doesn't seem to have an effect," a man shouted.

"Hit 'em again," Curl shouted.

"I've been gathering the symbols I could find on the web and the dark web," Mack said. "If these symbols are being handled as notes there's a mathematical value, right?"

"That's what I was thinking they'd done," Keon said.

"I've been through quite a few sources," Mack said. "I found a bit of data someone tried to erase from a server at one of the Groom's think tanks. I'm missing the last symbol. Wait a minute. I had a scan running. Looks like it was transmitted between a couple of sources recently… Looks like it's a fit with the others."

"They have some prototype portable 3D printer," Keon said. "They calibrated these loops on their staffs for the sounds and they sent the last symbol, my control symbol a little while ago."

"Let me just run a couple of programs. I should be able to re-create the values and then the sequence should be a matter of calculation."

"I could help with the order of the symbols," Keon said.

"Let's get this man a laptop," O'Donnell shouted off her mic. "Let's get you two in a huddle."

"Hold tight. We'll have you a version of the tune very quickly," Mack said.

As Keon fired up a laptop they had pulled from a cabinet set in the helicopter's bulkhead, Quinn shook his head.

"This looks insane where I sit," he said.

"From this angle, too," O'Donnell said. "Blowing a flute at a monster, but then everything looks insane just now. We're in the middle of a nightmare."

"Agreed."

Quinn put a hand against his earpiece, pressing into his ear, listening.

"Go ahead."

He turned back to O'Donnell.

"People are standing down."

"What?"

She looked out. Wind tore at the people on shore, pulling at hair and clothing, resisting their movement, threatening to topple them, fresh gale force or greater.

"The people on shore. They're putting their sticks down."

Quinn repeated that into his mouthpiece.

Keon stopped typing. "They must think it's finished. The opening is complete."

"We need your song!" O'Donnell shouted.

"Working with them," Keon said.

"I'm surprised anyone's able to stand up out there," Quinn said. "Another few minutes, this bird probably is going over."

"We're getting it pretty hard," an officer said from shore. "Wind's trying to pick the tourists up by their parka hoods."

O'Donnell turned toward Keon. "What happens next?"

"The gates are open. People on shore become the first meal, I guess. Then it moves inland."

O'Donnell turned back to Rees who'd been sitting silently, watching the chaos outside.

"Can we get them to scramble an air strike?"

Kaity had heard the phrase "the heart of midnight" in her lifetime. That seemed to define what unfolded before her as she guided

Vita Burke along the beach with Nelda and Alison assisting. She looked into the space in front of the abyss. In the channel where a sea floor had been, moving through mist and haze and showering water, writhing, towering, inconceivable forms approached. She caught hints of giant appendages, and yawning mouths, blisters of odd eyes and around the massive figures, she thought she saw winged, demonic forms and shapeless others with hints of more massive contours beyond.

The thrill inside her, even as wind whipped behind them and threatened to knock them forward was akin to orgasm mixed with shock and astonishment.

"It's incredible," she said, knowing the word to be almost a joke, an inadequate grunt.

She turned to Liam to see glazed eyes and an expression of amazement. He'd lost awareness of almost everything around him except the witching hour-vision, the death dream, the abyss in front of them.

Then he blinked.

His absent consciousness returned. And a new focus. Even with the hurricane winds that swirled around them, his body language suggested a sudden awareness of purpose. He grabbed Vita's arm, above the elbow, then stepped toward the crevasse in front of them and the sea of leviathans, tugging her along.

"Time for the offering," he shouted. "We've always known there'd have to be a sacrifice, something offered, an illustration of our submission and our regret for closing the door."

Though dazed, the girl tugged at his shackling fist with no luck.

"You're insane."

"No, not crazy, carrying on. My grandfather worked with Rottman," he shouted. "Compiled the research for Rottman's stories. Gave him the whispers that were in the tales, but he amassed much more knowledge. Happily, Keon came with the ideas to fill in the gaps, and he was easy enough to nudge in the right direction. Most of the time, until he hid things even from me. This is to be the final component. The sacrifice as invitation to step back into our world."

Vita tried to swing at him, strike a blow, but the force of the wind slowed her motion, weakened her strike. He barely felt it, and then he wrenched her arm behind her and shoved her forward.

Kaity had to admit he'd kept his secrets hidden well. If his grandfather had worked with Rottman, the old man at Clew Bay had been his father. She'd never known.

Vita tried to find purchase in the soft sand, but Liam kept pushing, and Kaity joined in, shoving her toward the maelstrom.

"We're bouncing pebbles off a stone wall," Curl said. "Even the incendiaries aren't doing any good. We need jets scrambling out of Baldonnel, but they're gonna take a while. What else can we hit it with, Professor? Do I try to push the whole ship through that wall and ram 'em?"

Before Bullfinch could speak, his tablet vibrated.

Mack was back.

"We almost have a tune," he said. "We get this worked out, you have a player?"

"I got blessed out the other day with the reminder of our Garda LRAD systems," O'Donnell said. "But we can't get a bird up over here anymore. Are they equipped on the OPV?"

Bullfinch looked to the captain. "I should have asked already. Sonic equipment?"

Hearing him, Darcy said: "They want to know if we have LRAD?"

Bullfinch nodded.

"We were fitted with a new system for the Mediterranean operation," Curl said. "Ships have used 'em against pirates but..."

Bullfinch put a finger in his right ear, pressing the bud in as he listened, trying to make out all of the words from O'Donnell, nodding. Then he looked toward Darcy and the captain.

"We're going to play a song," he said. "Something that may close the lid again out there."

"A song?" Curl asked.

"This brouhaha started with sounds, notes on shore. We're going to have to play the tune from here. We're going to ring Patrick's bell."

"And we have a long-range acoustical device, we can send a blast of it," Darcy said.

"Less showy than what the people did on shore but hopefully effective," Bullfinch said. "Something in the frequency created by these symbols intensifies energy from the elements."

"Have them get the speaker into position," Curl said. "Let's get your song beamed in if we can."

"We're ready for your mix tape," Bullfinch said into the tablet's small mic opening.

He was surprised he'd found that term in the back of his brain.

"Almost ready," Mack said. "I'm going to be sending you an MP3. In a few seconds. Watch your inbox."

Bullfinch stretched a thumb up to click his message box.

Then he waited.

Beyond the wind screen, as waves crashed across the deck, he watched crewmen heading along to the bow to the front railing, restraints around their waists to keep them from being hurled overboard.

Still nothing in his inbox.

He tried to think through the hops needed for the file transfer, plus the potential interruptions out here. Would it make it?

On the deck, connected, twin gray rectangles were being placed on the railing, clamped into place on a mount, the sailors ducking into the sloshing water as they worked.

And a message appeared.

Oghamfile.mp3

"Where do we put it?" Bullfinch asked.

"There's a player," Darcy said, pulling out a small box with rounded corners made of heavy gray plastic. "Heavy duty."

She yanked out connector cables as well.

"Can I see your tablet, sir?"

Bullfinch passed it over, wishing he had Mack on hand. Technical systems were second nature to him, and then Mack would have been just as comfortable securing the speakers on deck.

While Bullfinch's proficiency was improving, he was glad Darcy was on hand.

"I'm going to forward the file and then transfer it to the player," she said.

On deck, the sailors had the speakers in place. One turned toward the portal and raised a hand, thumbs up, while he kept his other hand curled around the railing.

"Are we close enough?" Bullfinch asked.

"For the sound to reach?" Curl asked. "Should be, but there's a lotta racket. This unit's supposed to be good for an audible message at eight thousand meters. That's, what did they say in the training session, Lt. Darcy?"

"It diminishes by distance, but the specs say eighty-one American football fields."

Bullfinch tried to remember sitting in U.S. stadiums accompanying friends. Then he looked at the wall of water and what he could see of the movement beyond.

"Environmental factors have their impact, but this should carry for a while," Darcy said. "It's ready to plug in. The big question is will the magic work."

"It may be some kind of physics we need, actually," Bullfinch said. "But as we're seeing, it'll seem damned close to magic."

O'Donnell ran, or pushed forward at least, in almost slow motion into the wind, shoulder to shoulder with Rees and the armored operatives from the regional squad, grabbing for the confused crowd members. Some seemed only dazed, but as they had looked forward, others, upon looking into the void, seemed to be driven instantly insane. They wailed and tore at their hair or tried to fold themselves into balls. She began pulling them back from the crevasse. If the professor couldn't work things out on the other end, the mission became saving as many lives as possible.

The dazed patrons complied with being urged in a direction away from shore, letting themselves be led inland as the armored team began to split the job up. The others were balls of agonized insanity.

"Take them toward the castle wall." Quinn motioned with a broad gesture, pointing with his entire hand as if he were on a runway directing a jet.

Then O'Donnell looked to the sea and caught sight of the long-haired man framed by the bipedal figures who had crouched in the water earlier. Then she spotted Kaity and the younger woman, a girl who struggled against his grip while incredible things loomed before them.

What the hell was he doing?

She handed off a man she'd been guiding to one of the team members and started toward the opening's edge, hand on the grip of her sidearm. Then she paused. She'd left the sword behind. Bullets had worked on the snake man Bullfinch had battled, but the professor had softened him up.

She changed direction and found herself in a wind that made her movement feel like a climb up a mountainside. She felt just like a mountaineer in a photo on Everest, frozen in a moment that looked immobile.

Her coat billowed around her like a cape. Her cheeks were slashed by wind, her hair follicles strained as her hair swept back from her face and the crown of her head.

She slogged on, forcing steps, compelling one foot to find purchase, then the other.

When she found the sword, she wheeled for the trip back to the beach. That did go a little faster, though crosswinds threatened to topple her first in one direction then another.

One of the gray things surrounding the man greeted her,

bulbous eyes staring, and just like before, an array of tentacles sprang from its back. Ignoring the pain in her shoulder, with the hilt in both hands, O'Donnell slashed, aiming a diagonal that took one tentacle tip off in a crackle of blue electricity before it raked across a shoulder and across the torso, driving the creature back.

She drew her sidearm then and fired two rounds, staggering it further before it fell back to the sand. She didn't risk more shots with the wind and the variables such as the girl on the far side of the opponents.

Behind the creatures, in fact, the girl continued to struggle as the man, Liam, forced her forward, his weight and strength compelling his steps. O'Donnell didn't shout. Words would be lost. She had to get to her before he forced her into the mass of nightmare that was a few meters after that.

47

The rugged MP3 player as it was described in the documentation had been plugged in. Kieran Darcy held a finger above the remote's large button, devised so that a person wearing gloves could still handle the controls.

"Are we ready?"

Bullfinch nodded.

"Like I said, it's worked on pirates. Let's hope," Curl said. "Fire."

Darcy dropped her thumb, and in spite of their ear plugs, the wind, storm, waves and the indefinable roar of the uplifted water and whatever was beyond, the shrill noise that broadcast through the LRAD speakers sounded and stabbed nerves, ears and consciousness.

More discordant than the wind through the staffs on shore, the noise blasted forward, and Bullfinch imagined it as a wave rushing toward the wall of water. For a second, there was nothing, but then the wall of water reacted, as if a wind had suddenly begun to push it.

No longer was it looking solid and immobile. It was almost straining.

"Are you at your maximum?"

"We've got a couple of decibels left," Kieran said.

"I'd up it. All the way." He gestured to the sky in case she couldn't hear him.

"Here goes," she said and thumbed the control.

No effect.

"Dammit," she shouted.

"No luck with Patrick's bell here," Bullfinch said.

O'Donnell had never used a sword, but she'd used a variety of batons. She shoved her sidearm into its holster and gripped the hilt with both hands again. The wounded shoulder was becoming excruciating, but she kept moving into the midst of the alien things, the blade raised high over her head.

They converged around her, and she swung, putting all of the muscle strength she had into the motion and trying to shift her weight into it as she'd been trained in hand-to-hand defense classes.

She raked the blade across a throat, blue tendrils of electricity crackling along the steel as it sliced. Then she stabbed the point into a figure's core, driving hard before yanking it out.

Another figure tried to move in on her, arms ready and tentacles flailing, and she had to remind herself these were possibly the source of the poison used in the serpent murders. A bite or perhaps a touch could be dangerous.

She raised the blade to a vertical position and slashed from side to side, giving the weapon a windshield-wiper motion, deflecting or slicing tentacles until she was able to change the blade's course.

She twisted the hilt in her hands and swung straight down. With new blue crackles and jagged tendrils around it, the steel sliced into the gray armor-like surface and bone beneath, cracking and separating.

She leaned in and forced weight and muscle into it, dragging it deeper, seeking brain. The thing staggered, tentacles from its back twitching wildly.

O'Donnell twisted and yanked, freeing the blade then giving a stomping kick to the chest to send the figure down. Then she looked into the dazed face of the girl Liam held.

"Vita Burke."

She was the girl from the office photo. No wonder the *Aisteach* hadn't found her.

"She knew all was lost, but if she could get her turned this way, she might help her help herself.

"Maybe we're un-ringing a bell," Mack said.

"Whatever it is, it doesn't look like it's working," Bullfinch said.

"The pulp stories talk about the song as opening," Keon said. "There's no mention of closing because the forces overwhelm…"

"But if we wanted to un-ring a bell, our notes are a mathematical sequence, maybe reversing the song sequence would do the trick," Mack said. "Any chance you could hit it from both sides? You have two walls of water out there, right?"

"Right."

"I'm told we can't get this chopper off the ground," Keon said.

"Where'd Ahlstrom go?" Bullfinch asked. "Can we try to reach him?"

Darcy stepped to a console and tapped a few keys.

"How long will it take you, Mack?" Bullfinch asked as she worked.

"Not long. Hold the fort, Geoffrey."

"Just work fast."

"Try not to sweat."

"Least of the functions I'm trying to control," Bullfinch said.

Black, winged things were fluttering above the towering water wall.

"I'm afraid that's not hope we're seeing," Curl said.

Bullfinch didn't want to agree, but he gave a nod. Mack had pulled off some impressive moves, but time was short and the belly of whatever world was out there was about to vomit its contents into this one.

Wherever he was sitting now, probably somewhere in the American Southwest, Mack would be surrounded by screens, keyboards, data, fingers thundering over keys if he didn't have something rigged to funnel his thoughts directly to a computer. Would even his feverish tenacity and brilliance be enough?

Closing his eyes, the professor summoned up a technique an aging Hindu sādhu with a painted face had imparted to him, one he claimed he'd perfected for pushing good thoughts from his inner being out to the universe.

Bullfinch sent those in what he hoped was Mack's direction and O'Donnell's direction as well, even as he gripped a counter edge on the bridge to steady himself and controlled his breathing while the ship shifted from side to side.

"Almost there," Mack said.

On the radar screen, the rectangles blipped closer and closer to shore.

The girl seemed out of it, not able to put up much resistance, even as O'Donnell shouted her name.

Two more figures stepped in to face O'Donnell. She recognized them too, Alison and Nelda. They placed themselves beside one of the tentacled figures and in O'Donnell's way as a barrier for their high priest. Or whatever the hell he was.

With a yell she'd been told could aid in focus and the tightening of muscle, O'Donnell charged. If a tentacle got her, so be it. She'd stop Liam's final ministrations or go down trying, and it would all be up to the professor after that.

Fighting the wind, she closed the distance between her and the younger women by forcing one foot in front of the other. She dodged a tentacle and feinted toward Alison now on her left. As Alison stepped back, O'Donnell slashed to her right, aiming for the point where a carotid artery ought to be on the reptile figure, aiming to pierce scale and skin.

The way the blood spurted around the blue electricity, it seemed to work.

A tentacle slapped her face before she could focus on the next. The impact felt heavy and strong enough to bruise, and her head jerked left, her balance thrown off.

She went down on an elbow.

Her body followed, and she lay on her side on the wet sand, brain not stunned but throbbing. From the corner of one eye, she could make out a wriggling array of appendages. Grips ready to coil and bind her to stop any further defense.

She turned her head slightly to stare into the thing's round, black eyes as it peered down at her, the slatted pupils spread wide, and the darkness in the depths of the thing's being threatening and beckoning.

Then the head exploded in a sudden burst of blood, skull fragments, brain matter and other gore that the wind quickly swept backward.

O'Donnell moved the sidearm away from her hip and pushed herself up on the sand.

For one opponent with a neck injury, it served just fine.

She found her way to her knees in a second, ejecting a clip and replacing it with another fresh load. She leveled the barrel toward Nelda and Alison and was getting to her knees. The Red Sea wasn't closing.

Tentacles from the abyss reached toward Vita and Liam.

"Aaaallllmoooost reaaaddy," Mack said.

"They're almost at shore," Darcy shouted. "Send it straight to my console."

She grabbed the tablet and typed an address for Mack.

"Okay, sending now," Mack said.

Nothing appeared.

"You rang," Ahlstrom's voice came through the com system.

"Another round," Curl ordered.

The rectangles blipped forward on screen, while the deck gun roared.

Bullfinch didn't harbor any hopes the shells would find some exposed weakness this time. The things would keep lumbering, and this corner of the world was about to be devastated. All because of some interrupted hop on an Internet route.

"Where are you?" Bullfinch asked.

"Sat down in a field I found a bit inland."

"Can you get in the air again?"

"Not sure it'd be the best idea, but aye, aye."

"Do you have LRAD on board?"

"Aye to that, too."

"We have an idea."

Then the mail icon blipped up on Bullfinch's screen:

Oghamfile2.mp3

"It's here," Bullfinch said, motioning over Darcy who began a repeat of the previous process.

"We're going to max it."

"Jimmy, I've got a song for you to play on the north side. Can you get there?"

"Piece of cake."

In front of O'Donnell, the women's hands shot to the sides of their heads as they tried to shut new sound out. The blast came from beyond the waves, shrill, horrible, somehow different than before.

O'Donnell pulled the scarf from her throat and looped it over her head, making sure her ears were covered as the sound began to impact her and reverberate through her skull. She forced her hands to work, to tie it in a quick knot at the base of her skull.

Then she pushed herself up and ran, grabbing for Liam, yanking him aside then grabbing Vita to drag her out of Kaity's grasp.

She was working to deflect arm movements when someone touched her shoulder.

Rees was suddenly brushing past her. He drove a fist into Kaity's jaw, shoved Nelda and Alison away and grabbed Liam's collar, tugging him aside and allowing O'Donnell to concentrate on Vita.

Looking into the girl's terrified eyes, O'Donnell jerked her head toward shore, and they turned and began the fight to reach some kind of refuge.

In a second, Rees was beside her, taking the girl's other arm. They managed to get her onto the beach, get her almost upright. Then, together they ran, heading for a crevasse in the castle ruins to hunker down.

"Here we go," Darcy said.

The speakers on deck blasted through the noise and roar outside.

The walls of water began to shimmy in a new way. It looked like a controlled fountain display about to a change pre-programed patterns. Perhaps it was. If this really worked, they'd be analyzing whatever forces and protocols might be at work here for some time. Mack would be heading over to apply his physicist side to the problem.

"Is it working?"

Bullfinch was jarred by Mack's voice from the tablet.

"Turn me to the storm," he said. "Can you see anything?"

Bullfinch moved to the console and picked up the tablet to aim the eye lens out the wind screen. No movement on the water walls.

"In the air," Ahlstrom said from the speakers. "It'll take us a few. I'm going to stay outside the worst of the wind spirals."

Bullfinch focused his gaze, searching for any sign of the walls relenting.

"Nothing yet."

"We'll keep the blast going at top decibels," Darcy said.

"Maxing my speed," Ahlstrom said. "Heading around the north side."

Bullfinch studied the shimmering water in front of him. It held fast, looked like a solid.

"In place," Ahlstrom said. "Can't see you, but we're firing up the speakers. Let's start the party over here."

With nothing else to do, Bullfinch counted Mississippis. When he was up to thirty-five, he saw a shimmer.

"It's starting to do something," he said.

He held his breath. More Mississippis ticked off. Then the tops of the waves were curling downward, spilling inward on the trench. In a few seconds, water showered around the massive figures, outlining them, as if they were draped in cloaks of liquid. Bullfinch took in the shapes, the odd, terrifying convolution of otherness as Rottman might have put it in a pulp tale.

Then they began to sink downward and the water continued to tumble and swirl.

"Are you seeing what I'm seeing?" Ahlstrom asked.

Bullfinch had to smile. "Good job, Jimmy."

"Full-throttle reverse," Curl said. "We don't want to go down with them."

"Guess we won't need to call the Brits for a nuke after all," Darcy said.

"Not this time," Bullfinch said. "Let's hope there won't be another."

He closed his eyes again and sent another wish O'Donnell's way, keeping his focus as intense as he could make it while they waited for the swirl and the waves to calm again to a still and silent sea.

The massive figures and the ancillary beings were caught in the downward onslaught and swirl. O'Donnell and Rees poked heads out through the wall's opening in Ballinskellig to watch.

A whirlpool looking like a fiercely tended stew began to spin, and hints of tentacles and black wings swirled as flailing ingredients.

"Looks like the professor did it," she said. Words were lost, she put her arm around Vita and rested her cheek against the girl's head. Someday they'd talk of fear and loss, but for the moment, it was time to weep and cheer.

48

The Liffey rolled in a steady ripple beside the railed sidewalk in Dublin, but it looked almost still in comparison to the waves they'd seen at Ballinskelligs Bay. O'Donnell leaned against the hard iron with the arm not in a sling and watched the flow, calmed by this movement and its familiar certainty.

"Looks constant and inevitable," she said.

"Not letting go of fatalism?" Bullfinch asked.

He was natty and perfect again, homburg sitting in a firm, faint tilt on his head, newly dry-cleaned overcoat crisp, creased and pressed into perfect alignment.

The doctors said the ringing that persisted in her ears would subside given time. She felt impatient, but that would have to do. She could make out the professor's words enough to shrug.

"It's ingrained, but I think we wound up doing some good," she said.

"You wound up doing a lot of it, Officer. You helped change the course of things. You are indeed a very special detective."

He leaned against the railing beside her and watched the water move.

"It's been a while since it's been an area of focus for me," he said. A corner of his mouth ticked up. "Other things demand attention, but when I read Aristotle and the philosophers, a point or two about fatalism stuck with me. Ultimately he rejected the notion that a proposition is always true or false. Memory gets fuzzy, but I believe when we're given two possibilities, great serpents emerge or great serpents don't, there are a lot of probabilities between the two. A determined woman at the center between the 'do' and 'do not' can mean a lot with those probabilities."

He turned toward her now and smiled again. "I'd say you had a good bit to do with eternity this week. You saved the world, dear lady, or a significant piece of it. We don't know what would have happened after the emerald isle was overrun."

"Saved it for now," she said. "I've never read the philosophers, but my mam used to read me Tolkien, and when things look bad there's a fellow who says '…in this hour I do not believe that any darkness will endure.' I'll give it an hour."

Bullfinch smiled.

"Then perhaps another after that?"

"After that, we'll see. There's work to be done. We keep getting mention of a pair of American brothers."

Bullfinch nodded. "They've been involved in think tanks for years, pulling political strings, shaping educational agendas, planting ideas where they can. They haven't managed to make the winds of change as chaotic as they'd like in the U.S. I think they were hoping to use destruction and rebuilding here as a cauldron for study, something that could be re-shaped into their vision."

"We can't actually prove that. They were on hand for some discussions; we show Liam Hennigan and his father pushed all the actual buttons. We can't pinpoint who was behind the deaths aimed at pushing Keon and acquiring his lost calculations and markings."

"Bright young man. I hope he does well in whatever he does next."

"We have him in protective custody for now. Freya is a little different story, a player in the mix though misguided. It's almost always the case that women bear the brunt."

"Perhaps at trial some truth will emerge," Bullfinch said.

"Maybe she or this Mike will finally testify. It's the brothers' heads that most need to be hoisted. They planned a long time."

"A long game."

"So, back to the U.S., Professor?"

"I must get back to O.C.L.T.'s efforts. Wherever I'm needed. You still have quite a few review boards and the like to face?"

"A few. I'll get through it. If I'm not going back to special detective, staying with *Aisteach* won't be too bad. Maybe the powers that be will feel a little more comfortable with me tucked away in a weird little agency. Clearly, I can do a bit of good here, too, Professor. I'll give you this as what I've learned. You do the good you can where you can, when you can, and hope it has an impact."

"Clearly." He tipped his hat. "Perhaps we'll meet again, perhaps under less cataclysmic circumstances."

"Or perhaps not." She smiled. "Maybe I did read a bit of Aristotle in school now that I think about it. He's the one who said happiness is related to the cultivation of virtue didn't he?"

"I think he might have," Bullfinch said. He took her hand to accept her hearty grip.

"Cheers to pursuit," he said. "Cheers and good wishes."

Report from the paranormal website Unexplained Oddities

Strange winged being spotted near ancient Irish ruin
by Shawn Drury

Amysterious winged figure, dubbed *Batswings* by Americans, has perplexed and frightened tourists and residents near the Ring of Kerry site at Ballinskellig Castle.

At dusk a number of people have recently reported seeing the figure either crouched on the top wall of the castle ruins or winging in wide circles across Ballinskellig Bay.

Harkening back to U.S. accounts of Mothman, the creature...

Want more O.C.L.T.?
Turn the page for a sneak peek at

O.C.L.T.

DIGGING DEEP

Aaron Rosenberg

Prologue

Far beneath the hustle and bustle of the crowds, the peaks and heights of the buildings, the ebb and flow of the traffic. Deep down, below pipes and girders and rails. A long, wide tunnel, towering cavern-like overhead but stretching on for miles in either direction. A smooth, solid surface, unworn by time or element—

—save where a crack ran through its center, splitting the dark gray with a jagged streak of pure black, like a negative of lightning forking through an overcast sky.

Near the middle of that crack, at its widest point, it was as broad as a man's hand, its sides razor sharp and plummeting into shadow. Impossible to see how deep the crack ran, or what might lie beneath it. It sat, fractured but immobile, a frozen tear in what seemed the very floor of the world.

Until that tear began to buckle.

It heaved upward, rock ripping with a terrible grinding sound as it was torn free and shoved aside, the crack widening, the bottom edge revealed as it rose, warping and twisting—

—and finally tore apart, shredded from the underside by an enormous, clawed hand that thrust through triumphantly, bridging the gap and stirring the still, cold air.

A second hand soon joined the first, rending rock and stone away to create a wider space. Then a long, lean figure thrust itself upward, those claws latching onto the unbroken portions of earth anchor it. It emerged from the hole, crawling onto solid ground before straightening.

It sniffed the air, its head swiveling about, testing this new world before it.

About the Author

Sidney Williams travelled to Ireland with his wife several years ago and fell in love with the land and people. Visits to Irish ruins and drives across the countryside piqued his imagination, and he had wanted to write about the land for some time when the opportunity to pen an O.C.L.T. title came along. Sidney is a Louisiana native who has worked as a newspaper reporter, reference librarian and more recently as a creative writing instructor concentrating on horror, mystery and suspense. He has also spent time in the corporate marketing world writing and editing web content and advertising and marketing materials. He earned an MFA from Goddard College in 2010.

As a reporter, he conducted a host of celebrity and author interviews and continues to write features on authors as a contributing editor of *The Big Thrill* newsletter for ITW, the International Thriller Writers organization.

His short stories have appeared in a number of magazines and anthologies including *Under the Fang* and *Hot Blood: Deadly After Dark*, and he has written comic book scripts and an audio-drama adaptation of *The War of the Worlds* by H.G. Wells. His serialized Lovecraftian story "Sleepers," appeared on the *Paper Tape* literary magazine website in 2014.

He currently resides in Florida with his wife, Christine Rutherford, and their cats. Find him online at sidisalive.com, on Facebook at www.facebook.com/SidneyWilliamsBooks, or on Twitter at @Sidney_Williams

Curious about other Crossroad Press books?
Stop by our site:
http://store.crossroadpress.com
We offer quality writing
in digital, audio, and print formats.

Enter the code FIRSTBOOK
to get 20% off your first order from our store!
Stop by today!

Made in the USA
Middletown, DE
30 April 2021